Before her death in July 1997, beloved lesbian-feminist author Chris Anne Wolfe published two Amazon adventure novels – *Shadows of Aggar* and *Fires of Aggar*. But these two volumes are only the first half of the four-part Aggar cycle. Chris Anne also published two stand-alone novels – a time-bending romance, *Annabel and I*, and a retelling of Beauty and the Beast, *Roses and Thorns*.

As her publisher and friend, I was honored to inherit the manuscripts of Chris Anne's remaining novels, short stories, poetry and songs. These hand-written volumes include both remaining Aggar books – *Sands of Aggar* and *Oceans of Aggar* – and more than a dozen retold fairy tales, and original fantasy and contemporary novels. Only Blue Forge Press has the right to publish Chris Anne's work and we take great pride in that mission.

Jennifer DiMarco
Publisher
Blue Forge Press

More by Chris Anne Wolfe

Amazons of Aggar

Book 1: Shadows of Aggar
Book 2: Fires of Aggar
Book 3: Sands of Aggar
Book 4: Oceans of Aggar
Book 5: Bonds of Aggar
Book 6: Wilds of Aggar

Annabel and I

Roses and Thorns

Talismans & Temptations

www.BlueForgePress.com

OCEANS OF AGGAR

Chris Anne Wolfe

BLUE FORGE PRESS

Port Orchard * Washington

Blue Forge Press is the print division of the volunteer-run, federal 501(c)3 nonprofit company, Blue Forge Group, founded in 1989 and dedicated to bringing light to the shadows and voice to the silence. We strive to empower storytellers across all walks of life with our four divisions: Blue Forge Press, Blue Forge Films, Blue Forge Gaming, and Blue Forge Records. Find out more at www.BlueForgeGroup.org

Blue Forge Press
7419 Ebbert Drive Southeast
Port Orchard, Washington 98367
blueforgepress@gmail.com
360-550-2071 ph.txt

OCEANS OF AGGAR

Chris Anne Wolfe

Prologue

Pallas looked out over the sea, her blue eyes flitting across the horizon as the moons crept into view. The sun was setting. Soon the stars would burn bright in the heavens and the distant planets would come into view, faded dots of light deep in the void of space. It seemed fitting that CX-12 would watch over her as she left her last mark on Aggar.

She took a step back, her old knees aching with the movement. She folded her soft, weathered hands as the wind tousled her silver-white hair. She wasn't sick or senile, but she could still feel her end was near. She felt ancient. She was one of the last on Aggar who still remembered the beginning, the first colonies, the first landings. She was one of the only ones who remembered a time when Aggar didn't have a name.

Her heart was heavy and weak. The attitudes and stories were changing. Countries were forming. The people were dividing. She could see bits and pieces of what the future held and it terrified her. She had to act.

"Are you ready?"

The ship rocked slowly as Pallas turned to the Circle. Five men and four women waited for her, standing around a metal canister the size of her head. Carmin tinkered with the device, working up until the end to ensure it wouldn't crack or erode.

"Yes." Pallas moved forward to join the circle.

She closed her eyes. Despite her age, her mind was perfect. Her memories were almost too clear for her liking. But there were some things she had tried to forget. Moments in time she'd have to drawn on again if she was to use the abilities she'd been gifted by Aggar to send her message.

Her fingertips trembled as she joined hands with the Circle. The young men on either side of her glanced at her with concern. She could feel their nervousness as they questioned what they were about to do. She grit her teeth and steadied her hands. She needed them to be as firm in their conviction as she was or everything would fall apart.

Carmin stood and closed the circle. She caught Pallas's eyes, sending her certainty and calm through their Sight connection. They had only met a tenmoon ago, but Carmin had quickly become the daughter Pallas never had. "When you're ready, connect with the lifestone core in the device. Focus on what you want to say. What you're feeling. What memories you want to imprint on the core. We'll use what abilities the Sight has given us to help you focus."

Pallas closed her eyes once more, calling on the Sight to help her go back. To remember what it was like before. She could taste the cold, processed air of the colony where she'd been born, a bloated pod floating in space, looking for a home. She could feel the gusts of a shuttle landing, the dust and and pine needles flying through the air and clinging to her hair. She could see the glint of the sun off the tin roofs of the temporary shelters. She could still see the glint in Athena's eyes when they thought they'd be safe.

She remembered everything in excruciating detail. She painted the memories with her thoughts and impressions. Her warnings and fears. Tears streamed down her cheeks and her breath came shallow and gasping to her lips. She started to lose control of her focus, her memories returning over and over again to Athena's face, her eyes, the feeling of her hands on her skin.

She fell to her knees, pulling away from the Circle and holding her hands tight over her heart. "I can't do this anymore."

Carmin kicked the latch to the capsule closed, sealing Pallas's memories inside as she fell to her knees, holding her friend.

"Pallas? Pallas, are you alright?"

Pallas held tight to Carmin's arms, but her senses of the other woman were quickly fading. Athena stood out in her mind. Her Athena. Her lost Amazon. "It's done. One day they'll know. One day they'll hear our whispers out of time." Pallas's words were slurred, barely audible.

Carmin held her tighter, but Pallas felt herself go weak. She didn't care as she lost all feeling in her body. She didn't see the tears flooding Carmin's cheeks or hear the frightened gasps of the Circle. There was only Athena. Finally.

The message was cast. She had given every bit of herself back to Aggar, and in return the planet had released her soul back where she wanted most to be. Somewhere in time, the future would find her last message of hope. Her greatest truth. She hoped it would be enough to stall the things she'd seen.

Athena smiled and reached out for her. Pallas took her hand, the wrinkles and age disappearing as they clasped hands. She couldn't care about the future anymore. She was going home.

PART ONE

SONGS OF DESTINY

Chapter One

The jungle threatened to swallow her whole. Long, wet vines tugged at her arms and legs, stinging her cheeks as she ran. The sky cracked overhead with a boom of thunder, sending an electric shock through the humid air, but there was no rain or wind. The Choir wouldn't allow anything as trivial as the weather to disrupt the chase.

Reve dodged sharply to the left, splashing and plunging into a thick swamp. The mud swallowed her to her neck, coating her pale skin and short, dark blonde hair. It masked the musk of her sweat, burying her in an earthy, sulfuric scent that seeped into her nose and coated her tongue.

She gasped for breath, her sides cramping and her muscles screaming as she allowed herself a moment to rest. The Song hadn't found her yet and there was enough living in the marsh to confuse it for at least a few breaths.

The wet soil was a blessing to her battered, bare feet. Her boots had worn out long ago and running through the rugged jungle terrain had left her soles bruised and bloody. It was easier to tread mud and swamp water than to race over spindly tree roots and thorny vines.

She closed her eyes, trying to refocus her thoughts. Her heart pounded wildly in her throat. Large beads of sweat rolled down her face, the salt stinging the shallow cuts across her cheeks and the broken skin of her dehydrated lips. Her stomach rumbled and ached, empty for days. She didn't know enough about the jungles of Karatan to safely forage for food and the last of her supplies had been used long ago. She was lucky to even find fresh water.

A soft, whistling melody echoed in the distance. Reve's pale blue eyes flew open, wide with fear as they flitted across the swamp. The jungle was too still. The animals had retreated hours ago, and with no breeze or rain to rustle the trees, the only sounds were the crackle of thunder and the deep, wet suck of the mud clinging to Reve's tattered clothes. But she had heard it, the approaching Song, spreading out across the landscape. Hunting her.

She couldn't rest anymore. She pushed forward, leaving heavy ripples across the swamp's surface. She didn't think of her empty stomach, her lacerated feet, or her steadily dwindling energy. All she thought about was the mountain, the crumbling ruins high enough to be surrounded by the buffeting winds that would keep the Song at bay. The mountain Reve had seen every night in her dreams since leaving the desert far to the north and trekking into the tangled wilderness of Karatan. The mountain that would take her one step closer to taking down the Choir for good.

She pulled herself out of the other end of the marsh, crawling like a beast on her hands and knees until she was free of the swamp. Her limbs trembled as she pushed off the ground. The whispers of the Song were growing louder. She glanced over her shoulder as a ghostly, white mist floated slowly across the swamp.

Reve didn't know anyone else who could see the Songs, the nanobots formed by the Choir to control everything from the weather to the minds of the people of Aggar. They were usually gentle, twisting and turning the forces of nature and human thought with a barely perceptible hand. Reve doubted such a painless fate awaited her if the Song reached her.

The cloud of Song traveled faster, catching her scent in the wrinkles of the mud. Reve sped into the jungle again, drawing into the deepest wells of her energy. The jungle became harder to traverse, the knotted, rolling roots of the ancient trees making the ground uneven and unstable.

The Song was getting closer, the mist engulfing the trees without slowing. Reve stumbled over an exposed root and nearly hit the ground. Her head ached. The muscles in her neck contracted as the Song drifted closer. The cuts in her feet and legs split, blood beading across the cracks and rolling down her skin in tiny rivulets. The mud on her back began to dry and harden from the heat of the Song. Reve wondered if it intended to set her on fire.

Reve turned sharply to the right, hoping to confuse or out-maneuver the nanobot cloud, but it had caught onto the fringes of her trail. It would continue following her until she could reach wind: the only natural phenomenon the Choir couldn't control and the Songs couldn't pass.

Reve pressed against the trees, willing herself to disappear, to be invisible. She wanted to meld into the shadows and pray the Song passed her by. She merged with the darkness, becoming silent and nearly untraceable. If her hunter had been a creature, even a human, she would have seemed to disappear. It was one of the many skills and gifts she'd had from birth.

Reve started to gain distance, the song finally growing fainter and eventually disappearing. She slowed her pace, fighting to catch her breath. She couldn't see the sky through the dense, leafy canopy but the shadows were deepening, stretching longer across the ground like ink stains. Night was falling, and while the Songs would stand out even better in the darkness, traveling through the jungle would become even more perilous.

The silence stretched on as jungle's elevation slowly increased, hills giving way to the base of her mountain. She was used to the stillness. Few living things would come near anyone marked for death by the Choir and the more sentient residents of Aggar would kill her on-sight for her eyes.

The silence didn't touch her except in the darkest moments of her despair. Reve had been used to the silence long before the Songs started pursuing her. She was born in darkness, in quiet. It was all she knew, all she trusted.

It could be a blessing: she rarely feared wild animals or poisonous insects. Even predatory plants shied away from her. Still, there were quiet moments, when she had evaded the Songs long enough for a night's rest or had found a patch of wind that would keep the Choir at bay, when she wondered what it would be like to have a companion. But it was a dream. Even if she blinded herself, clouding her damning blue eyes, the Songs wouldn't stop. No one would be willing to spend a life fleeing with her. A travel partner was a liability. She would only end up abandoning them when they inevitably couldn't keep up.

Reve stumbled over a thick, thorny vine and fell hard to the ground. She winced as the thorns tore through the thin cloth of her pants, slicing her shins. She carefully freed herself from the spines and sat hard on the ground. Her fingers probed the fresh cuts. They were shallow, barely bleeding, and she couldn't see any sign of discoloration in the dwindling light of day. If the thorns had been venomous, she'd know soon enough.

Reve smiled grimly, her thin lips quirked with dark humor. It would be a fitting end to her story to die in the depths of Karatan from a venomous plant. At least the Choir wouldn't have the satisfaction of being her end or pushing her to killing herself.

Reve turned to push off the ground and her hands grazed a broken shard of pottery. She hesitated, grabbing the shard and running her thumb over the sharp edges. She looked up into the darkness with an irrational glimmer of hope. Perhaps there was a settlement nearby with food, water, and a clean change of clothing. Perhaps even boots. Anything to make her climb up the mountain easier.

She struggled back to her feet and ran. She soon found a narrow trail, formed by hundreds of feet and machetes clearing back the jungle. She pounded down the carefully carved pathway through the towering, twisted trees until she reached the village. Her hope vanished, carrying with it the last of her energy. The village was long-abandoned. There was nothing to help her. No food, no water. Not even animals in cages to distract the Song.

She fell back against a slender, rough tree, her knees trembling, ready to buckle. She hadn't expected how hard losing such a tiny thread of hope would hit her.

This is why you don't hope. You don't think. There is nothing for you. There is only the mission.

Reve shook her head. She didn't have time for this. She couldn't be weak. She had to run. She'd already run so far. But she couldn't seem to find the strength. She was a shell of a woman, shattered and empty. If the Song found her, there would be barely anything left of her for it to take.

She clenched her hands into fists. This wasn't the time for self pity. It was never the time for self-pity.

Suddenly, a deep, vicious snarl echoed from the other side of the village. Songs were light and airy, mournful and distant. They lulled the populace into a false sense of security. They didn't growl.

Reve crept toward the sound, welcoming any sign of life, even an aggressive one. She paused. A Forest Wolf snapped at an ancient steel trap clamped around her paw. She gnashed her teeth and whimpered as she struggled to get free. Her ebony and silver fur stood on end, her slender ears pressed flat against her head.

"Calm down. Calm down." Reve's voice was infused with a deep calm, aided by her natural empathic abilities. The wolf watched her, the canine's deep golden eyes wary and full of pain. As the animal calmed, Reve patted her head, stroking between her ears and scratching her neck. Reve closed her eyes. She couldn't remember the last time she'd touched something so soft and warm.

Her touch whispered truths to Reve in snippets: the wolf was female, born far to the north. Her paw was sliced, but not broken. The trap was too dull to sever her limb, but she'd been stuck for more than a day and her struggling had only made her injuries worse. She was just as hungry as Reve, but she had no intention to attack her rescuer.

Reve knelt beside her and struggled to ease the trap from the creature's leg. The metal teeth were dulled from years of disuse, but they were slick with the wolf's blood. Reve tensed. She could hear a deep, sorrowful melody echoing in the distance. This one was different from the one in the swamp. A new Song. The melody was urgent, beckoning, willing her to stop running, to quietly wait for death.

The tune was clouding Reve's brain, weighing her down, like the blissful warmth before freezing to death or drowning. She bit her lip until she tasted blood, focusing on the pain. She had to get away. The new Song would soon call the other to join it, a pack instead of a lone wolf. If she didn't run, it would find her.

She grappled harder with the trap, the hinge slowly easing back. The wolf yelped with a mix of pain and relief as the pressure on her leg eased. She withdrew her paw and stumbled back, limping on away from the trap with another snarl.

The Song was getting louder. She could see the fog of the nanobots seeping into the village, lingering for a moment around the tree where she'd rested. The wolf whimpered, not from pain, but terror. Reve regarded her with surprise. No animal feared the Songs. The Songs only whispered to them, showing them where to nest or bidding them to clear away from populated areas. A wolf would have no reason to fear the Songs or even give them more than a passing notice.

Reve shook her head and fled once more, speeding toward higher parts of the jungle. As long as she continued to travel higher, she was on the right path. To her surprise, the wolf sped after her, keeping pace even with a wounded paw.

"You won't escape the Songs by following me." Reve's voice was soft and raspy with disuse, barely a whisper over the heady, beckoning Song. "If you run, you'll be safe."

The wolf regarded her slowly, almost as if she understood Reve's words, but her pace never slowed. Reve felt a flash of guilt in her stomach but she shook her head, casting it aside. It wasn't her fault if the beast wouldn't leave her. It wouldn't be her fault if the wolf fell behind and was consumed.

The rhythmic tones of the Song from the Marsh drifted toward her, its rolling fog spilling over the ridge in front of her. The tune melded with the Song from the village, creating a dark, warning melody as they sped after her.

The wolf howled once to the sky and took off away from the encroaching Songs. Reve had no choice but to follow. Reve felt as if she had lifted from her body as her focus narrowed. She couldn't feel the pain or the weakness in her lean muscles. There was only the race, one foot landing in front of the other, and a vague awareness that she had to keep moving higher.

Thunder crashed once more, harmonizing with the Songs as

they intensified. The Choir wasn't trying to lull her to them anymore. The facade of peace was abandoned: The Songs hissed, boomed, a roared threat about what would happen if they overtook her. Their message was simple: Give up. Give in. You can't run. We control everything. We control everyone. You are Chaos. You will be destroyed.

Reve's foot caught in an upturned root and she pitched forward, hitting the ground hard. She cried out in pain as she threw out her hands to brace her fall and the middle finger on her right hand snapped. Her body was fragile, too weak from malnutrition and exhaustion to absorb a blow.

The wolf spun back around, racing to her side and grabbing Reve's sleeve in her mouth. She pulled, desperate for Reve to follow. Reve locked eyes with the beast and was shocked to see fear and concern. Why would she already see Reve as worth saving? There was more to the Forest Wolf than met the eye.

Reve stumbled back to her feet, holding her broken hand in the other. The wolf growled at the oncoming Songs, her lips curled back from her teeth, defending Reve until she ran again. The wolf kept pace with her as they reached a path up the mountain, the ground leveling into a wide trail.

Reve's bare feet on the path filled her mind with the importance the dirt road had held for generations of pilgrims. She could see them hiking through the jungle, thousands of boots and feet pounding a path to the monastery at the top of the mountain. She could hear their whispered prayers, melding in dozens of different languages and dialects over hundreds of years. The monastery was now in ruins. There were no more religions on Aggar, nothing but belief in the Choir. But their faith, traveling along the nonlinear pathways of time and space, warmed Reve, blocking out the taunts of the Choir and her own strained gasps for breath.

Halfway up the mountain, the dirt path turned to stone steps. Pebbles and chunks of the stairs crumbled as Reve and the wolf bounded forward, but they held. Reve grit her teeth. She was going the right way. Her dreams never lied. If she could just reach the monastery, the winds would push back the Songs. She would be safe.

The Songs bounded after her. She couldn't avoid it anymore. It had found her. Now it was just a race to safety or death.

Tendrils snaked away from the clouds like octopus tentacles, reaching out to her in an attempt to throw her off the path. Reve cried out as a slender strand of Song wrapped around her leg, leaving a crimson trail of blisters across her skin. The wolf whimpered deep in her throat as another tentacle scorched her back.

The stone steps gave way to another dirt path, but the slope of Reve's path was leveling out. The first signs of wind tousled Reve's hair, licking at her filthy skin and rags. Her breath caught in her throat. She couldn't help but close her eyes. The wind was like the first breath of air after nearly drowning. Like sunlight on her face after an icy winter. The jungle canopy was thinning, dark storm clouds replacing shadowy boughs and vines. She was almost there. Almost safe.

The Songs climbed faster, no longer a rippling bank of fog but a creature with thousands of spider legs. It scuttled after her, the Song rising in pitch and intensity as it closed in on her.

Up ahead, the monastery came into view. Its dark stone towers stood out like a charcoal sketch against the violent storm clouds. A flash of lightning revealed massive, crumbling ruins surrounded by leafy trees, their branches swaying in the wind.

A fresh burst of hope filled Reve with enough strength to sprint the final few steps to safety. The wind became more violent, whipping at her skin and blowing even her muddy hair into disarray. The Songs shattered in the gale, torn apart and cast to the farthest corners of the earth. The winds were the one force of nature the Choir couldn't control, the one thing that could drown out and crush their destructive, manipulative Songs.

The winds died down as Reve staggered to the ruins. The ancient council room, now open to the elements after its walls and ceiling had collapsed, was the eye of the mountain's storm. A spot of perfect stillness surrounded by an unbreakable barrier.

Reve collapsed to the ground. With no Songs hunting her, she lost all will and ability to move. She could barely breathe. Every ache, pain, laceration and burn came screaming back to life, but they were nothing compared to her exhaustion.

I could die here.

The thought caught Reve off guard. It wasn't tainted with bitterness or hopelessness. It was simple fact. This was sacred ground. Holy. Safe. She had crossed continents, her search for vengeance taking her from the dank basement that had been her childhood prison to the top of a mountain on the other side of the world. She had evaded the Choir for twenty-one years, since the day she was born and first blinked up at the world with her sky-blue eyes. This could be enough for her. Perhaps this was all she was ever meant to do.

The wolf limped to her and carefully laid at her side. Her warmth and softness, the trembling rise and fall of her breath and the pound of her heart was a balm to Reve, something to bring her back to reality. Bring her back to life.

Reve reached out to her, running her unbroken hand over her coat. She had never been allowed a pet. They were too big a risk. But if the wolf wanted to stay with her, Reve wouldn't turn her away. Perhaps there was someone who could travel with her after all.

Reve's eyes slowly closed and her hand went limp in the wolf's fur. Still, sleep wouldn't come in the holy halls of the Triad monastery. Reve felt herself rising out of her body, her consciousness shedding her physical form. She was no longer encumbered by her injuries and pain. She was a ghost, a spirit with blue eyes. An astral projection walking the sliver of dimension between reality and dreams.

She stood over her own body. She was contorted like a broken marionette, covered in mud, dried blood, and mottled with deep purple and black bruises. Reve stared down at herself with disinterest. It was like watching her weakness come to life as a paralyzed lump of clay and injury.

Reve had been unimpressed with her own body and its limitations since the first day as a young adolescent she had dreamed herself into the spirit realm. Her mind, her will, was so much stronger than her prison of physicality allowed her to be. She could see the hair on her arms rise from the cold as her body slept, but even standing nude in her spirit form, she couldn't feel temperature. She had an awareness that the stones under her feet were chilled, but it didn't affect her.

Her eyes narrowed to a fierce glare. *Weak. You're weak.*

She turned on her spiritual heel, leaving herself behind, and strolled through the ruins. Every stone whispered to her, telling the story of the building's construction and destruction. Images and memories infused in the mortar came to life, layered around her like a dozen malfunctioning holograms. Generations of the faithful praying. Priests and Priestesses performing rituals and blessings.

Reve could see the faithful around her, transparent memories of men, women and children. There were Terrans, wise Changlings, and people of Aggar. She even spotted a few with blue eyes. They were peasants and royals, merchants and nomads. The Triad faithful didn't seem to have any prejudices among the believers. It was strict Triad law that all were welcome. These were the first centers of true freedom, where everyone was treated equally, regardless of gender, race, or station. Their doctrine had soon spread. Now, even under the thrall of the Choir, all residents of Aggar were equal.

The monastery had been a place of hope and peace. The theology of the Triads had always been a religion of acceptance, promoting education, charity, and spiritual enlightenment. It had been the only belief system to take hold in every region of Aggar. Belief in the Triad, the three separate yet unified Goddesses representing the people of Aggar, Terrans, and Changlings, had only existed for 300 years, but it had changed the landscape of the world.

It had been the Choir's first target when they came to power. The Choir had whispered to their faithful, urging them to burn and destroy the Triad temples and holy halls. The Choir's Songs had murdered the priests and priestesses. The Triad faithful had been hunted down and destroyed, massacred in their churches. The only reason the memory of the Triad still existed was the Choir had programmed people to kill any remaining believers on sight.

Reve circled the main chapel and the ruins slowly grew. Transparent bricks and mortar filled the holes in the walls while the debris of the ceiling disappeared. The memory of the building before the Choir's assault rose around her until she stood in the monastery as it had been at its prime. She turned in slow circles, marveling at the intricately painted ceiling and the ruins etched into the walls. Silk curtains and blown-glass lanterns cast the chapel in crimson, gold, and burnt orange. Silver trays bearing crystals, precious stones, vials of water and sticks of incense marked places of sacrifice and ritual. Lifestones were embedded in the walls, the fiery gems decorating hieroglyphs and providing places of prayer.

Reve ran her fingers over a stained-glass window decorated with the image of the Triad: a woman of Aggar dressed in crimson silk like a nomad, a blue-eyed woman dressed in a robe of shadow, and a Changling woman dressed in leather light-armor, ready for battle. They held hands, separate beings but only complete together.

Reve heard a sharp tap echoing in the distance. It was the steady scuff of footsteps. She followed the sound past the chapel, through the sparse living chambers of the priests and priestesses, and into the most ancient part of the monastery: The library.

The walls rose three times as tall as Reve. The ceiling was a glass dome allowing a cascade of pale, blue moonlight into the chamber. Massive oak shelves were filled with every book Reve could imagine, the leather-bound tomes detailing all of Aggar's history.

Despite their pristine conditions, Reve could smell smoke and ash. The books had all been burned at the command of the Choir. Possessing books that were unapproved by the Choir was punishable by torture and imprisonment. They were a sign of attachment to the past, and attachment — devotion — to anything but the Choir and Aggar was a sign of treason.

Books were holy to Reve. A sacred symbol of revolution and

rebellion.

The footsteps continued at the end of the library. The sound slowly scraped against the cold stones as a middle-aged woman paced before a large window looking out over the jungle. She was small, just shorter than Reve, her graying hair curling around her shoulders. Two other women sat nearby: an elegant, nomadic woman with silver streaks in her hair wearing a silk robe and a lithe woman with slender, ropey muscles leaning back against her chair with her feet propped up on the table. The memory was at least six hundred years old, more than twice as old as the monastery that must have been renovated or built around the library centuries later.

Reve instantly recognized them. The Triad. They were far less magnificent than the stained glass and the hieroglyphs had led her to believe. Reve paused and watched them, frozen in their activities: the Changling pacing, the nomad looking out over the jungle, the Terran-descended mage leaning back in her chair.

They were mortals. Not Goddesses or even demi-gods. Just women. Lovers. Teachers. Reve spotted lifestones embedded in their arms.

Reve had assumed as much. She had never believed in Gods and Goddesses — the Choir proved beings could exist outside of time and space without being creators or worthy of worship – but she had always loved the legends of the Triad. It had been a sweet story as she'd grown from infant to woman in the dark of her parent's basement. Later, stories of the believers, the last few who had stood against the rise of the Choir, had given her a sense of camaraderie.

Reve wasn't a believer. She was an agent of Chaos, dedicated to destroying the Choir even if it cost the delicate balance and forced-peace their brainwashing nanobots had brought upon the world, but she had always felt like a descendant of the Triad rebels. Those who had held true to their beliefs even in the face of death. It was somehow both disappointing and empowering to find the Triad had once simply been mortal women.

The moons rose high in the sky, both in Reve's vision and in the physical plain. It was midnight. In the distance, Reve could hear singing. She turned away from the imprint of the Triad and returned to the chapel. Two rows of priestesses passed among the faithful, their voices rising and falling in a gentle song of rebirth and renewal. They touched the sick and the broken-hearted, carrying intricate thuribles leaking jasmine, rose, and pine-scented incense.

Reve sat on the ground beside her physical body, crossing her legs and watching the women move around her. Reve hated singing. It reminded her of the Choir Songs, the melodies that had chased her across Aggar since her childhood. But there was something about the priestesses' songs that were truly soothing. Healing. They lulled her out of the present not to death, like the Choir Songs, but to somewhere warm. Peaceful. Somewhere her broken body would heal and her mind could be at rest.

The imprint of a priestess with short, black hair knelt beside her and touched her shoulder. Reve fell back in shock. Memories weren't intelligent. They couldn't see her. They were just a reproduction of the past. Still, the woman barely recognized her presence before moving on, leaving even Reve's astral form tired and warm.

Reve relaxed, closing her eyes. The singing continued, now a story about a sandstorm late at night, the first meeting of the Triad. The song brought a blush to Reve's cheeks as it detailed the romance, coupling, and bonding of the goddesses, how they become one in the depths of the desert. Reve wondered how the Triad, the mortal women who would become goddesses in songs and stories, had truly first met.

Reve could feel herself transcending even her astral form. She was changing again, her powers growing. It was why she had dreamt of this place, been drawn across two countries to find the monastery. If she released herself to the powers of the holy halls, she would grow. Become more powerful. She would be one step closer to the woman she needed to be to defeat the Choir.

Sleep.

The command was out of time, the voice neither male nor female. The voice wasn't threatening. It was gentle, almost as if spoken by the singing priestesses around her. Reve cocked her head to the side in confusion, her eyes still closed. She was sleeping. Her physical body was completely unconscious.

Dream.

Reve's lips pressed into a tight line. She didn't dream, she only traveled. Her mind was never at rest. Resting made her vulnerable, allowed the Choir a chance to enter her mind.

You are safe. Let go.

Reve felt herself rising above herself, her thoughts and focus drifting. For a moment she was gripped with terror. She couldn't let this happen. She was never safe. Safety was a lie.

The wind brushed her cheeks and swept through her thick hair. The Songs would never reach her through the breeze. She flexed her hand and could feel the wolf's thick fur, her muscles taut, ready to defend Reve in case of an attack. If Reve was ever going to relinquish her control and rest, it should be here.

Stop fighting.

Reve obeyed. She laid back, allowing the darkness of true dreams to close in, dampening her incessant thoughts until she knew true stillness. True peace. Moments later, for the first time in her life, Reve slept.

Chapter Two

The port village of Ristol sat on the edge of the desert, surrounded by sparse brush, mountainous dunes of sand to the east and endless seas to the west. It wasn't on any map. It was too far from every trade route to attract visitors and no one had the urge to explore the vast deserts of Aggar anymore.

Consisting of nothing but a large inn, a series of docks, and a scattering of houses, Ristol was a popular stop for marauders and sailors. A way stop for pirates. The last free people on the planet.

Nix leaned forward on the railing of her ship, the *Niachero*, and looked over the tiny settlement. The wind blew through her short, chestnut-brown hair. The few streaks of silver in her wild mane sparkled in the sun. She drew a deep breath, the salty sea air filling her mouth and nose, leaving a bitter acidic taste across her tongue. It mingled with her perfume, a heady mixture of pine and fresh herbs. Nix wore the expensive scent solely because of the way it combined with the brine of the sea. It was intoxicating.

Her family had already headed for the inn, anxious for a few days on land. Nix didn't long for the wide-open spaces off the *Niachero*. Her ship was her home. Her center. But that was what made her an Amazon. A captain. Leader of her own sorormin.

A dozen other ships swayed and creaked in the harbor. She recognized all their colors and crests. Many of the families had been allies for generations. A raucous swell of music echoed from the inn. The scents of cooking meat and ale tainted the breeze. Nix grinned. Perhaps there was some good on land after all.

She felt a sharp nip on her calf and glared down at the winged-cat. Enyo swished her ebony tail angrily, her golden eyes flashing a glare.

"We won't be gone long," Nix chided her obstinate pet. "And you're welcome to leave the ship. No one will attack."

Enyo leapt up to the ship's railing and dug her claws into the wood possessively. She'd never leave her post with no one else on board. Sometimes Nix wondered if Enyo was more Amazon than she was.

"Fine, have it your way. But I'm going to have some fun."

Nix sauntered down the gangplank, her hips swaying with each step. The tail of the crimson velvet sash around her waist slapped against her thighs in time with the click of her boots on the wooden dock. Her tension built with every step. Land always had that affect on her and she never felt it until her feet hit solid ground.

On her ship, she was surrounded by her family. Her children. Her crew. She had to keep her wits about her. She didn't have a lover on-board. Land was different. The possibility of letting go, if only for a night or two, was like siren's song. It made her blood burn, her breath quick and sharp. It made her muscles ache like a taut rope ready to snap.

By the time she reached the front door of the inn, her cheeks were flushed rosy red. She popped her jaw, relieving the tension. She needed a stiff drink. A willing partner. A day when she wasn't a mother, a sister, a daughter, a captain.

She stepped into the common room. The old, rickety inn trembled with laughter and song. It was a rare treat to have so many sorormins in one place, even more rare that the meeting was peaceful. Nix scanned the crowd, locating every member of her family before she allowed herself to wander to the bar. She tapped the counter twice with her trimmed, glossy nails. The innkeeper, a tough, wiry old woman named Constance, instantly delivered two mugs of strong, spiced ale.

Constance had been running Ristol for as long as Nix could remember, risking the Choir's wrath and living a life of isolation to provide a safe haven for the nomadic sailors. They kept her in business, bringing her supplies and food so she and the handful of sailor's children who had traded their ships for a life on the land wouldn't have to come into contact with merchants under the spell of the Choir's songs. It wasn't safe to be associated with the sorormins and their Amazon captains. They knew how to navigate the wind, and the Choir hated anything that was outside of their reach.

Nix took both mugs and leaned back against the counter. She took a deep swig of one, the spices barely covering the acidic taste of home-brewed ale that stung the back of her throat. It was rough, but it was strong.

"Didn't think you'd make it. You don't respond to most of my invitations. You're earning a reputation as antisocial."

Nix grinned into her drink and handed Hestia n'Vulcanis the other. "I was outvoted. Kana can be very persuasive."

Hestia wrapped zir arm around Nix's waist, watching Kana exchange stories with other bards and artisans near the fire. Her violet silk dress rippled molten in the firelight. Her hair fell in cascades of mahogany across her cinnamon shoulders.

"Shame she married," Hestia mourned.

Nix took another sip from her mug. "Shame she's monogamous."

Hestia regarded Nix carefully, zir expression an effortless mix of masculine and feminine. Nix always thought if she were to paint a picture of the perfect unfettered, those who rejected the label of man or woman, she would paint Hestia.

Hestia spoke slowly. "Must be lonely for you, after she left."

Nix shrugged. "We were lovers. Friends. But we never would have bonded and that was important to her. Volt's a good man. He loves her. She loves him. Now he's family, and I never begrudge my family their happiness."

Hestia snorted. "Bonding is so final. So boring." Zi looked up at Nix, zir plump lips twitching as zir eyes devoured Nix from head to toe. "I'm just after one great night."

Nix turned to Hestia, pressing tighter against zir. Hestia was shorter by nearly a head, zir green eyes sparkling mischief. She smelled of gun powder. Hestia was the weapons tech on the Vulcanis and always smelled of fire.

Nix ran her fingers through Hestia's long, blonde hair. "You grew your hair out since I last saw you."

"Twice. It's been a long time. Again, you're getting antisocial."

Nix tsked, setting her drink aside to wrap both arms around the younger sailor. Hestia was soft and warm, a new scar along zir brow since their last tryst. Nix couldn't help but wonder what else might have changed. "I promise, Hestia, I can be very social."

Hestia pouted. "You ignore my messages."

"Let me apologize."

They kissed, Hestia's embrace waking in Nix an insatiable hunger. The instant she had Hestia's sweet mouth, zir hot, wet tongue, zir softness mixed with hard muscle, Nix lost all appetite for liquor.

"I got a room here for the night." Hestia sighed.

Nix smirked. "I'm an Amazon, Hestia. I have a ship."

Hestia snorted and eased zir hand under Nix's tight leather vest. "I don't think your children should hear what I intend to do with their mother."

"My children are grown. They don't need to be protected from the realities of my world."

Hestia glanced over Nix's shoulder the opposite corner of the room. "Really? Because it seems your boy needs protecting from the inn."

Nix spun around. Her youngest child, Agwe, stood in the corner, his hand near his mouth, his dark eyes wide as they flitted across the room. He wouldn't speak or call out — Agwe was too shy — but Nix recognized his expression. His silent, anxious terror. The inn was too much for him.

She abandoned Hestia, pushing through the crowd to reach her boy. Agwe wouldn't look at her as she approached, he was lost in his head.

"Agwe."

He finally acknowledged her, his small, slender form, just barely out of adolescence, trembling. "There's so many people. I didn't expect there to be so many people."

Nix took his hand. "You don't have to be here if you don't want to. Home is just outside. It's nice and quiet."

Agwe's lips twitched, fluctuating between a tense, straight line and a sad frown. "I think I'd like that."

Nix took his hand and led him out of the inn, away from the heat and the noise. Night had already descended, the stars like flakes of diamond embroidering the sky. The lights from the inn dimmed their majesty. It was a sad side-effect of land. But Nix had memorized their constellations and patterns as a child. Her memories made them blaze brighter.

Agwe started to breathe easier as they left the confines of the inn. He smiled up at the moon, the wind ruffling his feather-soft russet hair and warming his fair cheeks. Like Nix, he was made for the sea.

Nix squeezed his hand. "Are you tired, coramee?"

"Kana told me coramee means daughter. I'm your son. I chose it."

"All the old Amazon words were about women. They cared more about gender then."

"There should be new words for men and unfettered, too."

"None of the words matter anymore. We don't even know if they used to mean what we think they mean now. The races are mixed. The settlements scattered. There hasn't been a segregated colony of Amazons in nearly a thousand years. As far as I care, Amazon means captain, my sorormin is my family on my ship, and you, my dear, beautiful boy, are my coramee. My child. Man, woman, or unfettered, I love you."

Agwe smiled wider and they reached the docks.

"M'Sormee!" Sirena, Nix's daughter, raced from the inn, her long, auburn-tinted hair waving behind her like a pennant. "I saw you leave. Are you alright, Agwe?"

"I'm fine. There are too many people in there."

Sirena nodded in understanding. "I was going to check on my garden. Do you want to help me?"

Agwe looked from his mother to his sister. "You don't have to watch over me. I can take care of myself. I don't like crowds. That doesn't make me a child."

Sirena's sculpted almond eyes squinted into a teasing glare. "Don't be vain. I actually need your help. Your herbs and plants are almost ready for harvesting. I don't know how to test their potency like you can, and some of them only bloom at night."

Agwe shot her a knowing look, but he nodded and continued toward the ship. "You're no good with medicinal herbs, Sirena. You're too rough with them."

Nix caught her daughter's arm. "You've been asking to land in Ristol for a ten-day. I can stay with him."

Sirena snorted. "I saw you with Hestia. You're like a bowstring pulled too taut. Get rid of your tension before you snap. Agwe doesn't need a minder. He needs space and something useful to do to take his mind off his worries. I need a hand with my hydroponics and I'll return to the inn when he's settled. I can take care of this. He's my brother. Now stop being his mother. Go be a woman."

Sirena jogged away after Agwe, leaving Nix alone on the shore. Nix watched her children go, a fleeting memory of them as infants flashing in the back of her mind. They didn't need her anymore. The thought was always bitter-sweet.

Nix strode back to the inn and nearly tripped over a pack of children, running and tumbling around the tables. She grinned at Doris and Pan, Kana and Volt's young children, leading the group. They were true children of the *Niachero*. Cunning and strong. Natural leaders.

Nix glanced around the room and caught sight of Hestia's hair in the lantern light. Zi was straddling a fellow weapons technician in a secluded booth in the back of the room. Nix leaned back against the wall and sighed. She couldn't expect someone like Hestia to wait around. If there was anything zi had less tolerance for than bonding, it was children.

"Is everything alright with Agwe and Sirena?" Tlaloc questioned as zi leaned against the wall beside Nix. Nix's quartermaster nursed a tankard, zir shoulder-length coal black hair falling into zir hazel eyes. Zir skin was a pale olive, betraying zir worry.

"Fine. Agwe grew tired of the crowd and Sirena went with him."

Tlaloc's skin returned to a light tan, zir worry gone. "And what about you? You seem off, Nix."

"I feel off." Nix watched Hestia kissing zir partner. She took Tlaloc's mug without glancing at her friend and took a deep gulp.

"That will disappoint you," Tlaloc warned, a hint of a laugh in zir voice.

The bittersweet brew was mild and warm on her tongue. Nix winced and handed the tankard back to Tlaloc. "Tea? You're too sober, Tlaloc."

Tlaloc set zir tea on a nearby table and adjusted the collar of zir shirt. "Perhaps. But someone must retain a clear head. Our family isn't known for our abstinence. Someone has to smooth things out with the other families when Lyr swings from the rafters or Kana is caught cheating at dice."

"Or Nix brawls or Volt sets something on fire. You're all troublemakers." Briza waddled to a nearby table, sitting heavily on a stool. Her stark-white hair was falling loose from her knotted bun and her leathery, wrinkled skin glittered with a thin sheen of sweat. She must have been dancing. Nix knew right away she was halfway to drunk. Briza was only wild after a half dozen ales.

"Says the biggest troublemaker in the family," Nix accused with a gentle laugh.

Briza tugged at her shoes, kicking them off beneath the table and wiggling her toes. "I'm matriarch of n'Niachero. Of course I'm trouble."

"M'Sormee, if you're sore, Agwe and Sirena can help you to bed. They're already back on the ship," Nix offered.

Briza waved her daughter away, her wizened features twisting in a look of annoyance. "Just resting my bones for a spell. I wouldn't spend a night of such merriment in bed. I'm not dead yet."

Nix patted her mother's shoulder. "Of course not."

Hestia rose, leading zir newest conquest up the stairs to zir room. She caught Nix's eye on the way and Nix rose a single brow in question. Hestia shook zir head. Zir new partner wouldn't be willing to share. Hestia sent Nix a teasing kiss through the air, zir message clear: better luck next time.

Nix crossed her arms over her chest and searched the room for any other potential bedmates. She spotted life-long friends and allies, most of them bonded or like cousins in Nix's eyes.

"I think you have the right idea about romance," Nix commented, leaning against Tlaloc's firm shoulder.

Tlaloc wrapped a friendly arm around Nix's waist. "I didn't choose a lack of desire, soroe. It's in my blood. Sometimes I believe it would be easier if I had the same urges as everyone else."

Briza took a sip of Tlaloc's tea and grimaced, setting it aside as

Nix had. "You don't drink, you don't lust. What makes your life worth living, Tlaloc?"

"I am quartermaster of the *Niachero*. Caretaker of the family. That's enough for me." Tlaloc gazed wistfully out across the hall, zir eyes lingering on each member of the family, laughing and singing, playing and dancing.

Briza slipped her shoes back on and hopped to her feet. Her head didn't even reach Nix's shoulder. "Well, I'll drink and dance enough for the both of us." She pulled Nix down for a hug and their eyes met. Briza regarded her for a long moment, her gray eyes searching Nix as if peeking into her soul. Finally, her lips fell into a disappointed frown. "Just pick one of them. It's only one night. It will be forgotten before the next meeting."

Nix blushed as her mother read her frustrations. Briza had always been able to see into her mind. "They're our cousins, m'Sormee. Our allies. We have to be careful."

"Half of them already wish to share your bed. Don't waste your energy on fear. You'll regret it when you're older."

Briza kissed her forehead and glided away, rejoining the other dancers. Lyr instantly scooped her up, his mottled gray and gold cat ears twitching with excitement against his curling, honey-colored hair as he danced with Briza.

"I'm grateful she isn't so blunt when she's sober," Tlaloc commented. "I think I prefer her usual vague allusions to the future."

Nix patted Tlaloc's shoulder. "She's not going to stop drinking any time soon, and you remember what happened last time she drank to forgetfulness. You'll have to watch out for her."

Tlaloc let out a deep breath. "I always do." Tlaloc nudged her. "But you don't have to. Get a drink. I'll watch out for the family."

Nix stepped again to the bar. If she couldn't take a lover to bed, she could at least give herself over to the ale. She downed two mugs and her head started to feel lighter and her thoughts drifted. The revelry around her seemed to fade into the background, the voices and music blending as one. For a moment, Nix truly felt like an outsider, separate from the joy around her. She felt the full force of her loneliness, separate from her desire but feeding it from the darkest places in her heart. Nix drank another tankard and her dark thoughts disappeared in a buzzing, drunken haze.

"You might want to slow down, Nix, the night is just beginning," Constance warned as Nix ordered another drink.

"She's n'Niachero. She can hold her drink." Nix turned to the familiar voice as Constance slid another tankard in front of her. Nix's eyes darkened, narrowing to slits. Gale n'Zephyr slid into the stool beside her, sitting facing away from the bar. Gale fixed Nix with a knowing stare. "Isn't that right, Nix?"

Nix didn't touch her next drink. She never would have started drinking if she'd thought the *Zephyr* would come to the gathering.

Gale leaned back against the bar, her long, raven hair sliding like a waterfall over her bare shoulders and the swell of cleavage peeking from her half-open black silk blouse. Emerald earrings dangled in layers, caressing the slender curve of her neck. Nix's eyes caught on the lines of her beneath her skirt and vest. A sash woven from netting, shells, gems, and beads created a glittering path from her narrow waist, over the swell of her hips and crashing along the bare skin of her dark thighs.

Nix swallowed hard, her eyes dilated with desire. She could already imagine in vivid detail how Gale would feel under her hands, how she'd taste in her mouth. She could already hear her voice, ragged with pleasure. It's what Gale wanted. She knew the affect she had on the younger Amazon and she relished it with an almost sadistic joy.

The only thing that tempered Nix's desire for her fellow Amazon was her seething hatred.

"I didn't think you'd be here," Nix growled. "I know no one here would have invited the *Zephyr*."

Nix could feel the people around her pausing, glancing between the well-known rivals. She became acutely aware of her family and Gale's family, everyone standing back, but ready to help in a fight.

"Oh Nix. I couldn't stay away when I heard you were coming." Gale touched Nix's arm, sending a shiver through Nix's body. "You have to tell me how you got off that island. No one seems to know the story."

Nix pulled away from her. "You stranded me."

Gale grinned and leaned on her elbows back against the bar again. "I could have killed you. You shouldn't have fallen asleep in my bed."

"You might regret letting me live."

Gale chuckled. "I'm not afraid of you."

"You should be."

Gale leaned forward again, keeping her hands on the bar but her lips nearly grazing Nix's ear. "Tell me how you got off my island. It couldn't have taken you long. There was no food or fresh water. The *Niachero* was at least half a ten-day away and they didn't know where you were. How did you escape? I'm curious."

Nix drew a dagger from her boot and embedded it in the counter between Gale's fingers. The heavy thud silenced the party, even the musicians pausing mid-song. Gale didn't even blink. Everyone stared at the two Amazons, their eyes locked in a death glare, the tension between them palpable.

"You tried to kill me, Gale. It wasn't a game or an experiment." Nix hissed through clenched teeth.

Gale pulled Nix's dagger from the counter and weighed it in her hand. "That was very impolite to Constance."

Nix pulled a bag of gold off her belt and tossed it to the innkeeper without taking her eyes off Gale. "Shame I missed your hand."

Gale sheathed Nix's knife at her own waist. "You've always had horrible aim."

"That's my knife," Gale growled.

Gale drew the dagger and slid off the stool. She slowly fell to her knees and tucked the knife back into Nix's boot, resting her cheek on Nix's thigh. Nix trembled at the weight of Gale's head, her hands running along her calf.

"I know what you're doing." Despite the venom in her voice, Nix couldn't pull away.

Gale ran one hand along the inside of Nix's thigh. "And you love it. I can feel you shaking. See the ache in your eyes. I promise not to maroon you again."

"You're a liar."

"But you want to take the risk."

Gale's eyes were so smug, so sure. Nix pulled away from her and turned away. "Don't be so presumptuous."

Gale sprang to her feet, her seductive warmth vanishing. She leaned over Nix, not touching her, the heat of her closeness more rage than lust. "How about you stop acting so noble? I stranded you because you fired on my ship in the night. You didn't even run up your flags or challenge us to a fight. You just fired. You could have killed my entire family."

"You kidnapped Kana."

"You burned Boreas."

Nix spun on Gale, her lips curling back from her teeth in a feral snarl. "You stabbed Sirena."

"And I'd do it again, if it finally put you in your place."

Nix punched Gale in the face, the force and surprise of the blow sending her toppling back to the ground. Nix rose from her stool as Gale jumped back to her feet. Gale wiped a trickle of blood from her nose, leaving a scarlet smear across her upper lip. She stared down at the trail across her fingers and her green eyes burned with rage.

She charged Nix, her fists flying. Nix blocked the first blow, but doubled over as a second caught her in the stomach, knocking the air from her lungs.

The n'Zephyr and n'Niachero families leapt up to help their captains, but Nix and Gale held up their hands, keeping their crews at bay. Nix stood as the pain in her stomach faded. She couldn't suppress the laugh that escaped her lips. What a perfect way to release her tension.

Nix and Gale launched themselves at each other, punching and kicking with deadly precision. Nix grazed Gale's jaw as she dodged and Gale swiped at her chest, leaving long, shallow cuts where her nails bit at Nix's skin. Gale smirked at her handiwork and Nix caught her by the throat, slamming her down onto a nearby table. The guests instantly scattered, knocking over their drinks. A pool of ale soaked Gale's sleeves and wet her hair.

Gale fought against Nix's grip, but Nix climbed atop the table, straddling her and squeezing her neck hard enough to choke her without completely cutting off her air. Nix blushed with the heat of battle and desire. Gale struggled beneath her and grabbed at her vest, her skin steadily growing darker with the same mix of emotions.

Gale laughed. "I knew you couldn't keep your hands off me."

A flood of memories and emotions returned. Nearly a decade of battle, kidnappings, injuries, sabotages and betrayal. Nix remembered a night of passion and waking alone on a sandy spit of land as Gale's ship sailed away into the night. She had never been so afraid of dying alone, of leaving her family without answers or a captain. After everything they'd done to each other, Gale had never before made her feel vulnerable. Afraid. It was unforgivable.

Nix squeezed harder, choking Gale for real, and Gale gasped in surprise, clawing at Nix's hands. Nix's words were acid. "This isn't a game anymore."

Gale hurled herself to the side, throwing Nix away from her and sending them both crashing to the floor. Nix released her throat in her surprise and Gale pinned her. Gale breathed in sharp gasps, a line of sweat rolling down her neck, her skirt riding high on her thighs. "Yield."

Nix looked up into her burning green eyes and bared her teeth, rebelling against the simple truth fighting through her rage and desire: in that moment, she felt alive. The numbness, the tension, the frustration was gone, replaced with an intense focus. With the thrill of fighting Gale, her only true opponent. Her match. The only person she knew could kill her and that thought excited her more than any heated gaze or familiar touch from a lover. For better or for worse, Gale was her addiction.

Nix bucked, tossing Gale. She rolled, grabbed a chair, and threw it. Gale scrambled away, narrowly dodging the chair as it crashed to the floor, one of the legs shattering, the other catching the netting of Gale's sash. As she pulled away, the delicate accessory tore, sending beads and shells rolling across the floor.

They both stood and gave in to their wilds. Their words turned to feral growls and screams as they fought, all formal training disappearing in their primal rage. Gale elbowed Nix in the stomach and Nix bit her shoulder hard enough to draw blood. Gale clawed at her face and Nix pulled her away by her hair.

They slammed into the bar again and Constance's sons grabbed them, pulling them apart. They fought against their captors, but Constance's shrill, no-nonsense voice broke through their rage. "Enough!"

Nix and Gale paused. Nix's heart sped in her chest. She was too full of adrenaline to feel her injuries, but she could already see bruises blossoming across Gale's skin and she doubted she was any better.

Constance looked from one Amazon to the other slowly and deliberately. "This is a place of peace. I'll not have you destroy everything I've built because of a grudge. If you want to kill each other, take to the sea. But while you are in my inn, you will be civil."

Nix and Gale pulled roughly away from Constance's sons, but they didn't attack again. Nix adjusted her collar and Gale smoothed her skirt before tossing her tangled hair over her shoulder.

"I'll help you make repairs, Constance."

Nix looked over her shoulder at Volt as he took a step forward, his bright blonde hair rustling across his brow as he sheathed his sword, his stocky muscles relaxing as the fight ended.

"No, Volturnus. No n'Niachero. No n'Zephyr. We can take care of ourselves," Constance huffed.

Nix winced. Constance was known for carrying grudges. It would take a long time and many gifts before any of her family would feel welcome in Ristol again.

The tension still hung heavy in the air, all the families anxious about how to proceed. Nix and Gale still eyed each other like vipers ready to strike. They both knew the instant they left the inn, they'd be coming for each other. Whether on land or sea, they weren't finished. They were never finished.

"A competition." Everyone turned to Briza as she stepped forward, the drunken joy in her eyes gone. "If I remember correctly, Cassandre n'Celestia was going to propose one."

Cassandre, the matriarch of the *Celestia*, took a hesitant step forward. "Yes. I thought it would be fun. A race to the Karatan peninsula. We could meet up again in the jungle caves."

Briza eyed her daughter, fierce warning in her eyes. "A fine substitution for burning down Ristol, don't you think?"

Nix turned to Gale, her chin raised in defiance. "Sounds good to me."

Gale spat a laugh. "You want to challenge the *Zephyr* to a race? There's no faster ship."

"Then you have nothing to worry about," Nix challenged. "Unless you're afraid?"

Gale studied her, clenching her jaw in determination. She raised one hand and snapped. Her family instantly joined her. "I'm not afraid of anything." As she and her family passed, Gale touched Nix's arm with one finger. "This isn't over."

Nix grabbed her finger and wrenched her hand back. "Touch me again, and I'll break your hand."

Gale pulled away with a feral smile. "You're welcome to try."

They left. Nix leaned back against the wall, seething. Briza waved exasperatedly at the musicians and they began to play again. The party slowly returned to normal, members of the other crews cleaning the mess of the fight.

Briza took Nix's hand and led her out of the inn toward the desert. "That was quite a show."

"I didn't mean for it to get so out of hand," Nix admitted.

"She gets under your skin in more ways than one." Nix didn't respond. She didn't have to. Briza stared out at the mountains of sand in the distance, the wind pulling at her long silver braid and rustling the dress against her small, round body. "You have so much turmoil inside you."

Nix shook her head. "It's just Gale."

"It's not. Ever since Agwe stopped needing you like he did as a child, you've gotten more restless. You brawl. You drink. You have more lovers scattered across the world now than you did in your youth. And all would be well and good with me if I didn't see the unhappiness in your eyes. I see you questioning your decisions. Your desires. You have to find your center, or at best you'll tear yourself apart."

Nix crossed her arms. "Your sight is slipping, m'Sormee."

"It's not and you know it. What do you want, Nix? What are you looking for? Do you want another child? Someone to care for? There are thousands of orphans across Aggar we could take in. If you're looking for a bondmate, I'm sure a few of your trysts would be open to exploring something more —"

"M'Sormee," Nix interrupted. "Right now all I want to do is beat Nix to Karatan. That's it. I'm not as complex as you like to believe."

Briza snorted and rounded on Nix, her hands on her hips. She looked her daughter over, reading her heart and perhaps her future. Finally, she nodded. "Fine. If you want to run away, we won't leave you behind. But one day your fate and weaknesses will catch up with you."

Nix shrugged. "I'll meet it when it does. Now help me get everyone together. Gale is casting off. We won't be far behind."

Chapter Three

Reve opened her eyes. The sky spiraled above her, glowing a mix of black, dark purple, and deep blue. Thunder ripped through the clouds, striking around the mountain. Reve knew she was dreaming. She couldn't feel the ground beneath her. She only noticed smells and sensations as she thought of them. Her mind wandered, the clouds forming various shapes in time with her thoughts. For some reason, she could taste the sea.

She pulled herself to her feet and looked around the monastery. The stone walls were translucent like ice. All of her visions from when she'd astral projected were layered together. The designs over the windows were a clash of chaos and the chapel was full of nearly a hundred people, constantly overlapping and passing through each other.

Soft, warm fur brushed against her legs and she glanced down at the wolf. The wolf sat, her golden eyes sparkling with understanding. Reve crouched down before her and scratched the top of her head.

"Why am I dreaming of you?" Reve's voice echoed, reverberating off the monastery walls.

The wolf shook her head and Reve heard her thoughts as if they were her own. She wasn't dreaming of the wolf. The wolf – Hecate – could walk with her in her dreams.

Reve stood again, her head cocked to the side as she regarded Hecate. "I suppose it doesn't matter how you're here. It wouldn't change anything. You can follow me if you want."

Hecate padded deeper into the ruins, her message clear: *I'm not following you. I already know where I'm going. Keep up.*

Reve slowly followed, unsure if she trusted the animal even in her sleep. The landscape shifted and changed with every step. The imprints of the past faded until only the transparent outlines of the ruins remained. The rippling colors in the sky consumed everything else until even the stone floor and the jungle surrounding the mountain were a swirling vortex of color and lightning. Hecate broke into a run glancing over her shoulder once, urging Reve on.

The confines of the ruins no longer mattered as Reve sprinted after Hecate. She didn't get tired or sore. She didn't breathe unless she thought about it. She had little awareness of her physical body at all. The landscape didn't change, even the swirling of the clouds had a rhythm and pattern to it. The only sound was the whistling of the wind, the sound playing on a loop.

She didn't know how long she ran. She felt suspended in a single state, nothing changing or moving. Then she heard it, rising above the gust of wind. A mournful tune, reverberating a swelling as if in a massive cavern. An electric chill raced beneath Reve's skin. It was a Song.

Reve had heard that the Choir could infiltrate the mind in dreams, that they existed in the dreamspace between dimensions. Was she dreaming of the Songs that had chased her for decades, or was it real? Had she somehow shifted into the Choir's realm, leaving behind the safety of Karatan's winds? Was there a way out of the limbo she'd found herself in?

Hecate arched her neck and howled and Reve ran, catching up with Hecate and keeping stride with her as they fled from the Song. The Song was getting louder, blocking out all other sound. Reve glanced over her shoulder. A tidal wave of Song swept toward her, rising impossibly high and wide. Reve ran faster, expecting it to crash around her at any moment, drowning her and stealing her mind for the Choir.

"Where do we go?" she screamed to Hecate. Hecate didn't answer.

Reve steeled herself. Then there was only one thing she could do.

Reve's mind went blank of everything but the mechanics of running. It was no longer strange that she didn't feel her body or the landscape was a vortex of storm clouds. Awake or asleep, Reve understood running. She refused to let the Choir have her without a fight. She would run forever just to spite them.

As she lost the last traces of herself, giving up any hope of a destination, she spotted a massive wall of ice in the distance, large enough to keep the Songs at bay. The translucent pennants along the wall twisted and danced in the wind. Wind meant safety.

Reve ran faster, reaching the wall faster than she expected it. It rose higher than she could see, splitting the swirl of clouds. Hecate raced to a small, wooden door only tall enough for Reve to crawl through, and grabbed the latch in her jaws. She growled as she opened the door and Reve dove, scrambling on her elbows and knees through the tight stone corridor.

Hecate followed, shuffling through the opening on her belly, the door closing hard behind her. Reve covered her head as the Song crashed against the wall, creating a violent earthquake that bounced Reve against the narrow tunnel. She gasped for breath, trying not to imagine the entire wall caving in on her, burying her in a pile of rubble and Song.

As the world around her grew still once more and the Song was silenced, Reve's panic slowly faded. She closed her eyes, searching with her mind for any remnants of the Song or the Choir, but she couldn't sense anything.

Her logical mind pushed away the last of her fear and she propped herself up on her elbows, continuing her crawl toward the distant light on the other side of the wall. She reached the edge of the tunnel and grabbed for the exit, pulling herself through the corridor.

It was like being reborn. The gales of wind and Song had been completely silenced, the wild colors and transparent walls had disappeared, replaced with the ancient oak walls of a library.

Reve stood, stretching her arms and legs as Hecate exited behind her. Reve's senses returned as if she was projecting, not dreaming. She could smell the ancient paper of the books mingling with freshly-polished wood. Her feet sank into the plush red and gold carpets. The flicker of candles and lanterns was the only sound.

Reve slowly walked around the room. It was only a handful of paces across. The wood walls and bookshelves were smooth, polished to a shine. There wasn't a spec of dust to be found. Reve picked up one of the books. The leather binding was supple with age, but the pages glowed a faint red and were cold and metallic to the touch. It smelled faintly of electricity and sulfur. Reve wondered why the rest of the room smelled like paper.

Hecate sniffed around the floor, her ears swiveling sharply, alert, but she didn't seem scared. Bolstered by Hecate's ease, Reve opened one of the books. The light glowed brighter and Reve was plunged into a torrent of sensation. She could feel flames at her back, smoke in her lungs. She heard fire crackling and spitting, around her, consuming thatch and wood. She could taste the flames on her tongue and her eyes stung as if she were trying to see through the flames. Her lungs were heavy, her mind spinning in a panic that was so foreign to Reve she knew the feelings weren't her own. She was dying. The thought filled her body and mind with helpless dread.

She snapped the book shut and everything disappeared. Her hands trembled as she slid the book back on the shelf and took a step back. For a second, she had lost all control of her mind and her body, consumed by something else. Reve had never felt so helpless. She didn't intend to repeat the experience.

Hecate nuzzled her leg and Reve scratched her back.

"I'm fine," she assured her.

It's an archive of memories.

Hecate's presence in her mind, made up of thoughts and impressions that sorted themselves into words, was becoming a familiar sensation. Reve couldn't deny the suggestion. She'd felt like she'd been thrown into someone else's mind. She wondered if all the memories were as intense.

She picked up another book, careful not to open it. The pages were deep violet and smelled of fresh bread. A third book was deep blue and smelled of salt.

Reve shook her head. "I don't like this."

Hecate padded to the tall, double doors on the far end of the room. *You came here for a reason.*

Reve grabbed the gold door handles and shook her head. "If it's in another book, I might as well wake up now."

She opened the doors and gasped. The library was massive, opening into a room that went on in every direction too far for Reve to see. She stepped out from under the wooden overhang over the door and looked up to see hundreds of stories or balconies and rooms, all filled with rows upon rows of bookshelves.

"What is this place?" Reve whispered, her voice echoing out into the ether.

Hecate refused to repeat herself and only wandered out into the stacks. Reve followed her, scanning the stacks for any sign of order. Every now and then she spotted a brass plate on the bookshelf, but she couldn't read the label. She blushed lightly and glanced away. She'd only ever learned the very basics of reading from her mother before she'd been separated from her parents. She couldn't even tell if the words on the labels were from Aggar.

Every now and then Reve would pick up a book and every time the pages glowed a different color and emitted a unique scent. When she put the book back on the shelf, however, the scent disappeared.

Reve had never been to a working library before and had no idea what one would smell like. There were very few left, all sanctioned by the Choir and run by Choir delegates. There had been one near her parent's house, however, and her mother would regularly sneak her books with pictures in them or read to her in the night. Reve wondered if the smell in the library was drawn from her memory of pouring through those old books or if this was really what a library smelled like.

"What am I supposed to be looking for?" Reve asked aloud. Hecate stared back at her.

It's your dream.

"If it was my dream, I wouldn't be surrounded by books. I don't know anything about words."

You obviously know more about them than you think.

Reve let out a tense breath and paused. If it was really her dream and it had been shaped from her experiences and thoughts to reveal some kind of truth, then there was only one way she knew to explore such a vast space.

She sat on the ground, her back to one of the massive bookshelves. Hecate jogged back to her, sniffing at her curiously. Reve closed her eyes and imagined the library, letting her mind wander. Slowly, the spaces she couldn't see started to fill into her mental picture, her abilities mapping out the space around her. The library was bigger than she'd expected, constantly expanding so she could never map out the entire thing.

She opened her eyes and stood, an overwhelming urge driving her forward. She knew where she was supposed to go, just like she'd known how to travel to Karatan. Hecate ran after her, but Reve barely noticed. Her concentration was on the path laid out like a golden trail in her mind.

She reached the end of one of the rows of books and found a spiraling staircase that led to the second story. She jogged up the steps, taking them two at a time until she reached the second floor. The library seemed to fade and blur as she ran, the dream rearranging itself around her.

Just ahead she spotted a door flicker into existence. It was older than the rest of the building, made of heavy, rough wood and brass hinges. Reve's heart pounded the closer she came to the door, her stomach turning with a mixture of excitement and fear. Reve carefully reached for the brass latch, the handle cold in her hands. Hecate let out a soft whimper, pressing her pointed nose into Reve's knee.

"It's alright," Reve whispered, touching Hecate's head. "I have to do this."

She opened the door and they were instantly consumed by a bright, white light.

Reve gasped and paused as the light receded. She was standing in a narrow tunnel. The stone walls were beveled, carved from a single piece of rock. She was underground. There were no torches or lanterns to light the way, but somehow she could still see where she was going.

A sharp, cold breeze swept through the corridor, setting her hair on end. She wasn't in the jungle anymore. She had only felt such a icy chill in the north. She hugged her arms to her chest and crept forward. Her boots didn't make a sound as she moved. She blended into the shadows, nothing but a pair of blue eyes in the darkness.

Hecate stayed a handful of paces behind her, sniffing at the air. Her padded feet tapped against the stones, but the sound didn't seem to draw any attention. Reve's heart tightened in her chest. Were they buried alive?

This is a dream.

Hecate's reminder rang in her thoughts. She slowly nodded and forced herself to relax. She wasn't really buried. She was sleeping in the ruins of the Triad Monastery in Karatan. No matter what she saw or found in these caverns, she was safe.

Reve could see a dim light in the distance, dancing across the walls like the flicker of a candle. Reve raced forward and the tunnel opened into a small cavern. The pocket of stone had been furnished like a sparse bedroom; a large bed, a bedside table, and three pine wardrobes were the only furniture. A woven blanket blocked the entrance to another tunnel and as Reve looked over her shoulder, she realized the tunnel she had entered through had disappeared.

Dozens of candles mounted on copper candlesticks lined every natural shelf and ledge. The flames cast long shadows across the walls, bathing the room in a soft golden glow.

Reve stood in the center of the room, bathed in candlelight. The room was warm, filled with floral and savory spiced scents she had only ever smelled in the desert. She silently sat on the edge of the bed, her fingers sinking into the silken fur blankets. Hecate laid at her feet, letting out a deep yawn.

Reve drew a deep breath, filling her lungs with the desert perfume in the air. She couldn't remember ever feeling so at peace.

She could hear the tap of boots echoing down the hall, but she felt no need to run or hide. A pale, slender hand pushed the curtain aside and three women stepped into the room.

They hesitated as they spotted Reve. Two of the women reached for knives, but the third put a hand on each of their shoulders. The chain of bells around her dark ankle jingled as she took a step toward Reve.

"Of course I'd dream of you," Reve muttered to herself. "You're the Triad."

The woman knelt in front of Reve, the deep green silk of her nomadic dress seemed to ripple in the candle light. She was younger than she'd been in the vision Reve had seen in the monastery library. Her hair was a wave of ebony. Gold bangle bracelets clinked against her arms, brushing the lifestones embedded in each of her wrists.

She smelled like the finest teas in the desert, a heady mixture of spices and herbs that made Reve lightheaded with pleasure.

"Who are you? Are you hurt? Do you need help?"

"Jacquin, be careful," the woman with blue eyes warned, her sword still raised. "She has the abilities of a shadow."

"Adrian." Jacquin's voice was soft but firm. "She's not really here."

"What do you mean?" the third, the smallest of the three, questioned. Her glass dagger looked molten in the dim light. Her eyes were sharp, searching. Reve recognized the Changling blood in her.

Jacquin glanced over her shoulder at her lovers. "She's a dream walker, Rox. She's asleep." She turned back to Reve. "Are you trying to reach the school? Are you in danger? Where are you? We can come to you."

Reve slowly shook her head. "This isn't real."

Jacquin smiled slowly. "It is. You're gifted with the sight. You've traveled out of your body to reach us."

"No. I've moved beyond projecting. I fell asleep while projecting."

Jacquin raised a sculpted eyebrow at Reve's announcement. She hadn't expected Reve to know about projecting. "Who are you?"

Reve hesitated. Hecate growled and nipped at her ankle. *Don't be stubborn.*

Reve jumped in surprise, moving her legs away from the wolf. The Triad watched her cautiously, Adrian and Rox holding tighter to their weapons. Reve realized they didn't see Hecate.

"My name is Reve.

"Where are you?" Adrian questioned.

"I'm sleeping on a mountain in Karatan, in the ruins of your monastery."

"She's speaking nonsense," Rox growled.

Adrian sheathed her sword, her fur cloak swaying with the motion. "No. She's using the sight. She's speaking out of time."

Reve looked between the three women, searching their eyes and energies. They were inseparably connected, communicating without words or even glances. Reve knew they were mortal women, but she could suddenly understand how they would come to be deified.

Jacquin touched her hand and they shared a glance of surprise when they made physical contact. "You said you were in our monastery. I don't understand."

"They made you gods. I don't know when. You've been dead for centuries, but the ruins of your temples and libraries are still there. I must be dreaming of you because I'm on your land."

Rox's brow furrowed. "Gods?"

"It makes sense. We're the only safe space for seers, Blue Sights, shadows, and changlings. More people are coming to the mountains every day. People are scared of us. If our institutions last for long, we're destined to be deified or demonized," Adrian stated matter-of-factly. "You've dreamed signs of it, Jacquin. I know you have."

Jacquin's lips pressed into a tight line and she nodded slowly. "I've dreamed a lot of things. That doesn't mean they'll come true."

Rox shook her head and sheathed her knife. "Dreaming out of time and seeing the future. Every day I'm grateful I have no gifts for seeing the future."

Jacquin smiled and reached back, squeezing Rox's hand without taking her eyes off Reve. "You must be very powerful to travel so far."

"It's a rare kind of sight. Maybe related to her shadow abilities," Adrian agreed. "Can you see the future, Reve?"

Reve shook her head. "What do you mean by sight?"

"You're a Blue Sight. Like me." Adrian indicated her eyes. "Do they call it something else in your time?"

Reve regarded them questioningly. Were they trying to trick her? Was there something cultural she didn't understand? "I've never heard of a Blue Sight. The Choir kills everyone with blue eyes."

A heavy silence settled over the room. The Triad tensed and Jacquin slowly closed her eyes in understanding. "I was afraid of this."

"What happens in the future?" Rox gasped.

"People have been targeting Blue Sights since they developed their powers," Adrian pointed out. "Obviously someone has succeeded."

"But she's never even heard of them. Blue-sights always come back, what could have eradicated them so permanently a Blue Sight won't even know her own history? It can't be nanobots again, because she's still alive." Rox turned to Reve. "Where did you grow up? Were you sheltered? Do you just not know about others with your abilities?"

Reve paled, a flood of memories from her childhood returning.

"Rox," Jacquin interrupted gently before Reve could answer. "You're being too brusque."

Rox paused. "I'm sorry."

"Jacquin, she might have been brought here to learn from us. That much power is dangerous unchecked. She needs boundaries and coping skills," Adrian suggested.

Jacquin studied Reve's eyes. Reve felt her shoulders rounding forward as she subconsciously backed away from the seer's gaze. She didn't want anyone in her mind. "She won't be here for that long."

Rox leaned back against the wall, her arms over her chest. "Then why is she here?"

"Only Reve can answer that," Adrian announced.

Jacquin sat on the bed next to Reve, still holding her hand. "What led you here? What were you thinking about before you fell asleep?"

"I've been traveling to your monastery for a tenmoon. I knew I was supposed to learn something that could help me fight the Choir. I didn't know it would take me to you."

Adrian took a step forward, studying Reve with narrow eyes. "Who are the Choir?"

Reve tried to find the words to describe the Choir and everything they'd done to Aggar. She looked between them and shook her head. Their world was so different. Was there anything she could say that would even make sense?

"Adrian, she said it's been six hundred years. We could talk for days and still not understand the position she's in," Rox pointed out as if reading Reve's mind.

"We could commune with her." Adrian and Rox stared at Jacquin in surprise. "She needs something from us and we need to better understand her position."

"We haven't communed with a stranger since the Changling raids," Rox argued. "I remember what that did to you and Adrian."

"That was years ago, Rox. We're all more powerful -- more in sync -- then we were then."

"That doesn't mean it will be any easier."

"What's the point of having a skill if we never use it," Jacquin argued.

"What do you want to do?" Reve questioned suspiciously, interrupting their argument.

Rox and Jacquin exchanged silent glances, trading concerns, but Adrian took a step forward, claiming Reve's full attention with her blue gaze. "Do you know why we're a triad, Reve? Why we were drawn to each other?"

Reve shook her head. "I never heard the story of your origin. The myths always speak of you as a unit, three parts of a whole."

"In many ways we are. We've each been blessed with various, complementary skills. When we're together, we have the ability to psychically and emotionally connect with any sentient being in Aggar. We used the ability to create peace between Aggar and the changlings. Now Jacquin wants us to use it to share your mind. In return, you'll be able to see into ours. It's the fastest way for us to understand each other."

Reve tensed. "You'll be in my mind?"

"Yes." Adrian answered bluntly.

Reve glanced down at Hecate, nearly ready to run. Only the Choir would want to access her mind in a dream. How did she know the Triad were really who they claimed to be? Hecate met her eyes.

Nothing worth knowing comes without risk.

Reve looked back up at the Triad. She couldn't deny that she wanted to trust them. Her instincts said they had crucial information she needed to have. She clenched her jaw. If they were the Choir in disguise, they would steal her mind. If they weren't and she refused to commune with them, the Choir would catch her eventually. She didn't have a choice.

"Fine." The word slipped past Reve's lips, hanging heavily in the air.

Adrian nodded without looking at her partners. "Sit with us on the floor."

Jacquin and Adrian sat on the floor and held hands. Rox joined them more hesitantly, sharing Reve's apprehension, but she slid to the ground next to Adrian and took her hand.

Jacquin reached out to Reve, a warm, gentle wave of calm flooding over Reve as their eyes met. She wondered if it was destiny confirming her decision or Jacquin's powers. "We won't hurt you, Reve. You'll have as much access into our minds as we will to yours. Our bond will be forged in mutual trust."

Reve cautiously joined them, Jacquin taking her right hand and Rox taking her left. "What am I supposed to do?"

"Nothing. Just relax. Keep yourself open," Jacquin instructed as she closed her eyes. The Triad relaxed, suddenly breathing as one, falling perfectly in sync with each other.

Reve felt a gentle tingle in each palm, but whatever magic they were invoking didn't seem to reach her. Rox and Jacquin closed their eyes, but as Reve looked to Adrian, she found the Blue Sight watching her. They met eyes and Jacquin gasped, instantly overcome.

She felt like she'd opened a book in the dream archive, her mind and personality completely consumed. She couldn't feel Jacquin or Rox. She had been cast adrift in Adrian's blue gaze.

A flood of emotions, memories, and sensations flooded Reve's mind. She was filled with centuries of history of the Blue Sights, powerful men and woman born with empath and seer abilities tying them deeply Aggar. Throughout history, they had shaped the destiny of Aggar and her people, bonding with the first Amazons, aiding and battling Terrans throughout multiple invasions, and acting as oracles and diplomats between various races and kingdoms.

Reve started to gain control over the endless flow of information. She latched onto every bit of information about herself she could. She studied shadows, the Blue Sights that shared her ability to meld with darkness and disappear. She saw eras ruled by Blue Sights and times of genocide. She saw Adrian's past. She had been cast out and hunted for her abilities just like Reve, but Adrian had known about her heritage. She knew she wasn't alone.

Reve was overwhelmed. She wasn't cursed or damaged. She wasn't wrong. She was a true child of Aggar, powerful and rare. She was gifted. She was strong. She was a shadow. She was a Blue Sight.

It made sense that the Choir would want her people destroyed. The Blue Sights were Aggar's first line of defense, created by the planet herself. The Choir had eradicated them. They'd wiped the legacy of the Blue Sights out of history and species memory. Now they wanted to destroy her, too.

Her connection with the Triad shattered. Jacquin and Adrian released her hands as if they'd been burned.

"Reve," Jacquin whispered, her voice heavy with sympathy and pain.

Adrian pulled her into a tight embrace. Reve clung to her just as tightly, still bound to her. She could read Adrian's mind, the Blue Sight lost in Reve's earliest memories of being locked in the basement, being chased by the Songs.

"I'm so sorry," Adrian wept. "I'm so sorry."

"They killed everyone. Our schools. Our seers and Blue Sights. Everyone." Rox's voice was strained. "Everything we're doing is for naught."

"No." Jacquin took Rox's hand. "The future needs us now more than ever."

"Everyone who believes in our work will die. They'll be hunted down."

Jacquin kissed her, desperate to calm her distraught bondmate. "Because they believe in freedom. Because we helped them."

"You have to kill them," Adrian hissed, holding tighter to Reve. "You're a hub. A Blue Sight born to change the world. You have to set Aggar free."

Reve felt the weight of her words, but it was nothing compared to the weight she put on herself. She wasn't just fighting for herself anymore. She was fighting for every Blue Sight who had been suppressed and killed so the Choir could keep Aggar under their thumb.

"I will," Reve promised. "I'll kill them all."

As the words slipped past her lips, Reve started to feel lightheaded. The stones beneath her started to grow paler and more translucent. She was waking up.

Rox took Reve's arm. "If you can find your way back to us, we'll do anything we can to help you."

"You need to travel to the coast." Jacquin's voice grew softer and distorted. Reve could see through her sight that Jacquin was caught in a seer's vision. "The next step of your journey lies on the coast."

Darkness closed in around Reve, swallowing the landscape until only the barest presence of the Triad remained.

"Kill them." Adrian's plea repeated, hanging heavily in the air.

"I will. I'll kill them all."

Chapter Four

ix bounded down the stairs into the bowels of *Niachero*. The heat from Volt's workshop slapped her in the face, a stark contrast to the frigid ocean air. The smell of brine and wood was overwhelmed by metal and fuel. The air conditioning system he'd built to use sea water to maintain the temperature in the room provided little relief. The generators buzzed and hummed in time with the whir of Volt's tools in mechanical harmony.

Nix climbed over a crate of spare parts and crept under the cords that connected to the kitchen and Sirena's hydroponic garden a floor above. The *Niachero*'s hold had drastically changed since she took control of her. She'd been hesitant to humor Volt's ideas when Kana first brought him aboard, but there had been method to his madness. His inventions had not only made life at sea safer and easier, but they had increased the *Niachero*'s speed and ballast. Still, Nix sometimes felt like there was a forge in the heart of her ship.

"How's it going?"

Volt slid out from beneath the old starship engine he'd repurposed into a thruster. His blonde mane was wild around his face, a smear of oil across his cheek. He lifted his goggles, an ecstatic smile on his face.

"Wait."

He leapt to his feet and threw two switches. The thruster rumbled to life and the ship bucked once before speeding forward. Nix could hear the roar of white water just outside the hull of the ship and the clatter of pots and pans being unsettled in the kitchen.

Nix cheered and pulled her friend into a tight hug. "You did it!"

"We'll catch up with Gale in a day. She'll be eating our waves by tomorrow night."

Nix shook her head. "Someone's going to try to steal you away from us someday."

Volt fixed his goggles back over his hazel eyes. "You have my bondmate and my children, Nix. I couldn't leave even if I wanted to."

Nix clasped his arm in friendship. "What do you want for dinner? I'll have Sirena make something special to celebrate."

"Kana has been lusting over the fresh fruit you picked up in Tsara. Make something with that."

"And some of Sirena's mead?"

Volt grinned. "You know me too well."

"We'll have a drink to celebrate. You'll be done by dusk?"

"A bit before. The thrusters are sounding smooth. I just want to run a few safety checks."

"Sounds good. Don't blow up my ship!"

Volt knelt on the floor, digging through his toolbox. "Never, n'Athena."

Nix smirked. "Kana would kill you for saying that."

Volt pulled out a diagnostic reader. "Historical accuracy be damned. The term fits you."

Nix patted his shoulder. "I'll see you at dinner."

Nix climbed back out of the cramped workshop as Volt wedged himself around the thruster, moving his muscular frame through the nooks and crannies of his invention like a contortionist. Nix thanked the winds once more for bringing him into her family.

"Volt got the thrusters running?"

Kana slid down the stairs, her feet barely hitting the steps as she raced toward the workshop. Her ebony braid slid over her shoulder, falling across her chest. The beads strung into the plait and her cerulean silk dress caught the light from the doorway above, sparkling like the sun on the sea.

"It's a thing of beauty," Nix announced.

Kana glowed with pride in her bondmate. "We have to be going twice as fast. This children think we're riding a sea serpent."

"Did Tlaloc have any trouble keeping us on course?"

Kana shook her head. "Zi's always so calm and responsive. I almost thought zi was predicting the acceleration."

"No one was. Volt didn't even tell me before activating the thruster."

Kana smiled gently. "He does like to surprise."

"We're going to celebrate tonight." Nix's smile turned evil. "Then again when we pass Gale."

"You think she'll even show up in Karatan when she sees us fly by?"

"I'll hunt her down if she doesn't."

"I don't doubt it."

The ship rumbled again and Volt cheered. Kana and Nix exchanged glances. Nix nodded to the workshop door. "Go celebrate with him."

Kana raced to her bondmate. Nix watched her go, the ghost of an old pain flitting momentarily through her heart, but it vanished at the sound of their shared laughter over the rumble of the thruster.

Nix jogged back up the stairs to the second floor, passing the tiny living quarters on her way to the kitchen. The sharp pound of Doris and Pan's feet racing along the main deck brought a smile to her lips. She should have known the moment the thrusters activated Briza would lose control of the children.

Sirena glared up at her as she entered the galley. She slowly stood, picking up the last of her fallen knives and cookware. Multicolored splashes of spices dusted the usually-spotless walls and floors. The scent of earthy herbs filled the room, the aroma heavier than normal. By the look of the kitchen,

Nix held up her hands in surrender. "I would have warned you if I'd known."

"I was in the middle of preparing for dinner." Sirena gestured to a lime green stain on the floor.

Nix leaned back against the wall. "Well, maybe it was for the best. I promised Volt we'd break into the fruits from Tsara and your mead stores. He finally got his thrusters up and running."

Sirena wiped her hands on a towel with a huff. "As much as I hate celebrating his lack of consideration for the rest of us, it will be nice to work with something fresh."

Nix watched her daughter in delight. She could see her mind spinning behind her eyes, combining flavors and textures into a culinary masterpiece. "I can't wait to try whatever you come up with."

Sirena's focus was already elsewhere as she shuffled into her back room after the fruit. Nix slipped out the door, leaving her daughter to her work.

The wind stung her face and whipped at her billowing sleeves as she climbed up to the main deck. The breeze took the edge off the blazing sun. Kana had been right: they were going at least twice as fast as before.

Doris and Pan leapt into the air, catching the wind in their coats to mimic the sails. Each leap sent them gliding back a couple steps on their tiny feet. Doris's wild, black hair flared away from zir face like the feathers of an owl.

"Don't fall over the edge," Nix warned with an affectionate smile.

Doris, barely three tenmoons, wrapped a protective arm around zir toddler sibling. "We never fall over the edge."

"That's because you're n'Niachero!"

Doris and Pan cheered with pride and took off across the deck again.

"You don't make teaching them humility easy." Briza stepped out of Nix's quarters where she'd been teaching Doris and Pan geography before the thrusters activated. Her long silver hair was wound up on the top of her head in a bundle of braids. The sleeves of her cotton dress were pushed up over her elbows. Her filed fingernails tapped on the soft, thin skin of her forearms. Her glare was almost as sharp as Enyo's, the winged-cat's glowing golden eyes glinting out of the darkness under Nix's bed.

"They don't need to be humble. They need to be confident. They're the future of our sorormin. Doris has all the markings of a future Amazon."

"Zi's three tenmoons and the child of an artist. Zi hasn't even come of age or chosen zir gender identity. You can't know what zi will become."

Nix laughed aloud and Briza's stony facade wavered. "That's funny coming from a seer."

Briza smiled, breaking the tension between them. "I don't see everything, Nix. I'm gifted, not a seer. If I was, I could have predicted Volt's stunt with the thrusters and kept order."

Nix shrugged. "Let them take pride in their father's accomplishment. They have years to study maps and compasses. They have one night of joy to celebrate an incredible advancement for our family."

"For our family or your race with the *Zephyr*?"

"That's not mutually exclusive."

"The *Zephyr* is on the horizon!"

Lyr's voice cut through the wind as he vaulted out of the crow's nest and scampered down the ratlines, his slight, wiry body moving with a fearless, energetic grace. He leapt from the ropes, landing with a dull thud on the main deck. His well-defined muscles glinted with sweat from being directly in the sun for so long. He flipped a golden curl away from his changling eyes, his cat ears turning, taking in the howl of the wind.

"Will they have spotted us yet?"

Lyr shook his head. "Even I had to use a telescope, and the *Zephyr* doesn't have anyone with changling blood. But we won't stay hidden for long. I give it a couple hours at most."

Nix glanced at the sky. The clouds were already dimming to blue, preparing for sunset. "Hopefully we'll be under the cloak of darkness before then. I want don't want them knowing we're here until we're right beside them."

Lyr's grin was feral. "Any chance we might exchange a few blows? I can think of a couple n'Zephyr I'd like to give a good thrashing. Dane was begging for a beating in Ristol."

Nix shrugged. "I don't plan on attacking them, but you can thrash to your heart's content once we reach Karatan."

"Lyr." Briza's voice was unamused.

Lyr glanced at Nix. "I couldn't make things any worse than they already are."

"You can escalate things. We have children on board, and I know it takes an emotional toll on some of the more sensitive members of the crew."

Lyr hesitated, his mischievous expression faltering at Briza's words. His eyes flitted between Briza and Nix. "I wouldn't want to hurt any of the family."

"Of course not."

Lyr ran his fingers through his tangle of curls and slowly walked away, deep in thought.

Nix leveled a glare down at her mother. "You need to stop using his love for Agwe against him. He's already afraid of unsettling him."

"I have to keep one of you in line. It's bad enough the way you and Gale go after each other. We don't need the weapons tech blowing us out of the water because Lyr bloodied his nose."

"Don't act like you don't have your own rivalries with the *Zephyr*."

"Of course I do! The *Zephyr* is full of arrogant louts, but I don't have a driving need to push them into a fight. We're just as obnoxious and troublesome. All sorormins are. It's one of the side-effects of being detached from the rest of the world. It would be better if we just left each other alone."

Nix considered her words. Perhaps Briza was right. Her feud with Gale and her family had danced along the edge of disastrous more than once, but the thought of forgiving and forgetting, of leaving Gale in her wake forever, turned her stomach. She didn't know what else she'd do. The prospect of such a purposeless life terrified Nix.

Briza watched Nix as she thought. Her sharpness faded and she squeezed her daughter's hand. "You'll find your way."

"I'm a bit old for changing, m'Sormee. My hair is already turning gray."

Briza laughed, full and hearty, the sound bursting from the depths of her heart. "Oh my dear soroe. If you're still foolish enough not to expect change, then you aren't as old as you think you are. You have no idea what's waiting on your horizon."

Nix crossed her arms and Briza walked away, probably bound for the galley to help Sirena with dinner. Nix watched her go, then turned her eyes to the sea. She didn't know what her future held, but she knew what stood between her and the horizon.

She grabbed her telescope from off the wall in her room and jogged to the helm. She scanned ahead, Gale's ship a grain of sand in the distance. "Turn two more degrees west," she instructed Tlaloc. "I want to catch her before dawn."

Nix leaned over the railing of the bow, sipping half-heartedly at a tankard of mead. The joyful sounds of her crew finishing dinner and dancing couldn't break through her stony demeanor. Briza's words had hit her harder than she expected, unbalancing her sense of self and purpose. She wanted to forget it, to drink until her uncertainty and questions disappeared, but Gale was close enough she could see the white of her sails flickering in the moonlight. She needed to keep her wits.

Enyo wove between her ankles and leapt up onto the rail, butting her head against Nix's shoulder. When Nix didn't pet her, the tiny eitteh scowled and flicked her wings, hovering for a moment before settling on Nix's shoulder and resting against Nix's hair.

A flash of light caught her attention. She turned to the *Niachero*'s ornate, sea serpent mast head. The moonlight had caught on the lifestones embedded in its eyes. The sparkling stones sent a chill down her spine, a physical testament to Briza's warnings.

The stones were set into the masthead of every Amazon's ship. When Nix had taken her oath of loyalty to her sorormin, Briza had told her the lifestones signified an Amazon's bond to her ship and her family. Where bondmates wore lifestone rings as a sign of loyalty and commitment, an Amazon was bound to her crew. Kana, however, had spun stories of a time before the people of Aggar had become one, when Amazons were still a separate race. When they were alien. In those days, the stones were set into the arms of Amazons and their bondmates. They were the tools of fate, drawing people together who were destined to change Aggar.

Nix couldn't help but fear the *Niachero*'s lifestones had intended more for her than mindlessly brawling across the oceans of Aggar.

Volt ran up behind her and wrapped his massive arms around her waist, lifting her off the ground. Enyo yowled in surprise and flew away, scratching Nix's shoulder in the process.

"You promised me a drink!" Volt declared.

Nix laughed, pushing her dark thoughts aside, and squirmed, pulling out of the shorter man's embrace. She gestured over her shoulder. "That will have to wait."

Volt raised an eyebrow. "We're getting awfully close. I thought we were just going to sail past. You planning to confront her?"

Nix adjusted her collar. "What's a little verbal sparring mid-competition? She should appreciate your work as much as the rest of us."

"She's not going to like it."

"She's not supposed to like it."

"I'll make sure the children are asleep before we reach them."

"Good idea."

Volt strode down the stairs back to the main deck and pulled Kana aside. Kana eyes widened in surprise and she looked up into the darkness, finding Nix. Nix didn't avoid her gaze. Kana understood what drove her. She didn't need to hide.

Kana nodded to Volt and took her childrens' hands, smiling and promising stories as she led them off to bed. Nix strolled to the rest of her family, setting her tankard of mead aside. They all looked up at her. They instantly knew what she intended to do. "Tlaloc. Take the helm?"

Tlaloc's eyes grew dark. Zi hated the *Zephyr* almost as much Nix. "Of course."

Sirena drew her short-sword, her jaw clenched. She'd never forgiven Gale for stabbing her not a tenmoon ago.

Lyr drew his knives, his muscles twitching for a fight and his eyes wild. Agwe, who had been standing with him, tensed and turned away. He started gathering the remains from dinner, finding a way to occupy his mind. Lyr's excitement disappeared and he rushed to help Agwe.

He gently touched Agwe's arm. "Don't worry. We aren't fighting. Just intimidating them."

Agwe moved away from him and took the plates Lyr had gathered from his hands. "Intimidation often leads to fighting." He turned to Nix. "I'll have my med kit ready and I'll keep an eye on the children."

He slipped away below deck. Lyr watched him go, uncertain of what to do, but Sirena took his hand as Kana returned to the main deck, fitting an arrow into her cross bow.

"We need your fire," Sirena whispered to Lyr. "He'll be fine."

"Coming up fast port side." Tlaloc's voice called them to attention.

Volt pressed a button on a mobile control panel in his pocket and the thrusters powered down. Kana pulled herself into the ratlines, her skirt doing nothing to impede her climb. Briza took up another ranged position, leveling her crossbow at the Niachero from the railing of the helm.

Nix sauntered to the port side of her ship and drew her sword. Lyr and Sirena stood beside her, looking menacing. Enyo leapt from the helm, her wings opening like a bird of prey and she settled on Nix's shoulder as the *Niachero* slid into place beside the *Zephyr*.

Gale was already waiting, her hands on her hips. Her best brawler, Boreas and Dane, flanked her. Gale's voice was clipped and fierce, her skin dark with barely-suppressed fury. "You've had an upgrade."

"You noticed. Having the best weapons tech in Aggar has its benefits." Nix sent an approving glance to Volt. "You won't beat us to Karatan. The *Zephyr* can't match us for speed anymore."

Gale's lips pulled back in a smile that was closer to a sneer. "Speed isn't the only way to win a race."

Without warning, Gale's cannons fired, ripping into the Niachero. The ship rumbled and threw Nix off-balance in shock. She looked around in a moment of confusion and shock. Her ears rang from the blast. She could hear Doris and Pan screaming. Her blood ran cold and then instantly hot as she cleared her mind and rounded on Gale. Sirena and Volt ran past her, racing for the gun deck.

"Too far, Gale!"

Gale lifted her hands, beckoning and taunting. "Come get me, Nix."

Kana shot at Gale, but Boreas pulled her away. Another round of canon fire shook the *Niachero*, but the canon balls rebounded off the reinforced hull and fell into the sea.

"I wonder how many rounds it will take to crack your precious *Niachero*," Gale snarled. "Or will you run away with your fancy new thrusters before we can find out?"

Volt and Sirena fired on the *Zephyr*, the cannons ringing in Nix's ears once more. Nix felt a moment of comfort; if Volt was manning a cannon, then Doris and Pan were safe.

Briza shot at Gale a second time, her bolt narrowly missing the Amazon.

In the fray, Tlaloc threw a grappling hook, stretching a rope between the two ships. Nix leapt up, crossing the rope at a run and launching herself onto the *Zephyr*. Lyr was directly behind her, landing in a crouch as the ships once again exchanged a round of cannon fire.

Nix immediately charged at Gale as Lyr took on Dane. Tlaloc secured the rope of the grappling hook and joined the fight, zir long limbs leaping elegantly onto the deck of the *Zephyr* as zi unsheathed a slender fencing sword and squared off with Boreas.

Nix and Gale met with a flash of steal in the moonlight, their swords sliding together as Nix swung and Gale blocked. The ship rumbled with another round of cannon fire and Nix grit her teeth at the sound of splintering wood. Both ships could only take so much at such a close range.

Nix bore down on Gale with a barrage of thrusts, backing her up against the port railing. She had always been a better fencer than the other Amazon.

She grabbed Gale's sword arm and crushed Gale with her body, leaning her back over the railing.

"You'll kill us all!" Nix hissed.

"Surrender to me and I'll stop." Gale threw her head forward, headbutting Nix just hard enough for her to stumble back, then punching her in the face.

Nix fell to her knees, momentarily disoriented. Her sword fell from her hand. She could hear the sharp whir and thud of arrows shooting from both vessels. The deafening roar of canons blended with Lyr's berserker growls and the ring of Tlaloc's expert swordplay.

Gale wrapped her arm around Nix's shoulders and leveled her blade at her throat as she kicked Nix's sword away. She pressed tight against Nix, whispering in her ear. "Surrender."

Nix seethed. "Kill me."

Gale pressed the blade tighter against her throat, drawing a thin line of blood. "I'd rather take you alive."

Nix barely heard the gentle flutter of wings before Enyo struck, descending on Gale with outstretched claws. Gale shouted in pain and surprise as Enyo clawed and bit at her face and arms. Nix pulled free of Gale and ran for her sword, grabbing the hilt Enyo yowled in pain, a crossbow bolt in her wing.

"No!" Enyo shouted, running for her dear companion as she stumbled back, her wing flailing and spasming in pain.

She scooped Enyo into her arms and ran for the *Niachero*. She had just reached the grappling hook, the rope now severed, when another round of cannon fire paralyzed her. She watched in horror as the first of Gale's canon balls breached her hull, sending chunks of wood and debris flying into the air. Nix trembled with rage and fear. Enough. She wouldn't sacrifice everything over one spat.

"Let me help." Tlaloc pulled Enyo gently out of Nix's arms. Boreas lay unconscious at the base of Gale's helm.

Another round of cannon fire sent a spray of carnage into the sea. Nix spun on Gale, her sword falling to the ground as she grabbed her in an iron grip, lifting her off the ground. "Make it stop. Now."

Gale struggled against her grip. Dozens of cuts and scratches from Enyo's attack left dots of blood across Gale's face. "You surrender?"

Nix dragged her to the starboard rail and pushed her forward. "Yes. Now stop it!"

"Cease fire!" Gale screamed. Both sides froze, the smoke from the gun powder rising through the air. Nix waited until Gale's gunmen had returned to the main deck and Sirena and Volt had ascended on the *Niachero*.

Sirena charged forward, ready to defend her mother, but Nix held up a hand and she stopped. Nix released Gale and turned on her, hissing between clenched teeth as she leaned less than a hair's breadth off her face. "Let my family go. You can take whatever you want. I'll yield the competition to you. But my sorormin is spared."

"You're hardly in a position to be making demands."

Nix flicked her wrist, a dagger falling from her sleeve, and she leveled the point at Gale's stomach. "I could kill you now."

Gale brushed the knife away. "There's no need for that." Gale flipped her hair over her shoulder and adjusted her skirt. "I don't want your ship or your supplies. Your sorormin goes free. You stay with me."

Nix snarled. "Fine." She turned to Tlaloc. "Take the ship ashore for repairs. The Karatan coast isn't far. I won't be here long."

Lyr leapt forward, still high on adrenaline. His shirt was sliced open, a long, bloody gash running from shoulder to hip. "Nix, we're stronger than they are. We can take them."

Nix held out her hand and touched his wound. It wasn't as deep as she'd feared. He followed her touch and his eyes widened. He hadn't even noticed. "Go see Agwe. I'll be fine."

"Nix—"

Tlaloc took Lyr's shoulder. "Come with me. We must trust our captain."

A board was stretched between the two vessels and Tlaloc, Lyr, and Enyo returned to the *Niachero*.

"M'Sormee?" Sirena stepped closer to the railing as Nix didn't move to rejoin her family as Tlaloc and Lyr reached the main deck. Gale kicked the board aside, letting it fall into the sea. "M'Sormee!"

Kana held Sirena back as the *Zephyr* pulled away, leaving the damaged *Niachero* behind.

Nix couldn't look away from her sorormin as Dane, bruised and bloody from his fight with Lyr, tied Nix's hands behind her back. Gale wrapped an arm around her shoulders and followed her line of sight. "Who do you think will be the next Amazon on the *Niachero*? Sirena seems strong. Who knows what losing her mother will do to her."

Nix whipped around, jerking forward to attack Gale, but Dane held her back. Gale laughed. "Take her to my room. Give her some time with her thoughts." She grabbed Nix's chin, looking into her eyes. "Be a good girl, Nix. Your ship isn't going anywhere fast and I can always turn back around."

Nix didn't fight as Dane pulled her into Gale's room and tied her to a chair at the shoulders and waist and left. Nix leaned back, her eyes flitting across the familiar chamber. Nothing had changed since the night Gale had marooned her. A desk. A feather bed, a couple book shelves and large, hand-drawn maps pinned to the walls. Moonlight streamed in through windows in the stern just over the bed. A small chandelier swung from the ceiling, the candles burned out.

Nix swore to herself she would get out. She wouldn't let Gale strip her away from her family again. Her ship was safe. It was no longer a battle of strength, but a battle of wits and time. She had to change tactics.

She tested the bonds around her wrists, tightening her hand into a point and trying to pull her hand free, but they were too tight. She slid her feet across the floor in an attempt to move the chair closer to something sharp, but the chair only teetered, nearly falling over.

"I don't know what to be more disappointed in: you already causing trouble or your failure at being successful."

Gale stood in the doorway. Nix glared up at her as she closed the door and walked in, sitting on the edge of her desk and resting a booted foot on Nix's thigh. "Be a dear and tell me where you're hiding the rest of your weapons? I don't fancy being stabbed in my sleep."

"I wouldn't need a knife to kill you in your sleep."

Gale shook her head and tsked, leaning forward over her leg and wrapping her hand in Nix's short hair. Nix grunted in pain as Gale forced her to meet her eyes.

"I would still sleep better knowing you don't have any weapons." Nix didn't answer, only glared. Gale released her hair with a shove and slid off the desk. She circled around to stand in front of Nix. "Well. There are the obvious places." She crouched low and ran her hands up Nix's calves, pulling a dagger off each leg.

Nix tensed under her touch, the familiar poison of desire and rage brewing in her stomach. This wasn't Ristol. Her family was safe. The moonlight, the scent of Gale, and the adrenaline of battle was making her seductive nemesis harder to resist.

Gale laughed to herself as she ran her hands up Nix's thighs and over her hips, rising and sliding forward to straddle Nix's lap. Her hands roamed beneath Nix's shirt, pulling a third knife out of the sheath at the small of Nix's back. She tossed it into the pile at Nix's feet.

She nipped at the sharp angle of Nix's cheek. "You're blushing."

"You think I want you after what you did?"

"Yes." Gale pressed tight against her, the lines, curves, and swells of her body pressed along every inch of her. Nix suppressed a groan. Gale ran her fingers over the rope tied under Nix's shoulders, securing her to the chair. "I should have tied you up a long time ago."

Nix's breath came in sharp gasps as she steadily lost the battle with her body. She wanted to punish Gale. She wanted to succumb to Gale. She needed to touch Gale.

The last of Nix's willpower went up in flames and Nix leaned forward, claiming Gale's mouth in a rough kiss. Gale responded instantly, grabbing Nix's face so tightly her nails bit into Nix's skin.

"Untie me," Nix demanded, breathless and desperate as Gale left a sharp trail of kisses and nips down her throat and chest.

Gale pulled at the ties of Nix's shirt, opening it to her navel. "I'm not stupid."

"Search me. I don't have any more weapons," Nix pled.

Gale looked her in the eye as her hands slid over the swell of her breasts, eliciting a guttural moan from Nix. "Beg me."

Nix's gaze grew dark. "No."

Gale pushed away from Nix and slowly undressed, unlacing her silk shirt and sliding her skirt over her hips. The sight of her took Nix's breath away. Her skin was flushed dark, the moonlight skating over the curve of her hip, the hollows of her stomach and swells of her breasts, and the arching curve of her back. She was strong, somehow still soft despite a life at sea. Her hair cascaded over her shoulders and down her back, nearly reaching the small of her back.

She was irresistible and she knew it.

"Beg me," she repeated.

Nix bit her tongue, refusing to give in to her again tonight. She'd already surrendered her ship and her body, she wouldn't surrender her pride. She didn't trust herself to speak, she merely lifted her chin in defiance.

Gale grabbed one of Nix's knives off the ground and straddled her again, the warmth of her skin pressed against Nix's bare chest nearly broke her. She pressed her lips against Nix's ear. "You know..." Nix's hands broke free as Gale's severed her bonds, first at her wrists, then at her waist, and finally at her shoulders. "I wouldn't have let you go if you'd begged."

Nix grabbed her, the ropes falling away as she tackled her back to the bed. Gale met her passion, both women devolving into their most animalistic selves. Gale ripped at Nix's clothes, shredding fabric and biting off buttons. They were still fighting, always on the knife edge between sex and brawl. Every fiber of Nix's body hummed and sang with release.

She pinned Gale to the bed, her anger feeding off the way Gale struggled against her in an effort to take control. "You're mine," Nix growled, licking a long line from Gale's navel to her collar. She could taste the gunpowder from the canons, the spray of the sea and the salt of sweat.

"I captured you," Gale argued.

Nix bit the crook of her neck, burying her teeth in the taut muscles. Gale's back arched and her knees bent, her feet pressing hard into the mattress. "But you're still mine."

"Take me," Gale whimpered.

"Beg me," Nix demanded.

Gale slapped her hard enough to make her see lights. "Never."

Nix growled. "We'll see."

Gale slept soundly beside her, her body limp and splayed across he bed. Nix stared up at the ceiling, her body exhausted, covered in sweat and Gale's scent. The pains of battling Gale all night were slowly returning. She felt every wound, every bruise, every cut from teeth and nails.

Even with the pain, Gale's body was finally at peace. The tension from Ristol was gone, but she still felt the deep, driving ache in the pit of her stomach. The hole in her heart that never seemed to fill.

She slowly, quietly crept out of bed, leaving the ruins of her clothes and her weapons behind. She couldn't swim with them anyway. If Gale wanted to cause trouble, she would wait another hour, almost dawn, to strike. Nix had to be long gone by then.

She slipped out of Gale's room, the sky just beginning to lighten with the first hints of dawn. Without a second glance back at her rival, she climbed the railing of the *Zephyr* and jumped overboard. She was caught in a moment of free fall before plunging deep into the sea. The cold of the water shocked her exhausted muscles awake and she swam toward shore.

Nix was a powerful long-distance swimmer, but she still had a long way to go to reach land and her family. She allowed herself to linger over the memories of Gale as she swam, to hold the intoxicating feeling of being powerfully, completely alive close for a few hours more. When she stepped onto the sands of Karatan, she'd have to cast those memories aside. She wouldn't allow her feud with

Gale to put her family in danger again. Even if she never felt fully alive again, at least the people she loved would be safe.

Gale's ship disappeared along the horizon by the time dawn broke. Nix imagined Gale's fury at finding Nix gone and grinned. She had lost the race, but Nix couldn't help but feel she had still won.

Chapter Five

Reve felt the tickle of a breeze across her cheeks and closed her eyes. She could smell salt, taste brine on her tongue. It wasn't real; the sensations were whispers to her Sight, but the message was clear. She was close to the sea. She'd reach the coast in a matter of hours.

The sharp slope of the jungle was steadily leveling off, the trees growing more sparse and bits of sky poking through the thinning jungle canopy. Reve nibbled at a fist-sized wild mushroom Hecate had rooted out of the undergrowth for her. Since leaving the monastery, Hecate had taken over the task of feeding them both, finding safe berries, roots, and once even traveling through the night to find fresh meat. It was more than Reve had found for herself since entering Karatan, but her stomach still cramped with every bite, crying for more.

Hecate trekked ahead, sniffing and pawing at the soil. Reve couldn't understand her thoughts outside of their shared dreams, but she could sense her intention, her emotions. Hecate was more anxious to reach the coast than Reve was.

Reve would run, but the breeze from the ocean was enough to slow and confuse the Songs and Reve was still weak. Slowing down made every injury spring sharply to life. Reve's feet stung with every step and her broken finger ached so badly it twisted her hand, making it nearly useless. Still, it seemed a special treat not to have to run for her life, even for just a few hours.

Hecate butted the back of her knee with her nose, urging her on.

"We're not in any kind of rush," Reve growled. "Save your energy for the next time we have to flee. Aren't you nocturnal?"

Reve glanced up into the trees as the leaves rustled. A cerulean bird hopped out onto a nearby branch and trilled at the sun. Reve's lips turned in a rare, genuine smile. She stood and watched the bird, entranced by the way it moved, the flutter of its wings, the sharp twitch of its neck as it glanced around the forest. It barely paid Reve any attention, concerned only with searching for grubs and singing its songs.

It had been so long since she'd seen another living creature that had no reaction to her. Most animals fled from her, subconsciously frightened of offending the Choir. Was it the breeze from the ocean that weakened the Choir's Songs?

The thought pleased and terrified her in equal measure. She had always had a deep, aching urge for companionship, but any living creature could turn on her with just a whisper from the Choir. Even in regions where it was hard for the Songs to follow her, Reve was sure the Choir could track her through the eyes of animals under their control. She wouldn't last long if she lost her anonymity.

Hecate growled, scaring the bird away. Reve glanced over her shoulder at the impatient beast and grunted. "You have no sense of beauty, do you?"

Hecate padded ahead into the trees. Reve followed slowly, finishing her mushroom. She reached out with her Sight, trying to understand what waited for her on the beach. Jacquin had sworn she'd find the next step of her journey on the coast, but Reve hadn't had any visions or impressions. It unnerved Reve. She usually knew what she had to do, the path laid out in her mind like a shining, golden path. But not now. All she could do was trust her dream.

As the sun reached the middle of the sky, the rainforest canopy had grown so sparse Reve could see it shining through waxy leaves. She stopped and stood in its light. The beams caught her golden hair and pale skin, so unused to standing still in the sun's warmth. The sun usually meant either potential discovery or oppressive heat to Reve, yet somehow today she could feel hope.

Hecate raced past her, plunging into the tangled foliage of a nearby bush. A moment later Reve heard it: voices talking. Machetes swinging. People were coming.

Reve dove after Hecate, laying flat on the ground amongst the tangled vines and thick undergrowth. She willed herself to merge with the darkness, to become unseen, undetectable. Her breathing stilled. Her heart slowed. She felt intrinsically connected to the soil, no longer human, but shadow.

"Yellow flowers with seven petals."

"Some of these have seven petals..."

"That doesn't look like his drawing."

"Looks good enough to me."

Two wanderers stepped into view, one holding a piece of parchment. The other, obviously changling in origin, followed close behind, a sharp machete in each hand. The changling crouched low beside a scattering of tiny, gold flowers growing out of the moss on a nearby tree. "What about these?"

The traveler with the drawing compared the flowers to the sketch, a single brow raised. "I'm not sure."

"What does Agwe want with the plants anyway? We can't grow them on board, the climate isn't right."

"He doesn't want to grow them. He wants to make tea. He has surprisingly refined tastes for such an undemanding sailor."

The changling frowned and severed a handful of the flowers from the moss with the sword, tucking them into a field bag. "At worst, he'll have new plants to experiment with."

Reve watched the pair carefully, her muscles twitching, aching to run. They didn't seem particularly dangerous, but no one did until they saw her eyes. She needed to know where they were from, how many were in their party. She needed to know how to avoid them, but most importantly she needed to know if they had any supplies she could abscond with unseen. The chance at finding new shoes and rations outweighed the danger.

They continued through the clearing for a time, collecting various yellow flowers until the field bag was full. Reve followed them with her eyes as they turned to go back to their camp. Once they were almost out of view, she crept forward on her arms and knees, sliding out of the foliage.

She stalked them through the forest, slipping silently between the shadows, always staying as far from them as possible, and Hecate even further back. They didn't sense her presence. It was obvious they weren't from the jungle. They stumbled over tree roots and spent most of their time complaining about the heat. The revelation eased Reve's mind. A band of travelers would be easier to evade than an established village.

The rainforest parted, revealing a long, slender stretch of sandy beach. Reve hesitated along the forest line, staring in wonder. Despite all the traveling she'd done since fleeing her birth home, she had never been to a beach. The ocean stretched out like a swath of blue silk, reflecting the sunlight like a dusting of diamonds.

A massive ship was beached, tipped on its side as multiple members of the crew patched various holes and made repairs with with sticky, black tar. The ship's furniture was laid out across the beach, surrounding a cluster of tents where the rest of the crew gathered.

Reve counted nine sailors, two of which were small children, and an eitteh with a bandaged wing. They were hardly a force to be afraid of.

The breeze was strong enough to push back Reve's hair, her golden mane dancing wild across her face and shoulders. Reve had heard of the Amazons and their sorormins, the last free people in Aggar. She'd assumed them to be stories or exaggerated, but feeling the presence of the wind just on the beach, Reve knew anyone who dedicated their life to the sea would be nearly untouched by the Choir's Songs.

With her eyes closed, a new sensation drifted on the breeze. She could smell cooked meat. The smell made her salivate, her stomach rumbling with need. She opened her eyes. Four birds were roasting over a spit on the fire built centrally to the tents. Reve instantly gave up hope of tasting them – here were too many sailors surrounding meal – but none of the explorers looked undernourished. They had to have other rations with them. She'd wait until nightfall, once they were all asleep, and then investigate. Hopefully she'd have everything she needed in a matter of minutes and could spend the rest of the night traveling further down the beach.

Reve shuffled deeper into the forest and climbed a slender, rough-barked tree, perching in a low branch, just high enough to glimpse the camp without being noticed. Hecate wandered deeper into the jungle, searching for a dark place to rest. Despite her impatience and seeming omniscience, Reve knew Hecate was still a nocturnal beast. She had to be exhausted.

The hours stretched on and Reve dozed in the sunlight. She had trained herself long ago to sleep absolutely still. She wasn't afraid of falling out of the tree. She let her spirit wander through the sailor's camp, examining each member of the crew. They were strangely unreadable to her, their emotions and thoughts cut off from her. All she could sense were their purest essences: their chosen genders, their general dispositions, their intentions. And she could observe them.

They were close. Family, despite being incredibly diverse in heritage. She could sense Amazon, Terran, Aggar, and Changling heritages in various degrees in each member of the crew, some of their lines more pure than Reve had ever seen. She sensed strong comraderie and love between them and, despite a heavy streak of pride and mischievousness, they seemed genuinely kind.

"Here Agwe." The changling handed a tall, willowy young man the field bag. "We weren't entirely sure about the plants we found, so we gathered you a collection."

The young man looked through the bag with a gentle smile and pulled out a thick-petaled blossom. "This one is poisonous."

The changling blushed and glanced away, his hands deep in his pockets. "I figured you could do something with the wrong ones even if they were next to useless. You can make anything out of nothing."

The young man didn't seem to notice the changling's discomfort, continuing to dig through the bag. "Ah. Here it is." He pulled out the small flowers Reve had seen the changling cut through from the tree. "This will work well. Thank you, Lyr."

Lyr reached out and squeezed the other man's shoulder. "My pleasure, Agwe. Anytime you want something, just ask."

Agwe nodded, his eyes bright, and walked away. Lyr watched him go and let out a deep breath, leaning back against a polished wardrobe sitting in the sand. The woman he'd been traveling with in the forest leaned on his shoulder and watched the young man as well. "That should distract him for a few hours."

"At least we found what he wanted, not just a collection of poisons and weeds."

"Honestly, I think he would have found something to do with anything we brought him. He's taking m'Sormee's capture hard. He needs a distraction."

"And what about you?"

The woman's face fell, her green eyes growing dark. "I deal with things in my own way."

"Do you think Nix will be able to escape?"

"She did it once before."

"You know that was pure dumb luck."

"She's not an Amazon for nothing, Lyr. She can escape a boatload of cowards like the Zephyr. And if she doesn't, I'll kill Gale myself."

"You'll take over for her? As our captain?" A long, uncomfortable silence settled around them. The woman's eyes fell, her auburn-tinted hair falling across her face. "I didn't mean anything by it, Sirena. I just meant we'd all support you. We've known since you came of age you were most likely to take over for your mother if something like this happened. You're the only one with the skills and drive."

Sirena looked up again, her face stony, her lips pressed in a tight line. Even observing her as a projection, the woman's will closed her off even further to Reve. Reve examined her even closer. It would take a tremendous amount of willpower to shut herself off so completely. Reve found herself intrigued by the beautiful young woman. She rarely came upon such a mystery. She didn't know if she liked it or not.

"Dinner is ready!" The old, plump woman tending the fire wiped her brow with the back of her hand and stood back, examining her feast with pride. Her companion, a slender unfettered, nodded approvingly at the meal as zi petted the eitteh purring in zir lap.

Sirena, Lyr, and Agwe rushed to her as the three members of the crew patching the ship carefully scurried and slid down the ship's hull, landing hard in the sand.

"Doris! Pan!" the woman called. The children, wild with the joy of being on a beach, didn't listen. They were caught up in kicking and splashing in the ocean waves. The woman touched the blonde man's chest. "Volt, would you grab them? I'll get them drinks and a couple apples for Pan. Zi won't eat meat anymore."

"Such a picky eater. How did my child become a vegetarian? Zi must get it from somewhere in your blood, Kana."

Kana shot him a good-natured glare. "You may eat meat, but the list of what you won't eat is longer than Pan's. I'll force Pan to eat new things when you start eating anything dug up from the ground."

Volt made an exaggerated retching face. "Fair enough."

Volt kissed Kana and dashed off down the beach, scooping a child under each arm. They screamed with delight as he spun them and bounced them, kicking hard enough at the waves that the spray reached their tiny, outstretched fingers.

"Time to eat, soroes!"

"I don't like bird meat!" the smallest child cried.

"You haven't tried every bird in the world," the other retorted.

"It's fine, Pan. Your mama has apples and berries and all the bugs you can eat."

"Ew!" Pan screeched.

"What, you don't like apples?"

"I don't eat bugs!"

"You don't like bugs? Not even worms? Slimy, wriggly, worms?"

"Ew!"

"You'll put them off eating altogether," Kana warned as she grabbed Pan out from under Volt's arm. "No one is eating bugs."

"I'd try a bug," Doris remarked.

Volt popped the child up into the air, zir hair and dress fluttering in the breeze in zir split-second of free-fall. Zir laughter was clear and ringing like a bell. "My warrior!"

"I will not eat bugs," Pan groused as zi munched on an apple.

Kana smiled at zir affectionately and brushed zir hair from zir eyes. "Neither would I, soroe."

Reve's spirit sat around the fire with them, watching as they laughed and ate. She felt a sudden deep ache for their life. For the love in their eyes, the companionship. Her mother used to tell her stories about Paradise, the afterlife. Reve had clung to the stories then, dreaming of a life after death outside of the darkness of her hiding spaces. Reve imagined paradise would be like this. Sitting around a fire with family.

She knew she should be scouting the camp, looking for supplies, but she couldn't bring herself to leave.

Night began to fall and the meal turned to stories. Kana wove tales of epic battles at sea, of Amazons taking to the sea in fleets, separating themselves and their families from the oppression of the Choir. She had a way with words and sounds that left Reve entranced, masterful images of endless ships, wild storms, and vicious sea serpents dancing through her mind.

Reve realized, once the Choir was defeated, she wanted to take to the sea. Perhaps she'd find a boat small enough she could crew it alone. She could sail away to an island, live out the rest of her days in the sun, surrounded by the wind, safe from anyone who would fear her eyes.

As the twin moons rose high, the family shuffled off to their tents, preparing for another long day of repairs that awaited them. Reve sat in silence for nearly an hour, staring at the ribbons of smoke drifting from the doused fire. The night had ended too quickly, leaving a bitter hole in Reve's stomach. She couldn't have expected it to last forever, but she was surprised how sad she was for it to end.

She allowed herself another moment to grieve, and then clenched her fists, steeling herself. She couldn't allow herself to become sentimental now. Sentimentality would get her killed.

She returned to her body, grabbing the tree as she swayed. She wiped the tears from her eyes. Hecate looked up at her in concern from the forest floor. Reve grit her teeth. It was time.

She scurried down the tree and crept through the forest, keeping a careful eye on the tents as she moved. She had seen the general area where Kana had retrieved the apples. She reached the stack of barrels, separated from the camp by a line of wardrobes and trunks. Hecate stayed behind. She had no interest in stealing.

She carefully lifted the lid to one and her entire body trembled. It was full of fresh fruit; apples and berries,citrus and melons. She grabbed a bag of clothing and emptied it in a pile in the sand. She filled the bag with everything she thought she could eat before it spoiled.

She turned to another barrel, this one filled with salted meat. She ate a handful immediately, the savory flavor overwhelming her. She would have to remember to pace herself. It would be so easy to gorge, but the food would be useless if her tender stomach heaved all of it back up again.

She added as much meat to her bag as she could, knowing it would hold. She tested the weight of her treasure, determining she could run with it without too much trouble. Now all she needed were shoes and perhaps a change of clothes.

She stood to leave and felt a firm hand grab her arm. She instinctively dropped her bag and spun around to kick at her captor, but he caught her leg with his other arm. It was Agwe, the winged-cat perched on his shoulder, his eyes sharp and fierce.

"Who are you?"

Reve panicked, fighting back as hard as she could, but Agwe was surprisingly strong and agile. He blocked her blows, never releasing her arm, but his blows weren't sharp or vicious. He wasn't trying to hurt her.

He swept her legs out from under her and pinned her in the sand. When she realized she couldn't move, she started to tremble. She was terrified of being captured, of the moment he'd look into her eyes and his efforts to capture her would turn to attempts to murder her.

"Don't kill me." The words slipped from her lips unbidden, a nearly inaudible plea.

Agwe looked her over again and instead of filling with rage, his face fell in pity. "You're hurt. And starving." It wasn't a question. "Were you going to hurt my family?"

Reve shook her head hard. It was the truth. She had no desire to hurt anyone.

Agwe's grip on her wrists relaxed and he slowly moved away, still crouching beside her. She sat up in surprise, rubbing her wrists where he'd held her.

"What's your name?"

"Reve."

Agwe smiled gently and offered his hand. "Agwe."

She tentatively shook it. After watching the gentle man all day, yearning to have his life, she was starting to feel the pangs of friendship deep in her heart. Perhaps he was someone she could trust for a time.

"If you steal this way, they'll know right away. They'll come after you. Go back to the forest. I'll bring you supplies later."

Reve looked him over in disbelief. "Why would you help me?"

"Why wouldn't I?"

"Agwe?"

Sirena's voice drifted through the camp. Agwe paled. "You have to hide."

He pulled her to her feet and tried to lead her back to the forest, but Sirena was blocking their path. Without a word, Agwe opened a large chest and urged her inside. The moment he closed the lid, throwing her into darkness, Reve felt her heart pound wildly. She didn't like being trapped in tight spaces, she didn't like hiding. She struggled not to hyperventilate, to meld with the shadow, but her mind was too panicked to allow her to relax.

"What are you doing?" Sirena's voice was suspicious.

"I was looking for something."

"In Tlaloc's clothing bag?"

"I must have gotten confused in the dark."

A long pause settled between them and Reve tensed. Did she know? Had she seen Agwe hide her?

"Come back to bed, Agwe."

"Alright."

Reve heard them walk away and, once there was silence again, she reached for the lid of the trunk, pushing up. It opened less than a finger's width and then stopped. It was stuck.

Reve panicked, pushing up against it with all her might, but she was too weak. The lid wouldn't open. She was trapped until Agwe let her out. Instantly, everyone of her muscles cramped, desperate to move, to stretch. Reve forced herself to sleep, to allow her astral self out of the box and escape her physical body. She stared down at herself, tiny and hidden away in the dark. She had to find some way out.

Reve sat in the sand against the boat as the sun rose. Near dawn, just before everyone else woke, Agwe rushed back out of his tent to her.

"I'm so sorry," he whispered as he attempted to pry the sticky lid open. It had just opened wide enough for Reve to stick her arm through when Agwe turned to the beach. Someone crawled out of the waves onto the shore, vomiting water.

"M'Sormee!" Agwe screamed as he raced for her, pulling her out of the sea.

She trembled and stumbled, her bare skin pale with cold. Her short black hair, tinted with silver, clung to her face and neck, a thread of seaweed trailing from her crown to her shoulder. "Agwe!" She whispered, pulling her son into a tight embrace.

The rest of the crew were instantly awake, running out of their tents as Agwe threw a blanket around his mother and helped her stand. She was quickly regaining her strength, but she was obviously weak.

Sirena ran to her mother, wrapping her in her arms. Nix held one of her children in each arm, kissing their brows, her eyes closed in gratitude.

"Nix, did you swim here?" Kana exclaimed.

Even halfway dead, Nix managed to shoot her a cocky grin. "I escaped. That's what matters."

"You look famished. I'll get you something to eat," Briza announced.

"Thank you, m'Sormee."

Doris and Pan shot away from their father and clung to Nix's legs. Agwe and Sirena stabilized her as she nearly fell back.

"Welcome back!" Doris cheered.

"Children," Kana gasped. "Nix is very sick."

Nix only smiled. "It's fine, Kana." She looked down at Doris and Pan. "I'm happy to see you both, too."

"The ship is nearly repaired. It's not a perfect fix, but she'll hold," Tlaloc reported, awe and respect for Nix's strength shining in zir eyes.

"We'll save up and head to Port Marik. There's a ship builder there who will work with Amazons."

"You don't plan to go after Gale?" Volt questioned.

Nix shook her head. "Gale is dead to me."

As the family reunited, a soft padding caught Reve's attention. Hecate stalked out of the forest, sniffing at the air. Reve tensed. She should have known her companion would come looking for her.

Reve fled back into her body as Hecate reached her trunk, thrusting her nose into the narrow crack between the lid and the box. Reve pushed her nose away, trying to tell her without words that she needed to flee. People were just as scared of wolves as they were Blue Sights. Reve couldn't bear it if they shot Hecate out of fear.

Reve heard footsteps and her heart froze. Hecate growled and backed away. Reve closed her eyes tight, waiting for the snap of a crossbow string of the yelp of her only friend being slaughtered. Instead there was a violent creak as the chest was pried open. Sunlight streamed across Reve's fragile body.

"Who are you?"

Reve opened her eyes in fear as Nix looked down at her, all signs of weakness gone, replaced with sharp suspicion. Reve cowered under her glare, her presence overwhelming.

"M'Sormee, please. She's lost. I caught her stealing food. I was helping her," Agwe pled.

"Helping her? Why would you hide her from your family?" Nix demanded. She turned to Reve. "What have you been telling my son, thief?"

"Please." Everyone watched Agwe in shock as he begged, his voice more adamant and demanding than ever before. "Look at her. Is she really a threat to any of us?"

Nix looked down at her, her eyes never losing their hardness.

"Nix, don't be stubborn."

Briza stepped forward and reached down for Reve, helping her out of the trunk. Her grip was solid for such an old woman, her hands callused from work. Briza looked her over, lingering on her eyes. Reve shrank back, but Briza only grunted and turned, placing herself between Nix and Reve.

"We should take her with us."

Reve's breath caught in her throat and many of the crew gasped at the suggestion. Agwe turned to his family, his arms outstretched. "We can't leave her here. She'll die."

"Absolutely not." Nix's voice was final. "All we know for sure about her is that she'd steal from us."

"You'd steal in her situation, too," Agwe accused.

The sharpness in his voice caught Nix off guard.

"I wouldn't mind." Sirena's voice rang from the back of the group. She looked Reve over, a very different expression in her eyes than her mother or her brother. "She seems interesting."

Nix turned on her daughter, her eyes wide. "Sirena!"

"At least half the crew vouches for her, Nix," Briza pointed out.

"Why do you care, m'Sormee? You're not a bleeding heart."

"I sense destiny on her." Briza's response was swift and casual, but it sent a shock of fear and understanding through Reve. This was what Jacquin had wanted her to find. These people. But how would they possibly help her?

The rumbling of a purr echoed across the beach and Nix turned. The winged-cat had nestled on Hecate's back, her wings folded back and her eyes closed blissfully. Hecate didn't seem to mind, even turning to lick once at the cat's broken wing.

"Enyo?" Nix approached her pet and attempted to pick her up, but Enyo swiped at her, leaving shallow scratches across her arm. Nix pulled her arm back in shock.

"That's the majority," Briza announced.

Nix spun on her mother, her face twisted with frustration and pride. "Fine. She can come." She pulled a length of rope out of a stack of supplies. "But she's coming as a prisoner."

PART TWO

LUCID DREAMING

Chapter One

Reve skidded hard on her feet, sliding down the slick, stone chute deeper into the roots of the mountain. She felt the cold chill of the stone walls. A metallic scent floated through the nooks and crannies of the stones despite the fact that Reve could feel she was deep underground. The tunnels weren't supported like in a mine: they were hewn directly from the stone. The walls were decorated with the short, textured strokes of a chisel.

Hecate wasn't with her. It made Reve pause to realize that in a matter of days she'd already come to expect the wolf to follow her into her dreams.

She slowly made her way through the twisting, narrow tunnels. For a moment she thought she was in the Triad's mountain, but there were no veins of lifestone, no buzzing warmth across her skin. She didn't feel like she'd traveled through time or memory. She didn't even feel like she was on Aggar anymore. She was somewhere else entirely.

Reve closed her eyes and moved by Sight. She could see the labyrinth of trails spiraling ahead of her like a slithering snake. She could hear a violent hiss in he air, like steam escaping a pipe. The scents of sulfur and copper grew stronger the further she traveled, coating her tongue and filling her nose.

Reve traveled for hours, but the tunnels never seemed to change. Her Sight never showed her anything but stone. She started moving faster, fleeing into the unknown in search of anything else. Her body cramped. Her heart sped in her chest. The walls felt like they were closing in around her. She was trapped.

Reve heard the low hum of a Song in the distance and she panicked, running faster. If the Songs swarmed, she'd never escape. The stone floors were rough against her feet, biting at her injuries, but she couldn't stop. She turned a sharp corner and screamed as the floor disintegrated beneath her.

She was falling into a deep, all-consuming darkness. She couldn't feel the mountain around her anymore. Instead, she felt as if she were drifting in space, surrounded by an endless expanse of nothingness.

She hit water, sinking like a rock beneath the surface. Her hair floated around her face. The water pressed heavy against her skin. Her lungs burned as she ran out of air, but no matter how hard she swam, she couldn't reach the surface again.

As her vision blurred and she started to fall unconscious, bright lights flashed beneath her. They sparkled like stars. Faint, inaudible whispers fluttered through the deep rumble of the waves. Reve strained to hear what the voices were saying, but just as she started to make out words she could understand, the dream disappeared.

Reve gasped, waking with a start, and slowly sat up. She drew a deep breath, her lungs still aching as if she'd been drowning. She curled her knees to her chest. The *Niachero* swayed slowly like a child's cradle, the ship creaking and groaning with every motion. The brig sat in the bowels of the ship, too deep for a window. The only light in the room was a small lantern swinging from the ceiling.

The sharp hiss of steam from her dream echoed in the distance, the run-off of the ship's thrusters.

Hecate yawned and stretched, her front paws slipping through the bars of the brig cell. Reve glared into the darkness, her good hand balled into a tight fist. She couldn't think too long about where she was. If she accepted the darkness, the tight cell, the rush of the ocean against the wall at her back, she would drive herself crazy.

She didn't want to be brought aboard the *Niachero*, let alone as a prisoner. She didn't feel any draw to the sea. She couldn't fight the Songs if she couldn't reach them. Every moment on the ship was only taking her further from her goal.

Hecate, however, barely seemed to noticed anything out of the ordinary. She'd spent the last two days sleeping, only waking to be fed or when the ship's winged-cat came to visit. While traveling through the jungle, Reve had started to think her animal companion never needed sleep. It turned out Hecate had been running herself just as ragged as Reve had.

The sharp tap of boots on the nearby stairs echoed through the room. Sirena carried in a tray of meat, bread, and cheese. A bag was slung over her shoulder. "How are you doing today, Reve?"

Reve didn't answer, just followed Sirena with her sharp, cold glare. Reve hadn't said a word since being locked in her cell. That didn't stop the various members of the crew from constantly visiting and trying to comfort her. Their guilt was obvious, but none of them had the courage to stand up to their captain.

Sirena sighed and slid the tray under the brig bars. Reve stopped it with her foot, her eyes never leaving the captain's daughter. Hecate woke enough to grab a meaty bone from the tray. The smell of braised meat mingled with the briny scent embedded in the wooden walls. Reve's stomach let out a desperate growl, but she didn't acknowledge it.

Sirena crouched down, grabbing the bars. "We're working on a way to get you out of here. M'Sormee is... stubborn. But she isn't cruel. We just have to convince her you aren't dangerous."

Reve clenched her jaw. Sirena's face fell for a moment, but she glanced away before Reve could see her disappointment. She slid her bag to the ground and pulled out fresh clothes and boots. "They'll probably be a bit big on you, but I figured they were better than the rags you have now. I wish you'd let Agwe examine you. Your hand looks awful. You could be sick."

Reve clenched her jaw in defiance.

Sirena slid the clothes through the bars. She waited a moment longer, hoping for some kind of response, but eventually stood with a sharp sigh. She tucked a strand of her auburn hair behind her ear and turned away. She stopped in the doorway. "I'm sorry for what's happened to you. You have every right to be angry. I'll be back with dinner."

As she disappeared up the stairs, Reve let her gaze wander. She slowly picked up the clothes. She ran the soft cotton between her fingers and over the silky leather of the boots. They were a world away from what she was used to.

She glanced out the brig doorway up the stairs and slowly stood. The clothes were baggy on her starved frame, but the boots fit like a glove. Hecate glanced at her over her bone, her eyes glinting in the darkness.

"You have no right to judge me," Reve growled as she grabbed her share of the meal and tore into a hunk of bread.

Reve stood, leaning back against the bars. She had no way of telling time in the brig, but when Hecate started to stir and finally woke, Reve assumed night had fallen. Reve closed her eyes and searched the ship with her Sight. Most of the inhabitants were already asleep. Even the spastic energy of the small children had calmed.

Reve could see Kana and Volt wrapped in each other's arms. Sirena relaxed in her hammock, reading by lantern light. Agwe tended his plants, his mind completely at ease. Briza meditated, her mind soaring so far into the ether Reve couldn't sense her thoughts. Tlaloc dreamt of sailing.

It was nice for a moment, the quiet and the warmth of the

family. Reve remembered sleeping in her mother's arms, warm and safe in her embrace. Reve's nostalgia didn't last long as she shifted and the bar of her cell dug into her shoulder.

"Are those Sirena's clothes?"

Reve's eyes flew open and she fell back a step. Nix was standing just outside her cell. Reve looked her over in shock. She hadn't felt her near. No one had crept up on her in years.

Enyo leapt off Nix's shoulder and squeezed through the bars, fluttering her wings and settling on Hecate's back. Hecate turned and licked the tiny cat once before laying down again.

Reve stared at Nix, her eyes burning. Nix met her gaze without flinching. "I guess it was foolish of me to assume she'd let you stay in your rags."

Nix leaned back against the wall, her arms crossed over her chest. The gold and sparkling green of an emerald amulet around her neck and the strands of metallic silver in her hair glittered in the lantern light. She didn't wear boots, her bare feet steady on the paneled floors. Reve spotted a thin, silver ring on the second toe of both feet.

"Sirena has been begging me for days to talk to you. She thinks you can be trusted. Judging by the fact that I can count the words you've said to anyone in my family on one hand, I assume her determination stems from somewhere other than your delightful conversation." Nix looked her over. "Yet somehow, you have half my crew believing you're already family. Sirena I could understand. But Agwe? Briza? They aren't so easily swayed by mystery and a pretty face. There's something off about you and I don't want you on my ship."

Hecate stood and brushed against Reve's leg. Enyo flapped her wings in frustration.

Nix pushed off from the wall and took a step forward. The movement rustled the billowing white sleeves of her shirt. "But I'm an Amazon. I'm not a dictator. My family puts their faith in me, but we make decisions together. I won't send you away. But I won't leave you free to wander my home and cause trouble."

Reve's lips curled back from her teeth and for an instant Nix's face changed, growing older, more fierce. The face of her hometown magistrate, the Choir's eyes and ears who had discovered her in her parent's basement. The woman who had tried to offer her up to the Songs.

Nix turned to leave, walking toward the stairs. Reve threw herself at the bars closest to the door, her words escaping through clenched teeth. "I didn't ask to be here. You could have let me go.

You brought me on board."

Nix turned slowly, a triumphant glint in her eyes. "You didn't try to leave."

They stared into each others' eyes, a battle of wills with an unspoken truth neither wanted to admit: they were curious about each other.

Nix took a single step forward and reached out, grabbing Reve's broken hand. Reve tried to pull away but the taller woman held tight, her grip like iron. "Don't think you know me, Reve."

With a quick, sharp thrust of her wrist Nix snapped Reve's ring finger back into place. Reve let out an involuntary whimper of pain, but the sensation faded. Nix grabbed Reve's middle finger. Reve was ready this time, gritting her teeth and meeting Nix's eyes with a fiery gaze as a second finger was realigned. She didn't allow herself any more sounds of pain. For the first time, Nix regarded her with a hint of respect.

After a moment of sharp pain, the sensation dulled and finally disappeared. Reve carefully curled her fingers, her dexterity restored.

"Stop moving it. I'll send Agwe to splint you so you heal properly. I won't let my prisoners turn into cripples on my watch. Even if I wasn't the one to break them."

Nix turned away again. She called down to Reve as she walked up the stairs. "We're sailing north. When we next make port, you'll have the choice to stay or go. Choose carefully."

Nix's footsteps disappeared. Reve took a step back and nearly stumbled over Hecate. Enyo hissed. Reve glared and sat in the opposite corner of the cell, holding her broken hand close to her chest.

Reve's breath caught in her throat as she ran, her side cramping as she bounded through the stone tunnels. She could hear the Song behind her, growing louder and more insistent as it poured through the mountain trails after her.

The walls were growing tighter, closing in around her until she had to hunch and then crawl forward. She forced herself to breathe, to ignore the rapidly narrowing space. She could smell fresh air ahead. The tunnel had to open up somewhere.

She could feel the Song closing in. Her feet stung as the air tingled with the Song's intention. She cried out in shock as an electric sting lashed out at her leg, making the limb jump involuntarily.

Her fingers scraped at the stone floors as she dragged herself forward. Just ahead she could see a light. She could fit. She had to.

Her hands grabbed a stone ledge just ahead of her and she pulled herself forward. She popped out of the narrow passage into a giant cavern, her momentum throwing her over the slender ledge at the mouth of the tunnel. She fell, bracing herself for impact, but instead of shattering against the rocky cavern floor she dove into a pool of dark water.

She twisted and turned, fighting for air.

"Closer... Closer..."

A multitude of voices chanted the word over and over, whispers of something else jumbled in the distance.

I'm dreaming. I must be dreaming.

Reve closed her eyes and forced herself not to be afraid of drowning. She couldn't suffocate in a dream. Her primal instincts didn't apply here.

Instantly, Reve realized she could breathe again. She floated, weightless in the void, and tried to understand what the voices were saying to her.

"Closer... Closer... Come..."

Reve could see lights in the distance, twinkling like stars. She watched their pattern carefully, something odd about the design. Where was she?

Hecate kicked Reve in the stomach, instantly waking her. Reve's heart pounded as her eyes opened and she pushed herself up onto her hands. Hecate stilled. She was dreaming.

Reve trembled, still shaken by the hyper-realistic dream, and rested once more on Hecate's stomach. Even though the wolf was lean, her soft, warm fur and the steady rise and fall of her breath was comforting.

Reve's hand ached. She'd let Agwe splint her the night before, but healing seemed to be more painful than letting it stay broken. She was surprised she'd been able to fall asleep in the first place.

Hecate let out a deep, rumbling snore. Reve glared at her and sat up. She wouldn't be able to rest again.

A tray of food sat on the cell floor. Sirena must have delivered a meal while she was asleep. She reached for the apple and leaned forward in interest. A folded piece of paper had been hidden on the bottom of the tray.

Reve carefully opened it and stared at the words. The note was short, written in an artistic hand, but she couldn't read it. She strained to remember any of the words her parents had tried to teach her. She could make out a few of the individual letters, but not enough to even attempt to sound out the words.

Sirena had never been shy about trying to talk to Reve. What could be so important that she would have to hide it in a note in Reve's meal?

Short, light taps of feet creeping down the stairs echoed in the brig. Reve looked up in surprise as Sirena and Agwe padded down the stairs, casting nervous glances over their shoulders.

"Are you ready?" Agwe asked.

Reve looked them over in confusion. Sirena pointed to the letter in Reve's hand. "You got my message?"

Reve's lips formed a tight, straight line. Agwe's eyes lit with understanding. "You can't read."

Sirena looked between Reve and her brother, a deep blush rising to her cheeks. "Oh. I didn't even think... I'm sorry, Reve."

Agwe pulled a ring of keys from his belt and unlocked Reve's door. Hecate turned and stood, instantly waking. Reve followed cautiously, looking between the siblings.

Agwe shut the door behind her. "We can't let you out for long. M'Sormee won't like it, but she's sleeping. I'm sure you'd like some fresh air. We'll race you back if she wakes."

"M'Soremee won't wake," Sirena grunted. "I drugged her."

Agwe turned to his sister in shock, his delicate mouth opening in surprise and horror. "Sirena!"

"She's being a brute." Sirena stomped up the stairs.

Agwe turned to Reve, his soft eyes beseeching. "She's not dangerous."

"I never thought she was."

Agwe smiled in shock at Reve's voice. Reve sent him the ghost of a grin in return. She decided she liked the gentle healer.

She followed Agwe through the layers of the *Niachero*, moving on silent feet. As she reached the main deck she paused. The cold sea air licked at her cheeks. The night sky stretched endlessly above, not a single cloud blocking the clusters of stars of the brilliant light of the full moon.

Reve drew a breath deep into her lungs and closed her eyes, tipping her head back to the open air. For a moment she forgot that she was still on a ship – a floating prison – and just adored being free once more. She didn't belong locked in a cage. She belonged out in the wild.

"Thank you." The words escaped her lips, full of genuine gratitude. When she opened her eyes again, the siblings were watching her, smiling wide.

"I knew it would make you feel better," Sirena cheered softly.

Reve moved to the railing, staring down at the waves. There was no land in sight and Reve had never learned to swim. Still, she wondered what would happen if she jumped over the side. Would she be able to flounder back to land before she drowned? Was it worth the risk.

Reve felt a feather-light touch on her shoulder. "I can't let you do that."

She turned to face Agwe. He didn't look aggressive, but there was determination in his eyes. He knew what she'd been thinking. Reve cocked her head to the side. His grandmother claimed to be a seer. What else could Agwe see?

"Stay out of my mind," she whispered as she pulled out of his grip.

He only smiled. "I can't read minds, Reve. It wasn't hard to see what you were thinking. You'd drown. We're far from land and you have a broken hand. Even if you were as good a swimmer as m'Sormee you wouldn't make it."

Hecate yawned and stretched, padding dragging her claws along the floor. Enyo swept down from the helm and landed on the main deck. She swatted plafully at Hecate and bounded across the ship to the prow. Hecate followed, her feet thudding hard on the wood floors.

"Shh! You two..." Sirena raced after the animals.

Agwe leaned back against the railing and watched the animals play as Sirena tried to calm them. "I've never seen Enyo take after anyone like that. Is your wolf telepathic?"

"She's not mine. She just follows me. And I have no idea what she's capable of."

"It seems wrong to keep a land animal like her cooped up on a ship. It seems solid ground would be a better place."

Reve met his eyes and knew he wasn't talking about Hecate. Reve glanced out at sea again, the ocean breeze tousling her hair. Reve couldn't remember a time she'd gone so long without hearing a Song. "You don't know what land is like. There is no better place. There's only whatever path our destiny demands we take."

Reve walked away before Agwe could say anything else. She couldn't let herself care for the young man who fought so hard to keep her safe. She couldn't get used to days without running. This wasn't where she was supposed to be. She had to leave the moment she could. Hopefully, she'd leave Agwe behind so quickly he wouldn't catch the Choir's eye. They wouldn't take kindly to anyone helping her.

Sirena raced to her and took her arm. Reve stumbled back a step in surprise. "I want to show you my favorite place on the ship."

Sirena's eyes sparkled with delight. She raced to the ratlines and swung around the edge, climbing half-way up the rope ladder like a squirrel. "You're not afraid of heights are you?"

Reve watched Sirena scale the ratlines to the crow's nest, nestling high in the Niachero's ghostly sails. Reve wondered how far she'd be able to see from such a high location.

She whipped around the ratlines and slipped her feet into the rope rungs, careful not to put too much weight on her splinted hand. Agwe watched her carefully as she rocked forward, sent off-balance by the wind and rock of the ship. She quickly found her footing and followed Sirena.

Sirena's eyes were locked on the sea. The wind was stronger here, sending Sirena's skirt and hair rippling and whipping back in the breeze. She turned with a bright smile as Reve climbed into the wooden basket just big enough to hold three people. The moonlight tinted her skin blue, catching on the auburn of her hair until it glowed violet. Her joy radiated from her like the warmth of the springtime sun. Reve couldn't take her eyes off her. She was like a goddess formed from the wind.

"I love being up here. It's like flying. I thought... I thought maybe you'd appreciate that."

Reve joined Sirena at the rail of the basket. She looked as far out to sea as she could. Agwe had been right. There was no land nearby. Still, with Sirena standing so close, so full of joy... for a brief moment in time, Reve wasn't desperate to run away.

"Thank you."

Sirena smiled wide. She hesitantly reached out, her fingers brushing Reve's hand. "We'll keep you safe. Nix takes a while to cool down, but she's already rethinking putting you in the brig. She talked to you. She's been unsettled all day."

"She thinks I'll be a bad influence on you."

Sirena snorted. "At the end of the day, m'Sormee will always see Agwe and I as children. She's come to trust me in battle and at the helm. She doesn't care when I take a lover for the night. But she'll never trust us with a stranger we want to bring home, friend or otherwise."

"And why do you trust me, Sirena?"

Sirena blushed at the sound of Reve saying her name and tucked a strand of hair behind her ear. "Agwe trusts you and he doesn't trust anyone." Sirena turned, leaning back against the rail, boldly looking Reve over. "And you have the most beautiful eyes I've ever seen."

The warmth Reve had felt for Sirena evaporated at the mention of her eyes. She rapidly scanned her face for signs of the Choir's influence. She expected a sudden shift, she waited for her eyes to grow bloodthirsty, her smile to be replaced with a sneer. She would try to strangle her or throw her from the nest. No one looked into Reve's eyes and didn't try to kill her.

Sirena reached forward to stroke Reve's cheek and Reve flinched. Sirena instantly pulled back, her smile fading not with rage, but sadness. "I'm sorry Reve, I didn't mean to come on too strong. I would never —"

"No. It's fine." Reve took a step back, shaken by the entire encounter. The wind must be too strong to allow Sirena to be tainted by the Choir. Reve didn't know if the realization was comforting or unsettling. "The Amazons have sailed their sorormins outside of the Choir's grasp for generations. You just don't know what it's like on land. What it's like under the Choir's thumb."

"Reve, I know what it's like on land."

Reve shook her head and turned away. "No you don't."

She slid back down onto the ratlines, sliding down the ropes. The instant her feet hit the main deck, rough hands grabbed her shirt and threw her back against the wall. Nix glared down at her, wild-eyed and disheveled. "What are you doing here?"

Reve reacted instinctively, punching Nix hard in the face. The Amazon fell back in shock and Reve tried to run away, but Nix caught her around the waist, pulling them both to the ground. They struggled, but Nix was stronger and healthier than Reve. She quickly had the younger woman pinned to the ground, completely immobile.

Reve still struggled, growling snarling as she tried to fight off the Amazon. Hecate bounded across the ship and crouched low, baring her teeth, ready to attack.

"M'Sormee!" Agwe screamed as he ran across the deck. Sirena leapt down from the ratlines and raced to her mother, grabbing her arms.

The other members of the crew raced up the stairs at the sound of a fight.

"She hit me!" Nix shouted to her family.

"You pinned her," Sirena accused.

"She escaped."

"We let her out," Agwe argued. "She was going mad down there."

Nix looked between her children, her eyes lingering on Sirena. "You drugged me? For her?"

Sirena's lips twitched, her eyes shifting between her mother and Reve. "She doesn't deserve to be locked up. She's not dangerous. You're being proud."

Briza stepped forward. "Listen to her, Nix. Reve doesn't deserve your wrath just because you're afraid."

Nix slowly released Reve and stood, her eyes darting between the different members of her family. None of them spoke to argue with Briza and Sirena. Nix's eyes targeted Reve. "Fine. You have all of our attention. Tell me why you should be trusted."

"I don't have to prove anything to any of you," Reve hissed.

"You do if you don't want me to throw you overboard."

"M'Sormee!" Sirena and Agwe cried as one.

"They want you here. They already see you as family. But I won't allow it unless I can trust you."

Reve glanced over her shoulder, wondering once more how bad it would be if she leapt into the sea. Hecate moved to her, laying at her side and resting her head on Reve's shins. She looked up at Reve, her eyes glowing in the darkness. For an instant they connected like they only had in dreams, Hecate's thoughts and intentions laid bare.

Reve's panic ebbed and she looked back up at Nix. For the first time she didn't see rage and anger, but fear. She didn't want to hurt Reve. She was protecting her family. Reve could hardly fault her or it.

"Fine. I'll tell you my story. But I can't promise it will make you trust me any more."

Nix sat before her, crossing her legs. The rest of the crew followed suit, sitting and listening intently. Nix raised one hand. "Try me."

Chapter Two

Nix watched her waif-like prisoner as she chose her words, her eyes hard as steel, her expression unreadable. Reve's forest wolf nestled against her leg and Enyo preened herself standing on the wolf's back.

Nix's lips curled back from her teeth. Even her winged-cat seemed to prefer the newcomer. Nix didn't understand her family's attachment to the woman. What kind of person wanders Karatan alone with no supplies? The only emotions she'd shown were contempt and frustration except the moment Nix had fixed her broken hand and seen a flash of pain and determination. Everything else about her was a mystery.

There was something about her unnatural eyes that unnerved Nix to her core. Monsters and sea serpents, shifters and tricksters had blue eyes, not people. But somehow her children weren't unnerved by Reve's gaze. She could tell Sirena even found it attractive. They didn't see the signs.

"I was born in Opal Ridge, about a ten-day on foot north of the desert. Opal Ridge is a Choir hub It houses and trains Choir enforcers and agents. So when I was born with blue eyes my parents panicked."

Sirena leaned forward. "Why would the Choir care about your eyes?"

Reve hesitated. She let out a sharp breath of disbelief.

"Stories say demons have blue eyes." Briza's voice was heavy with disgust.

Reve flinched. "That's what the Choir whispers, yes."

"That's ridiculous. There are no such things as demons," Agwe countered.

"That doesn't stop the people from killing anyone born with blue eyes on sight." Agwe and Sirena fell silent in shock. Reve looked away, refusing to meet their eyes as she spoke. "You grew up surrounded by the wind. The Choir can't reach you." Reve's eyes caught on Nix. "They didn't have the chance to fill you with hate and fear."

"I didn't realize it was so different on land." Sirena's voice was soft, almost ashamed.

"The fear is ingrained in your minds from birth. It's whispered in the Songs that blanket you when you sleep. Monsters have blue eyes. Beasts have blue eyes. Murdering Blue Sights becomes instinctual. Primal. My mother told me my nurse tried to smother me before my first cry. Most parents throw their blue-eyed children down wells. I don't know why my parents kept their urge to protect me. Everyone else I've ever met has tried to kill me the instant they saw my eyes. Everyone but you."

Kana reached out and touched Reve's shoulder. "Reve."

Nix narrowed her eyes, but her stomach turned. She knew how insidious the Choir's control over the people of Aggar could be, but she had been on the sea for decades. The Choir didn't have any sway over her mind anymore.

"My parents did everything they could to keep me safe. They hid me, telling everyone I'd died in my crib. I spent half my life living in their cellar, in the dark. I started hearing the Songs just after I came of age. They'd drift through the night, blanketing the city, seeping into everyone's minds. I used to think they were beautiful. I didn't realize what they were." Reve hesitated before continuing, the words falling stiff and clinical from her lips. "I climbed out of the cellar one night. I wanted to listen to the Songs. My Mother had told me about the dangers of the Choir, but she had never warned me about the Songs. My parents couldn't hear them. I watched as they rolled over the hills and into tow like morning fog."

"That's impossible. No one can see Songs," Nix interrupted.

"I can." Reve glared at her out of the side of her eyes, her expression too genuine and intense for Nix to argue. "The Songs found me instantly. I'm lucky the Choir hadn't expected to find me, or they would have killed me. Every Choir agent was alerted about my existence. The entire town stormed my house. My parents tried to save me, but they were beaten to death on our front doorstep. I ran. I barely escaped. I started dreaming of a monastery on a mountaintop in Karatan that night. I ran through the hills, the desert and the jungle, the Songs always just behind me."

Nix's eyelids grew heavy as Reve spoke, her words infused with power. She could imagine Reve's journey in vivid detail: years of struggle, starvation, and fear. She could feel the oppressive heat off the desert and the poisonous wilds of Karatan.

Nix heard a deep hum on the breeze and turned to her mother, her eyes closed, Agwe half-asleep leaning on her shoulder. She looked around in shock. Her entire crew were held mesmerized by

Reve.

"My travels have made me who I am. They've crushed and pounded and wrung me out until all I am is my will to destroy the Choir. The Songs tell the world the Choir gives us peace. They've eradicated wars and monarchies. They control the weather, the seasons, pestilence and famine. But they took our free will. They took our minds." Reve's words became more heated, her defenses crumbling as she revealed her true self. Briza and Agwe breathed in sharp gasps, tears rolling down Agwe's cheeks. "I am an agent of chaos. I am the wind. And I'll see the Choir destroyed."

Agwe cried out, caught in a vision woven by Reve's story and Nix charged, knocking Reve to the ground. "What are you doing to them?"

Reve fought back, pushing Nix away and struggling to escape. Nix grabbed her around the waist, holding her down. "I'm not doing anything!"

"Look at them!" Nix grabbed her hair, turning her to face the crew, everyone still mesmerized by Reve's story. Briza and Agwe were nearly unconscious. "You rail against the Choir for controlling our minds. How are you any different?"

Reve twisted around, grabbing Nix by the throat, her eyes burning and her teeth bared. "I am nothing like the Choir."

The moment they met each other's eyes, Nix plummeted into the depths of Reve's mind. Reve's blue gaze bound them together, overwhelming Nix until she couldn't feel her ship or her family around her. She couldn't feel the wind or the roll of the sea.

Instead she scrambled across an old wooden floor. She could feel hot, wet blood under her palms as she watched through Reve's eyes as her parents were crushed beneath the mob.

She ran from the Songs, her body screaming as the billowing storms of Song chased after her.

She crept, too hungry to stand, through the desert. She felt a moment of hope as she crossed a trader, the feeble, elderly woman smiling down at her with kind eyes. The woman offered her bread, her gentle smile turning to a frown as she noticed Reve's blue eyes. The grandmother grabbed an ax, flinging it at her as she ran away.

In a matter of minutes, Nix felt the weight of Reve's nearly eleven tenmoons, the emotions and memories coming so fast she could barely comprehend them. Details faded, replaced only with the pain, the fear, the determination.

Nix cried out and was plunged into darkness. She couldn't breathe. She was stranded weightless, floating as if she were deep under water. Lights flickered behind her eyes and she felt herself passing out.

"Nix!"

Tlaloc pulled her away from Reve, breaking their connection. Nix gasped for breath, struggling wildly as she was pulled out of the darkness. She calmed as her home became her reality again, Tlaloc's protective embrace giving her something to focus on beyond the crushing darkness of Reve's past.

"What are you?" Tlaloc demanded.

Reve stumbled and tripped as she tried to flee. She was obviously still just as dazed as Nix. Lyr, Kana, and Volt grabbed her, pinning her to the ground and holding her still.

"Stop." Nix's voice was weak, but it caught her crew's attention. She pulled herself to her feet, swaying once before regaining her balance. "She's not a threat."

Reve breathed hard, her eyes wide in shock at Nix's announcement. Kana and Volt slowly released her.

"Are you alright, m'Sormee?" Sirena gasped. "You looked like you were dying."

"She was allowed to see the truth." Briza ran her fingers through Agwe's hair as she looked up at her daughter. Nix instantly knew Reve hadn't been bewitching them. She had triggered their latent seer abilities. Whatever Agwe had seen had sapped the last of his energy.

"Reve is a Blue Sight. She has..." Nix shook her head in confusion, the visions she'd seen in Reve's mind already fading like a dream. "Abilities. She was trying to help us understand, but I pushed her too far."

"You've changed your mind about her, then?" Lyr questioned, still crouched low in a fighting stance, ready to tackle Reve again if necessary.

Nix hesitated, her emotions still a tangle. "Yes, I think I have."

The family stepped away from Reve, slowly sitting again. Hecate circled Reve. The Blue Sight grabbed the wolf, burying her face in the creature's neck. Her long, delicate fingers curled in the beast's fur. Her hands were shaking. Nix remembered the endless stream of people who had turned on her, trying to kill her. Being thrown to the ground three times in one night had obviously triggered old fears.

"No one else will touch you tonight," Nix promised, her voice soft while addressing Reve for the first time.

Reve looked up over Hecate's neck, her hypnotic eyes flashing. "I told you my story, Nix n'Niachero. Now you tell me yours."

Nix sat again. She could only imagine what Reve had seen when they connected. "Fine." She turned to Kana. "You tell stories better than I do and you've been with me since the beginning."

Reve looked between the two of them, but she didn't argue with Nix's request.

Kana started telling the familiar story, her words flowing like strands of an intricate tapestry. Kana could do with words what Reve had with her Sight and Nix found herself traveling back in time, to before she had taken to the sea. Back when she was Agwe's age, living in a tiny village on the edge of the desert.

It had just been Nix, Kana, and Tlaloc then. Briza was still young, spending more time sailing in Nix's youth than at home with her daughter. Life on the sea had been harder then and Briza had thought her daughter would be safer on solid ground. She'd never admit it, but Nix had always known Briza hadn't planned to be a mother.

Nix could still feel the desert sun on her skin, feel the sand beneath her toes and smell the sharp aroma of desert roses. Kana had been pure magic then, dancing and spinning under the endless desert sky. Tlaloc had been an accountant, running the village storehouse with meticulous care.

Like every other village in Aggar, Nix's home depended on the weather cycles created by the Choir to survive. The Choir's rains allowed their farms to thrive and provided plenty of water. Nix had trusted the Choir then, believing the lies that the Choir created the perfect cycle, keeping Aggar thriving and peaceful.

A flood of faces, long dead, flashed across Nix's mind. Friends and family that had raised her in Briza's absence. She had watched all of them whither away. The Choir had diverted the rain, leaving Nix's home in an endless drought.

As the strongest members of the village, Kana and Nix had traveled more than a ten-day to the nearest Choir oracle. They'd begged her to speak to the Choir on their behalf, to find out why the rain had stopped. There had been no pity in her eyes when she told them the rain was needed in more important parts of the world.

Nix had lost her faith in the Choir that day. By the time Kana and Nix had returned, more than half the village had perished from heat, starvation, or thirst. They had abandoned their land and home, intent on traveling to the coast to seek the aide of the Amazons and their ships.

By the time they reached the sea, less than a dozen of them were left. Lyr had been born on the beach, stealing the last of his mother's strength. Nix had delivered him with her own hands and buried his mother the same day.

Briza had found them, nearly dead. In less than a tenmoon, only

Kana, Tlaloc, Lyr, and Briza were left alive from their home village.

"Agwe, Sirena, Doris, and Pan were born at sea. Volt joined the crew when we bonded. We haven't lived on land since." Kana's voice hung heavy in the air.

Reve turned to Nix. "You hate the Choir as much as I do. I felt it."

"They killed everyone." Nix's voice grew in strength as she spoke, old rage she'd been repressing for decades returning. "They deemed us worthless and abandoned us. I swore my family would never be under the Choir's control again."

"Your story isn't unique. The Choir doesn't feel. They don't care about us. They only care about keeping their power. If that means massacring blue sights or letting villages turn to ash and dust, so be it. No one is safe in their world. No one has the power or ability to control their own destinies. They must be destroyed. The people of Aggar must take their planet back into their own hands."

Nix clenched her jaw as she thought, trying to make sense out of everything she'd seen and felt in the last couple hours. She glanced at Agwe as he shifted against Briza's knee, slipping from unconsciousness into regular sleep.

"We all need rest. A lot has happened tonight."

"Are you sending me back to the brig?" Reve's voice was almost a challenge.

Nix shook her head. She didn't have the strength to fight the wild Blue Sight anymore. "You're our guest until we figure out how we want to proceed."

"You can share my room. I have an empty bunk," Sirena offered.

Nix glanced at her daughter. It had been a long time since Sirena had been so obviously interested in someone. The thought broke Nix's heart; Reve would never allow herself into a relationship. With her focus so firmly rooted in her mission, Nix doubted Reve even noticed Sirena's interest. Still, there were no spare rooms on the ship and Sirena had the most free space and the only free bunk.

"Anything is better than a cell," Reve agreed.

Sirena smiled wide.

Nix stood. "We'll talk again in the morning."

Her family nodded and parted ways, Briza helping Agwe down to his room. Sirena led Reve to their room. Reve glanced over her shoulder at Nix before disappearing down the stairs. Their eyes met briefly, a moment of familiarity and understanding passing between them. Nix nodded. Reve's eyes flicked, looking Nix over anew. Quickly, almost imperceptibly, she nodded in return and followed Sirena.

A shock of electricity raced up Nix's spine as the younger woman left. It unsettled her how connected she felt to her when she hadn't even decided what she thought of the Blue Sight.

She shook her head, brushing her discomfort aside. She was in no place to be making decisions. She needed a good night's sleep, that was all. A few hours of rest and she wouldn't feel so unnerved.

Still, as she shut herself in her cabin, stripped out of her clothes, and laid in bed, she couldn't forget the bond they'd forged in the furnace of Reve's Sight. She struggled to forget the vivid memory of Reve's parents being murdered and the suffocating feeling of drowning in the dark. She wondered what she was going to do, if she could let Reve go knowing how violently the Choir would pursue her the moment she stepped foot back on land.

She fought to quiet her mind. She grounded herself in the moment even as she let the stress of the day wash away. As she slowly drifted into dreams, every thought disappeared but the memory of the fire in Reve's eyes.

Nix gasped and grabbed at her sheets in tight fists. Her sweat-soaked clothes clung to her body like a second skin. Her heart pounded wildly in her chest and her breath came in quick, sharp gasps.

She couldn't remember what she'd been dreaming. She could only remember Reve's eyes, glowing out of the darkness. She wasn't scared of the Blue Sight. She wasn't ashamed of whatever Reve's supernatural eyes could see in her mind and soul. But Reve affected her in ways she couldn't understand.

She stood on trembling legs and forced herself to calm down. It made sense that she was dreaming of Reve. They'd just been in each other's minds. She'd experienced a glimpse of Reve's most traumatic experiences. It would be strange if she didn't dream of Reve.

She dressed quickly and ran a wet towel over her face, breathing deeply into the hot, wet fabric as she steeled her nerves. She wouldn't let her family see her unsettled.

The sun was already high in the sky and the crew of the *Niachero* were going about their daily tasks as Nix walked out onto the main deck. She looked up at the sun in a daze. She hadn't realized it was so late.

"You look drunk." Briza eased her way down the stairs, her log, silver braid hanging over one plump shoulder.

"Hard night."

"I'd imagine it would be. Did you dream?"

Nix glanced at her mother, her eyes angled knowingly. "What have you seen?"

Briza crossed her arms over her chest. She watched Agwe and Sirena teaching Reve to tie knots. Nix felt a knot of worry untangle in her stomach at Agwe's smile. Whatever visions had tormented him the night before hadn't clung to him.

"I've seen Reve."

"Seems everyone has lately."

"Does she still upset you?"

Hecate raced circles around Reve, Agwe, and Sirena. They laughed, Reve's face splitting into a genuine smile. Nix shook her head. "There's something... off-putting about her. Something I can't explain. But she isn't dangerous to us. Not unless we get in her way."

"Perhaps you feel uncomfortable around her because you still carry whispers of the Choir."

Nix glared at her mother, clenching her jaw. "The Choir doesn't control me."

Briza held up a had in surrender. "I didn't mean to upset you. I only meant that you were raised on land. Your earliest fears and beliefs were influenced by the Choir's Songs. It would make sense that you have an inborn fear of blue eyes."

"Are you calling me prejudiced, m'Sormee?"

"We're all prejudiced, Soroe. The only way our minds will ever be free is if we accept and fight our ugliest feelings and beliefs. I sensed parts of Reve's past and I saw glimpses of her future. Only you walked her path. After everything you've seen of her, you still think there's malice behind her eyes?"

Sirena touched Reve's shoulder as she examined her knot. Her gaze was warm and affectionate. Agwe smiled and patted Hecate. Despite her motherly concern, Nix knew her children weren't bad judges of character. Sirena was very particular about her lovers and Agwe rarely took to anyone.

Briza patted her daughter's hand. "They were never touched by the Choir's influence. They don't see the bad in Reve. They aren't scared like you are. That has to mean something, Nix."

Briza took two steps away, heading for the living quarters to teach Doris and Pan their history lesson.

"M'Sormee," Nix called. Briza glanced over her shoulder at her daughter. "Tell me what you saw in her."

Briza hesitated. "I saw her changing everything."

Nix leaned back against the door to her room as Briza left. Perhaps Briza was right. Nix was well aware of how stubborn her pride could be.

She pressed her lips into a hard line and let out a low, steady breath. She had to talk to Reve.

The sun was steadily sinking behind the horizon when Nix spotted Reve standing alone at the prow. The rest of the crew were still eating dinner. Agwe had suggested Reve pace herself, eating small meals throughout the day to expand her stomach slowly as she recovered from malnutrition.

"How are you feeling?" Nix stepped beside Reve and leaned forward against the rail.

"Better. Hecate likes it here."

Nix snorted. "That's because Sirena sneaks her bones."

"And Enyo massages her back."

Nix scowled. "That cat has never been sweet to anyone before. Now she's practically purring over a wolf."

"Maybe she just doesn't like people. I can understand that."

Nix tensed. Their conversation was already taking a turn. "I've always found the sea soothing."

"I wasn't looking at the ocean, I was looking at your masthead," Reve admitted. "I never realized there were lifestones aboard the ship."

"They're symbolic of my bond with my sorormin. Of our bond as a family."

"Blue-sights and Amazons have been using lifestones for bonding for ages. It's where current marriage traditions came from."

Nix shifted uncomfortably. "I'm not one for bonding."

"I know."

Nix stared down at her hands, Reve's eyes still locked on the masthead. "I don't know what you saw in my mind when we connected, but if it was anything like what I saw..."

"I'm fine, Nix."

"That's not what I meant. I saw your hatred for the Choir and I know what brought you to that place. I respect that."

"I saw your trek through the desert. I watched your friends die and I buried them. I felt your anger at your mother for leaving you. For not foreseeing the Choir turning on your village."

Nix closed her eyes. She felt a tug at her waist, like a golden thread binding them together through their shared experience. She suddenly knew she'd never have any secrets from the Blue Sight.

Nix turned around, leaning back against the railing and looking Reve in her eyes. She wouldn't let the Choir dictate her fears. "Then you know how much I hate the Choir. I thought taking to the sea was the most rebellious thing I could do, but Briza thinks you have a part to play in their demise, and her visions have always been trustworthy. Perhaps by taking care of you, I can do my part to see them wiped off Aggar for good."

The same fire that had lit Reve's eyes when she allowed Nix to reset her broken fingers returned. Nix's breath caught in the back of her throat and she could hear her heart pounding behind her ears. "You'll help me? Knowing who I am?"

Nix nodded. "As long as you want us, the Niachero can be your home. Your family."

"I don't have a home, Nix. My journey, my life, will end with the death of the Choir. Your family can't count on me."

Nix offered her hand. "Just tell me how I can help you and I will. Whatever happens will be worth it once the Choir burns."

Reve glanced down warily at Nix's offered hand. Nix could read her hesitance in her eyes. Finally, she took Nix's hand in a firm grip and nodded. "Thank you."

Nix clasped Reve's shoulder and smiled. "Tell me the next time you have a vision. My rudder is at your command."

Nix turned and walked away. She could feel Reve's eyes on her back, but for the first time the sensation didn't unnerve her. She felt steady. Stable. She was doing the right thing and soon she'd watch the Choir fade away to nothingness.

She felt Reve smile and couldn't help but smile as well. Perhaps it wouldn't be so bad to have a Blue Sight on board.

Chapter Three

Reve laid awake, staring at the wooden slats of the ceiling. Her woven rope hammock swung with the gentle rocking of the ship. Hecate slept beneath her, the wolf's fur brushing against her back as the netting of the hammock swayed. Hecate had stalked around the ship all night, coming back to Reve just as the sun broke across the horizon. It seemed peacetime was making her nocturnal again.

Reve rested one hand on her stomach. She couldn't remember the last time she'd been so full. She wondered if she'd get the chance to grow fat in her contentment. She smiled. She'd always wondered what it would be like to touch her stomach and feel more than bones and wiry muscle.

Sirena slept on the opposite end of the cabin, burrowed in a pile of furs and blankets. Reve watched her, the young cook's dreams pleasant and still. She looked so peaceful, a soft smile on her full lips, her auburn hair splayed across her face, shading her eyes. For a moment Reve closed her eyes in disbelief. She'd been on the *Niachero* for a couple ten-days, but everything still felt foreign. It didn't seem natural that a woman like Sirena would share a room with her. That she wouldn't flinch at the sight of her.

Reve rustled, kicking her blanket away with her feet. No matter what she did, she couldn't rest. She hadn't had any impressions of visions about the next step of her journey. Every time she dreamt, it was of the same stone passageways, the same heavy darkness that drowned her until she woke in a cold sweat.

It was clear she was where she was supposed to be. Everything about the ship felt solid. Right. Hecate was adamant about staying. Reve knew her Sight wouldn't have bonded her so tightly to Nix's mind if she was straying from her path.

Still, despite sailing across the coasts of Aggar, Reve felt like she was standing still. Her muscles ached to run, to press on. She didn't know what to do with herself when she wasn't being chased by the Songs.

Reve drew a deep breath, the familiar tang of brine in the air dancing across her tongue and filling her lungs. She ran her fingers through her shaggy blonde hair, her locks growing faster and thicker on the ship than it ever had on the run.

She tried to project, but the ship was so still. Everyone slept. Even the creatures of the deep seemed to be at peace. Reve's spirit had wandered the rooms and spaces of the *Niachero* dozens of times since her arrival, but over time she'd started to feel like an intruder. It didn't seem right to sit with Doris and Pan as Kana told them bedtime stories or to lounge on Tlaloc's couch as zi read late into the night. They had welcomed her as a guest. They didn't fear her or hurt her. She didn't need to resort to spying.

"Reve?" Reve opened her eyes as Sirena climbed out of bed. "Are you alright? You've been tossing and turning all night."

"I'm fine," Reve muttered. "Just thinking."

Sirena smiled and brushed her hair out of her eyes. "I'm going to start breakfast soon. Is there anything you want?"

Reve grinned. "Anything with eggs. And fruit. And maybe jam?"

Sirena laughed. "No one appreciates my food like you."

Reve propped herself up on her elbows, her eyes warm. "You eat enough raw roots and the occasional rat and jam will taste like paradise."

Sirena's eyes flashed. She walked to Reve, bent over her hammock and kissed her cheek. "You know how to make a girl feel appreciated."

Reve smiled up at her, but made no move to touch her. Sirena only waited a moment before slipping out of their shared room into the kitchen. Reve tucked her hands behind her head. Sirena wasn't shy about her attraction to Reve, but she made a point never to push Reve's boundaries.

Reve had learned about sex and love from her parents, but she'd never considered it a possibility for her future until she'd met Sirena. Part of her knew it was selfish to even entertain Sirena's flirtations – Reve wasn't going to fall in love with her, and she wasn't going to take Sirena with her when she went after the Choir – but it felt good to have her affection. Perhaps Reve was more of a pack animal than she'd realized.

A sharp knock echoed on the door frame and Agwe called into the room. "Can I come in?"

Reve sat up. "Yes."

Agwe strolled into the room, his medicine bag over his shoulder. Reve smiled at him. The expression seemed to come more easily every day.

"How's your hand today, Reve?"

Reve swung her legs over the side of the hammock, the edge of the oversized sleep shirt Volt had given her bunched around her thighs. She held out her splinted hand. "It itches."

"It's healing," Agwe commented. He opened her bag and pulled out fresh bandages. "I suspect most of your body itches by now. Your feet still hurt when you walk?"

Reve shook her head. "I've never felt so strong. Your poultices worked wonders. You're amazing."

Agwe snorted and knelt in front of her, carefully undoing the knots that held her splint in place. "You've don't have many healers to compare me to. Our bodies are the real wonders. I just ease the process."

He finished unbinding her splint and gently moved her wrist through a full range of motion, easing the tension in the tiny muscles of her wrist and hand. "Still. Thank you."

Agwe nodded, all his focus on her injury. "You're coming along well. I want you to leave the splint off today. Let me know how you feel by dinner time. Don't do anything too intense, but let your fingers move again."

Reve grinned. It was good to have her hand back. "I will."

Agwe stood. "I found my first medical journal. There are a few easy poultices and recipes I could teach you if you're still interested in learning."

Reve slid to her feet. Hecate licked affectionately at her ankle before falling asleep again. "I'd love to."

"Meet me after breakfast, when the children have class. We can work together then."

"I look forward to it."

Agwe slipped out of the room to allow Reve to get dressed. Reve crouched down before the small, wooden chest Nix had given her. Everyone in the crew had pitched in to provide her with basic necessities. A small, sapphire pendant swung around her neck off a copper chain. Kana had pressed it into her hand with a change of clothing and whispered in her ear that it was because everyone deserved to have something beautiful. It was the exact color of Reve's eyes, but somehow it warmed Reve to keep it near her heart despite its offensive color.

She sifted through the small collection of shirts and breeches, pulling out a soft, white shirt and tan breeches. Her fingers lingered over a warm, quilted vest from Nix. She'd avoided wearing anything the Amazon had given her.

She dressed quickly and pulled on the boots Sirena had given her in the brig. She patted Hecate's back. "I'll get you a bone," she promised. Hecate snored.

Sirena was slicing warm bread as Reve stepped into the kitchen. She swiped at a bowl of jam with her finger. Sirena swatted at her hand and Reve spun away, licking the sugary treat from her hand.

"Already so spoiled," Sirena teased.

Reve only laughed and walked out of the galley toward the main deck.

Doris and Pan, still dressed in their nightclothes, ran around Reve as they raced up the stairs. Lyr chased after them, swinging around the ratlines and grabbing a child under each arm.

"Good morning, Reve," Lyr greeted as Doris and Pan kicked and giggled. "Breakfast almost ready?"

"Sirena's just finishing now."

"Good, I'm starving," Lyr grunted as he bounced the children and carried them back down to their room."

Reve stepped out into the early morning sunlight and drew a deep breath. She was becoming more accustomed to ocean air. She barely even noticed the wind anymore unless Volt activated the thrusters.

Reve swung around the ratlines and climbed to the crow's nest. She'd made the climb every day since Sirena had first shown her the lookout. It gave Reve peace when the energy and chatter of the crew became too much to bear. She was getting more accustomed to the company, but sometimes she longed for the quiet.

Reve leaned back against the wooden rail of the nest and stared up at the sky. Sirena had told her they'd reach Nix's shipbuilding friend in a couple days. He'd be able to fix the ship, but they'd have to be on land while the repairs were made. Reve knew she'd have to make a decision. The Choir would find her instantly. The shipbuilder was likely to attempt to put an awl through her skull and even if she escaped, she knew the Choir wouldn't hesitate to massacre Nix and her crew for giving her shelter.

Perhaps everyone would be safe if she stayed at sea, adrift in a life boat until the *Niachero* returned for her? Maybe she should run away, leap into the sea when they approached land and draw the Choir away from the crew. She needed answers. She needed direction. Perhaps there was something about the wind that hindered her ability to find her path as much as it kept the Songs at bay.

Reve closed her eyes and let her Sight wander. Sirena was serving breakfast. The rest of the crew were already lined up in the galley. Reve could feel Sirena looking for her, wondering where she was. Nix lingered in her quarters, pacing her room. Reve kept her thoughts and energy at bay. Ever since they'd connected, Reve had intentionally left the Amazon alone. Even when she wandered the ship as a projection, Reve was quietly afraid she'd be consumed by the older woman's presence again.

"There you are." Reve opened her eyes. Agwe climbed into the nest with her. "Sirena's made breakfast. Said it was special for you."

Reve nodded. "I know. I just wanted to clear my head. It always gets so busy in the galley at breakfast time."

Agwe sat beside her. "I know what you mean."

They sat in comfortable silence for a long moment. Reve and Agwe rarely needed to talk to each other. They both appreciated the quiet as much as the warmth of a friend.

"Have you had any dreams about where you're supposed to go next?"

Reve glanced Agwe, a single brow raised in question. "Have you seen anything?"

He laughed. "My visions aren't like your Sight, Reve. I can't control them. I can't even interpret them like Briza can. I just know you're confused."

Reve let out a deep breath and watched the clouds pass overhead. "I have no idea where I'm supposed to go or what I'm supposed to do. Whatever force or visions that were guiding me before have gone silent. All I can See now is in the present."

"Maybe that's a message in itself. Maybe you're already where you're supposed to be."

Reve ran her thumb over her bottom lip, deep in thought. "Maybe."

"Reve? Agwe? Are you coming to breakfast?" Kana's voice cut through the howl of the ocean breeze and the rustle of the sails.

Agwe glanced over the edge of the crow's nest and nodded. "We should go. We don't want to make Sirena upset."

Reve grinned at the thought and followed Agwe out of the nest and down the ratlines to the main deck.

"Now, carefully cut away the skin from the leaf."

Reve glanced at Agwe and slowly ran the edge of her knife just under the waxy outer shell of the wide, pale green leaf Agwe had harvested from his garden. The leaf was as long as Reve's forearm, but the slender blade Agwe had lent her made quick work of the succulent's skin.

Agwe beamed at her with pride as she revealed channels of sticky, pale green gel just under the leaf's surface. "The gel can be used to seal and soothe all kinds of minor injuries. Burns. Cuts.

Headaches. Sores."

Reve shook her head in disbelief. "I saw hundreds of these in the jungle."

"They could have helped your feet and scrapes." Reve offered Agwe his knife back and he shook his head. "Keep it. If you find yourself alone in the jungle again, I'd like to think you could patch yourself up a bit better than last time."

Reve held tighter to the knife and smiled softly. "Is it safe for wolves?"

"Should be. Enyo used to try to eat my succulents when I first brought them aboard. They didn't even make her sick. That's why I keep the door closed."

"You know of anything that could cure a fever?"

Agwe pulled open his field journal and flipped through its yellowing pages. "Depends on what causes the fever. Are you prone to fevers?"

Reve shook her head. "I caught a few crossing the desert. I nearly died three times."

"Probably heat exhaustion. Do you know how to harvest cactus for the water?"

Reve shook her head. "Teach me?"

Lyr and Volt stumbled inside. Volt supported Lyr, his arm under the changling's shoulders. Lyr held his side, his face twisted with embarrassment and pain.

"What happened?" Agwe leapt to Lyr's side and helped Volt carry him to the examination table.

"It's nothing," Lyr grunted as he sat on the table.

"Let me see." Agwe gently moved Lyr's hand from his side, revealing a bloody gash along his waist.

"He cut himself in my shop," Volt explained.

Lyr glanced away from Agwe. "It was stupid. I tripped. I shouldn't have been standing so close to Volt's tools."

"We all make mistakes." Agwe's voice was soft but distant, his focus clearly on the injury. "Reve, get me a warm towel?" Reve rushed to do as she was told. Agwe glanced at Lyr. "Take your shirt off?"

Lyr squirmed and blushed as he pulled his shirt over his head. His lean, sculpted muscles twitched in pain. Reve returned with the rag and Agwe set about cleaning the wound. Lyr watched him work, his cat-like ears laying flat against his head. Volt squeezed his shoulder sympathetically.

Agwe stood and dug through his medical bag.

"Is it bad?" Volt questioned.

Agwe shook his head. "Not at all, just bloody. A few stitches and all will be well."

Agwe's hand was steady and his stitches even and tight. Reve could tell he had a natural talent for healing. Within moments, Lyr's wound was a slender line of embroidery. Agwe knotted the stitch and clipped the rest of the thread, carefully setting the bloody needle in a small bowl for disinfecting.

"Thank you, Agwe," Lyr muttered.

Agwe stood and shook his head with a smile. "I'm just glad to help. Try to be a bit more careful where you step."

Agwe turned to a water basin to wash his hands. Lyr's lips twitched as if he wanted to say more, but instead he only slid off the table, grabbed his shirt and slunk away.

Agwe glanced over his shoulder. "Did Lyr leave already?"

Volt chuckled and shook his head as he turned to leave. "You poor, blind fool."

Agwe turned to Reve. "I don't understand."

Reve smiled gently. "It's fine. Can you teach me to stitch like that?"

Agwe wiped his hands on a dry rag and dug a clean needle from his bag. "Have you ever embroidered before?"

Reve sat in her hammock, carefully stitching a line of thread through a square of thin leather. Her stitches were nowhere near as precise and even as Agwe's. Her fingertips were dotted with blood from pricking herself, but she was confident with a bit more practice she'd be able to stitch her own wounds when the time came. At the very least, her time on the *Niachero* was proving educational.

Hecate sniffed at her boot, watching her as she struggled with the finishing knot that would secure the stitch. "It's not as easy as it looks," Reve grunted. Hecate nudged her arm and Reve smiled, scratching between Hecate's ears. "I might have to stitch you up one day, too."

The door between the bedroom and the galley swung open. Reve jolted upright, instinctively holding the needle out like a weapon. Nix looked her over, almost amused. "A needle?"

"It's all I had," Reve muttered.

"No one will attack you on my ship, Reve."

"Old habits die hard."

The light of Reve's lantern caught on the gold amulet hanging low over Nix's heart. Reve's breath caught in her throat as her eyes caught on the lines of the Amazon's body. She forced her eyes to Nix's face. Their connection through the Sight was playing tricks on her mind. She suddenly wished they were on the main deck, not alone in a tiny room.

"Have you seen Sirena?"

Reve shook her head. "Not since breakfast."

Nix hesitated. "We've never talked about where you want to go. I offered you my support, but I don't know what you want me to do."

"I don't know where I'm supposed to go yet. I haven't had any dreams."

"Does it usually take so long for you to know what to do next?"

Reve shook her head. "I think the wind might be interfering with my Sight."

"Well, we'll know once we make port."

Reve clenched her jaw. She wondered how much Nix knew about her plans. Every now and then Reve could still feel Nix's emotions or sense her dreams through their bond. Could Nix sense her confusion as well?

"Is everything alright, Reve?"

Reve's head cocked to the side in surprise at the question. "Why?"

Nix chuckled. "It wasn't an accusation. You've been with us for some time now, but you still seem withdrawn."

"Agwe is just as reclusive," Reve pointed out.

"By choice, yes. I want to be sure your solitude is also by choice."

Reve glanced away, pondering Nix's question. "Sometimes I find people overwhelming."

Reve could feel Nix's eyes on her, not entirely believing her. Reve was sure she was a terrible liar. She hadn't had much experience hiding her feelings from other people.

"Just know you're welcome among us. We can help you."

"Thank you."

Nix's eyes lingered over Reve a moment longer, sending the hair on the back of Reve's neck standing on end. Finally, Nix turned and left, closing the door behind her.

Reve let out a deep breath and leaned back in her hammock. Her skin felt tight and her blood pounded behind her ears. She still didn't know what to make of the brusque captain. In the time Reve had been on the *Niachero*, Nix had imprisoned her, broken her hand, attacked her, and tried to send her away. She'd also walked in Reve's mind, provided her with food, shelter, clothes, and promised her a home. Reve didn't know what to expect next.

The Blue Sight balled her fists in confusion and frustration. She had always been so focused, so sure. She didn't like being confused.

Tlaloc carefully lit the kindling in the large, iron fire basin. The excellerant caught immediately and Tlaloc added more wood to the fire as it blazed to life. Doris and Pan cheered, the fire casting their long shadows across the main deck. Sirena laid three fowls over the flames, already plucked and threaded on a spit. The sun had already set, the stars blazing in milky-white patterns across the sky.

There was an air of joy on the *Niachero* that night. A lightness of being that cracked through Reve's hard exterior. She remembered hiding in the trunk the night she'd met Agwe. She remembered the deep longing to be a part of the family. It seemed like a dream to be included in their happiness.

Volt and Kana danced in the moonlight while Lyr chased the children from bow to stern. Tlaloc and Nix threw darts at a wooden target, testing their aim in the dark. Agwe sat beside Briza and read, but his eyes flicked up from the page often, a contented smile lighting his face.

Hecate howled at the moons in glee as Enyo flew above her, the cat's wings casting flickering shadows across sails.

Reve was suddenly caught by a deep sadness. She didn't want to leave them, but this wasn't her life. This happiness, this contentment, was like a different reality.

"You're more quiet than usual tonight."

Briza eased herself to the ground to sit beside Reve. The top of the tiny woman's head barely reached Reve's chin.

"I like watching," Reve answered honestly.

"That's because you're a shadow."

Reve turned to her sharply, her eyes wide. "How do you know?"

Briza laughed, the sound weathered and deep. "My visions have never given me the whys or the hows. I just know things, whether they make sense or not. I know you are shadow, like I know you are Blue Sight. I have no idea what exactly that entails, and honestly I don't care. I'm too old to think I know everything. A little mystery keeps me on my toes."

"Is it always like this? Dancing and laughing together?"

"Sometimes Nix gets drunk and Volt catches fire. Sometimes we fight. But most of the time we're happy. We're chosen family. Nix invited you into the family."

"She did."

"You won't take her up on it? She wouldn't have offered without good reason. Especially not just days after she'd tried to convince you to leave."

"My path doesn't include families. But I'll never forget this. I think I want this to be my last thought when I die."

"So dark for someone so young."

Reve met Briza's eyes and saw the wisdom there. Of everyone Reve had ever met, Briza knew what it was like to See with more than her eyes. "Sometimes the thought of death is a peaceful one."

Briza patted her shoulder. "Well, my dear, if I've learned one thing in all my years it's that only a fool thinks she can predict the future. You're touched by fate. No telling where your path will take you."

"Briza, help me?"

Briza turned to her granddaughter and nodded. She used Reve's shoulder as support to stand. "Just think about what I said, Reve. You deserve a little happiness." Briza crossed the deck to help Sirena with dinner.

Reve watched them work together and curled her knees to her chest. Perhaps Briza was right. Maybe her future did hold some kind of happiness. But hoping for it was more dangerous than fear or allowing herself to succumb to pain. If she found happiness, if she had something she wanted outside of destroying the Choir, she could be distracted. The Choir was powerful, ancient. She'd never questioned that destroying them would take the ultimate sacrifice. She couldn't afford to balk at that responsibility because she had other things on her mind.

Still, it couldn't hurt to have one night of laughter. One night warm by the fire. It couldn't hurt to sit close to family if she didn't allow herself to become part of one.

"What story do you want tonight, my children?" Kana sat against the railing of the ship and gathered her children close. "It's almost time for bed."

"Tell us about the sea snakes!" Doris cheered.

"Again?"

"With their metal scales and glowing eyes." Pan opened zir eyes as wide as zi could, zir deep brown irises glowing in the light of the fire.

"Always monsters with you two," Volt sat beside his bondmate and Pan crawled onto his lap. "Don't you want to hear of something more pleasant? An adventure story? Or a poem?"

"They're not monsters. They're guardians," Pan argued.

Volt shrugged. "They're giant snakes that sink ships. They sound like monsters to me."

"M'Sormee tells the stories better," Doris grunted.

Volt feigned insult. "Well."

Kana touched his shoulder. "You're not entirely wrong, darling."

Reve sat her dinner plate aside. She rested her arms on her knees as she watched the little family with interest.

"M'Sormee, they aren't monsters, are they?" Pan questioned.

Kana wrapped an arm around each of her children, her voice low and husky as she spoke. "It's true that some of the serpents have gone wild. They've been guarding their treasures and secrets since the beginning of time. A few were bound to lose their minds."

"Those are the ones that attack ships?" Doris questioned.

"Yes. They rise out of the sea like mountains of steel and lifestone, sinking ships and dragging their treasures back to their lairs. Some of the greatest Amazons in history were serpent hunters."

"I'm going to slay a serpent someday," Doris announced. "I'm going to cut off its head and make it my masthead."

"Doris!" Volt gasped in shock. Kana only smiled.

Pan took his mother's hand. "But they're not all wild."

Kana shook her head. Of course not. The oldest and wisest of the serpents never leave the depths. They guard the most precious secrets in all of Aggar. Stories, histories, treasures that not even the Choir can touch. They are the guardians, born from our planet's core. Their veins are pure lifestone, binding them to Aggar like the stones of our ship bind us as a family. Stories claim that if you meet one of the ancient ones and prove you are pure of heart, zi will tell you zir secret."

"That's what I want to do. I don't want to kill anything." Pan's eyes were already dropping with exhaustion.

Kana ran her fingers through zir hair. "You can do whatever you dream and work for, my love."

"Do you think a serpent will ever attack the *Niachero*?" Doris questioned.

"The sea is vast and impossibly deep. Even a serpent as large as a mountain could go centuries without meeting another of its kind. If we ever encounter a serpent, it will be because destiny wills it."

Doris and Pan nodded off in their parents' arms. Within moments they were limp with sleep. Volt gathered Pan into his arms and carried zir to their cabin before quickly returning for Doris.

"Are they real?" Reve called.

Kana glanced up at her in surprise. "The serpents?"

"Yes. Have you ever seen one?"

Kana smiled gently. "No, I haven't. But that doesn't mean they aren't real. Stories of the serpents have been passed down for ages, never changing. I like to think there's some truth to them."

"That's why you're not an Amazon," Nix commented as she sat beside her friend. "I could live my whole life never seeing a serpent and it would be just fine with me."

Reve felt her mind wander and she was suddenly overcome by her Sight. She felt her head fall back, gently hitting the wall as her spirit left her body. She turned in a quick circle, breathing fast in a panic. No one seemed to notice her sudden shift. She looked like she was asleep.

Reve walked slowly across the deck. She couldn't feel anything against her bare skin but the gentle flick of the ocean wind. She'd never projected involuntarily before.

She moved to the rail of the ship and all sound faded. She felt as if the ship had turned to steam. She could feel the lapping of the waves against her ankles and deep, deep beneath her she could feel something massive shifting and rolling, waking from its slumber.

Without a second thought, Reve dove over the edge of the ship, slicing through the water like a knife through butter. She didn't need to breathe here. She couldn't feel the crushing pressure of the sea as she swam. There was only darkness and the absolute certainty that she had to continue on.

Reve became aware that she had shifted from projecting to dreaming. She couldn't feel the Niachero above her anymore. In the distance she could hear a long, mournful song, but it wasn't quite the same as the Choir's Songs. The tune was deeper, longer, sadder. The Choir's Songs were a pale imitation.

Reve could see bright lights sparkle far below her, a mirror of her recurring dream. She swam faster, harder, but they always seemed just out of her reach. As the vision began to fade and disappear, the lights twinkled, momentarily reflecting metal and gemstone scales. A massive serpent, curling and coiling in an endless tangle, wrapping around the lights like a dragon guarding its horde.

Another long, piercing note of the serpent's song cut through the deep and Reve's vision vanished.

Reve's eyes fluttered beneath her closed eyelids as she woke. She felt a gentle hand draw a blanket over her chest and linger on her shoulder. She could smell pine and salt, the scent familiar and entrancing. She swayed slightly and realized she was back in her hammock. Her eyes flickered open and she watched as Nix slipped out the door back to the galley.

Reve sat up stiffly and caught her breath, making sure not to wake Sirena. The sounds of merriment had dissipated. She must have been asleep for a while.

She held her head in her hands. Her vision of the serpent and the lights stood out in vivid detail in her mind. Her heart pounded against her ribs but she wasn't afraid. The familiar intensity of her focus returned. She smiled, the expression fierce and determined. Finally.

She slipped out of her hammock, her bare feet silent on the cool wooden floors. Nix had removed her boots when she'd carried her to bed, but she was still dressed in what she'd worn the day before.

She padded through the galley and up the stairs to the main deck. In a few long strides she'd reached Nix's door. She knocked lightly and Nix instantly answered.

"Reve? What are you doing here?" Nix's brow furrowed in shock and concern. "Is everything alright?"

"I've seen a vision. I know where we have to go."

Chapter Four

Nix held her face in her hands. The rough texture of the map brushed her elbows and the feather of her quill brushed her ear. She'd spent hours charting and researching. Her mind swam and her eyes burned from sorting through atlases and journals.

She was exhausted. She hadn't slept since Reve had visited her in the middle of the night, claiming to know where they needed to go for the next step toward defeating the Choir. There was something about Reve's insistence, the power in her eyes, that made it impossible to do anything until a course had been charted. Nix wanted to take down the Choir more than anything, but she found herself even more driven not to disappoint the Blue Sight.

Briza brushed her shoulder. "Did you find anything?"

Nix rubbed her eyes and looked up at her mother. "Nothing. There's nothing there; not an island, not even a reef. I'd understand if the area was uncharted, but it's been sailed numerous times. It's just open sea."

"Maybe Reve's dream was off a bit?"

Nix shook her head. "She was exact in her coordinates. She says her dreams want her to go here." Nix indicated a black 'x' on her map. "It's far away. Right in the middle of the Great Sea."

"Perhaps something will happen there. Dreams don't always indicate the location of something."

"An expedition this far out will be dangerous. We'll have to restock the ship. If anything happens, we'll be too far from land to survive. What if Reve was just dreaming? She hasn't had a vision since joining us. She could be desperate for guidance."

Briza leaned over the map, her thoughts spinning behind her eyes. "Do you doubt her?"

Nix's breath caught in her throat as she tried to answer. Everything about Reve was complicated. "I don't know what I think about her."

Briza grinned. "Yes you do."

Nix glared at her mother. "I'm not talking about this."

"You have feelings for her."

"She's a child, m'Sormee. Younger than Sirena."

"Why would that possibly matter?"

Nix dropped her quill and leaned back in her chair. "Sirena likes her."

"I have eyes."

"I won't compete with my daughter for the affections of a stranger," Nix grunted. "I'm not completely ruled by my libido."

Briza raised an eyebrow. "You're attracted to her?"

"She's too skinny for me."

"I see the way you look at her when she's with Agwe or Sirena. They way you watch her eyes, the way she moves. You've always been more attracted to intensity than body. You know she's more like you than she's like Sirena."

Nix's hands slapped her desk hard. Her lips curled back in frustration. "How could you possibly know that? She's barely said a dozen words to me. She spends most of her time alone in her room or with Agwe. We don't really know anything about her. How could I possibly have any feelings for her?"

Briza was unshaken by Nix's anger. "You saw her past. Into her mind. Whatever you felt in her left you shaken."

Nix hesitated, memories of her shared memories and feelings with Reve flashing through her mind and body. Her voice was soft as she responded. "Knowing someone's past doesn't tell you who they are now. I saw her trauma. I felt her pain. That doesn't tell me who she is now."

"And if Reve shares your feelings? Isn't this as much her decision as it is yours?"

"She doesn't."

"You're so sure?"

"Reve doesn't see anything but her mission. She enjoys our company. She's watchful. But she doesn't think about a life outside of the Choir. We're a pleasant ride toward the next step of her journey. She'd leave us in a second if she thought it would get her closer to the Choir. She doesn't feel anything for us."

Briza leaned back against Nix's desk, crossing her arms over her ample bosom. Her long, silver braid draped over her shoulder. She seemed to look older every time Nix glanced at her, but the look of disappointment in her eyes was ageless. "You know my visions aren't detailed. I get impressions. Impulses. But never the entire story. I don't know the state of Reve's mind, but I do know her energy. She cares about us. She's even been contemplating leaving not for the mission, but to keep us safe."

Nix's brow furrowed in confusion. "How could she protect us?"

"The Choir isn't a forgiving entity, soroe. They want her. If they discover we gave her safe passage, do you think they would overlook it?"

Nix frowned. "I never thought of that."

"To the rest of us, the Choir is a presence. A force. They are everywhere and nowhere, affecting change without anyone noticing. The only way we can communicate with them is through conduits and agents. But for Reve, they are physical. If we're going to keep her safe, if we're going to keep ourselves safe, we'll have to change the way we think of them."

Nix ran her hands through her mane of hair, her heavy rings clinking with the movement. "What do I do, m'sormee?"

Briza grunted. "That's not for me to decide, Nix. I haven't had any visions about where we need to go. You're our Amazon. Our captain. If there are any Gods still watching over Aggar, they'll work through you. Do you trust Reve?"

Nix searched her heart, her stomach sinking as she accepted the truth. "I do. Gods help me, I do."

"Then you seem to have your answer. We've crossed the Great Sea. We can do it again. The crew is with you." Briza patted her arm. "Now sleep. It's late. You'll feel better when you're rested."

A shrill cry echoed through the depths of the cabin. Nix was instantly on her feet and out the door to the main deck. Lyr met her by the stairs to the crew's quarters. "It's Reve. She won't wake up."

Nix raced down the stairs and through the galley to Sirena's room. Sirena knelt by Reve, holding her shoulders, tears streaming down her face. Reve convulsed and shrieked in her sleep, sweat rolling across her skin in fat drops, her hands clenching and unclenching in tight fists. Her hands were already bruising from pounding the floor and her lip was bloody from biting it.

Hecate crouched low to the ground under Reve's hammock, whimpering and clawing at the ground until her nails left long scratches in the wooden floor. Her eyes were wild, her teeth bared. Whatever was happening to Reve, Hecate was unable to help her.

"She fell out of bed. She won't wake up," Sirena wept, helpless to wake her friend.

Agwe ran into the room and cleared the area around Reve. "You need to stay away from her. She could hurt both of you." He pulled Sirena away. "How long has she been seizing?"

"A few minutes," Sirena answered.

Agwe's eyes hardened. "That's a long time."

Reve's convulsing calmed for a moment and Reve turned on her side, weeping and curling in on herself. Her muscles twitched as if in pain. Nix fought the urge to go to her, afraid she'd hurt Reve if she stood too close. Her stomach turned and her hands balled into fists. There were a thousand things she'd seen in Reve's mind that would leave anyone else weeping on the floor, but Reve was different. Something had to be horribly wrong to affect Reve so completely, even in a dream.

"Briza, can you help her? Use your abilities?" Nix's voice trembled as she spoke.

Briza shook her head. "You know I can't call on my abilities at will. Only you've been able to interact with her abilities."

Nix took a cautious step forward, her eyes locked on the trembling shadow. "M'Soremee, be careful," Agwe warned. "She could still seize again."

Nix raised a hand, acknowledging his fears, but she didn't stop. She slowly circled Reve. She didn't seem to sense anyone's presence. Nix carefully fell to her knees and placed a hand on Reve's shoulder. "Reve, wake up. You're safe."

Reve didn't respond to her touch or her call, but Nix felt her muscles start to calm. Encouraged by even a small sign of change, she continued. "Reve. You're dreaming. It isn't real. Whatever you're seeing, whatever you feel, it's just in your mind. You're on the *Niachero*. You're with friends. Come back to us. Please."

Reve's legs spasmed, kicking out at the air and she cried out again, falling deeper into her dream. Nix felt tears in her eyes, panic seeping through her veins. She pulled Reve into her arms like a child, cradling her "Reve. Come on. Don't do this. I know you can break out. You're strong." Nix held her face in her hand. She didn't want her family to see her cry. She never cried. "Come back to me."

Reve gasped, her hand wrapping around the back of Nix's neck, holding so tight her nails bit into Nix's skin. She reared up, a hair's breadth from Nix. Her eyes opened, clouded with dream and tears.

Nix was instantly overwhelmed by her emotions, her wild Sight filling Nix with Reve's terror and pain. She didn't see into her mind, but the emotions were familiar, tainted with memory Nix had seen in their shared memories.

She spoke through gritted teeth, her breath hot on Nix's lips. "Help me."

Nix held her tighter, shocked by her sudden awakening. "What do I do? How can I help you?"

Reve's words were choppy and broken, her voice fading in and out of her dream. "The wind. I need the wind."

Nix instantly understood. The Choir. She adjusted her grip,

scooping Reve into her arms and lifting her off the ground. Reve's eyes closed again, but her grip around Nix's neck remained tight, assuring Nix, at least for the moment, she was present.

Nix's crew parted as she ran through the galley. As she reached the stairs, Reve started convulsing again, nearly knocking Nix to the ground. The Amazon struggled to keep her still and climbed the stairs to the main deck. The sails rippled in the cold breeze, the night lit by the light of both Twin Moons.

The moment they stepped outside, Reve began to calm. The wind caught at her hair, blowing it over her shoulders and ruffling her nightshirt. Nix carefully laid her on the deck, taking Reve's hand from her neck and holding it tightly between both of her own. Nix felt her crew at her back, climbing up the stairs after her.

After a moment, Reve's convulsions and cries stopped and she laid still. Sirena took a step forward. "Is she alright? Is she dead?"

Nix shook her head. She could still feel Reve's heartbeat shallow in her wrist. "She just needs to find her way back out."

Time passed and neither Reve nor Nix moved. As the moons drifted across the sky, Briza and Agwe urged the rest of the crew back to bed. Reve was breathing steadily again. There was no telling when she'd wake.

Sirena was the last to go, her eyes wide and her hands clasped in front of her chest. Agwe wrapped his arms around her and tried to guide her back to bed. "She's fine now. Probably just sleeping. You need to rest."

"I don't want to leave her," Sirena protested.

Agwe sighed gently. "I've never seen you so upset. You're pale and clammy. You're cold. You could get sick. You could get another headache."

Sirena's eyes flashed. "Don't be ridiculous, Agwe. I haven't had anxiety headaches since I was a child."

Agwe hugged her tight. "Alright. But consider it. And come see me if you start to feel off." He slipped back down to his room.

Briza touched Nix's shoulder. "Nix, you can't help her anymore." Nix jerked her arm out of Briza's grip. "Nix."

"The Choir has her mind, Briza. I'm not leaving her until she finds her way back."

"You don't know how long that could take."

"It doesn't matter."

"You still doubt your feelings for her?"

Nix clenched her jaw. "Briza, stop."

"I can tell —"

Reve coughed and gasped, trembling as she woke. Her back

arched and her feet skidded against the deck. Nix instantly grabbed her, helping her sit up. She seemed so fragile to Nix, more than when she'd been in the brig or even in her dream. Her breaths started to even and her muscles relaxed. She slowly opened her eyes.

Nix held her tighter. "Reve?"

"I'm awake," she whispered. "I'm awake."

"What happened?"

Reve closed her eyes tight, shaking her head as if she had a headache. "They caught me in my dream. They know where I am."

"But you're safe here. We're protected by the sea. By the wind."

Reve nodded, opening her eyes again. "I think so."

"Reve?" Sirena crept forward.

Reve smiled up at her. "Hello, Sirena."

Sirena's shoulders sank with relief and she smiled, her eyes sparkling. "I'm so glad you're alright."

Nix tensed and her heart sank at the look in Sirena's eyes. She released Reve and let Sirena help her to her feet. Reve doubled over once, but quickly regained her balance.

"Is it safe for you to go back to our room?" Sirena questioned.

Reve nodded. "I think I'm safe now."

Nix stood stiffly, her knees sore. She turned away. She couldn't look at them anymore. "I'll let you two get back to bed, then."

Briza took a step toward her daughter. "Nix?"

"Good night, Briza."

Nix returned to her room and shut the door. She leaned back heavily. She was being ridiculous. She had left Gale because her obsession had become dangerous. Now she couldn't push Reve out of her thoughts and the woman had never even shown interest in her. It was irresponsible. It was wrong. Reve was young. She had been Nix's prisoner and was clearly being victimized by the Choir. Nix vowed to herself not to add to Reve's struggle.

She sat heavily at her desk and stared at the map once more. She knew she wouldn't be able to sleep. She stared at the circle around Reve's coordinates until the image swam and her eyes burned. She pushed away from her desk with a frustrated growl. She couldn't concentrate. She needed a stiff drink. She needed a brawl. Her thoughts drifted back to Gale and she frowned. She was always going back to old addictions.

Enyo purred loud from the bed, too tired to be perturbed by Nix's anger. Nix glanced at her dear friend and Enyo slowly blinked, a classic sign of affection. Nix sighed softly and sat on the edge of the bed. She absentmindedly stroked between Enyo's ears until her wings stretched out in contentment.

Nix brushed her fingers over Enyo's still-bandaged wing joint. "How could I think of Gale after what happened to you?" Enyo bumped her brow against Nix's palm. "So affectionate when you're sleepy. We should keep you drugged."

Enyo batted at her hand and Nix laughed.

A soft knock at the door caught Nix's attention. She frowned and stood. She didn't know if she had the energy to see anyone, even her family. She opened the door slowly and her breath caught in her throat.

"Reve?"

"Can I come in?"

Nix mutely stepped aside and Reve walked into the room. "How are you feeling?"

Reve sat at the end of Nix's bed, her arms wrapped around her stomach. "Still a little off, but better. Thanks to you."

The wall felt hard and rough against Nix's back. She kept the door cracked open. "I didn't do anything."

"You led me out. I felt you in the darkness. I wouldn't have escaped them without you."

"I don't even know what I did."

"Neither do I. But I... I had to thank you."

Nix nodded. "I'm just glad you're safe."

Reve refused to meet Nix's eyes. She ran her fingers over the threads of Nix's quilt, toying with a frayed piece of cloth. She frowned. "Did you see anything? Did I pull you into my dream?"

"No. I just carried you to the deck. I didn't see anything."

Reve let out a breath of relief. "I don't have a lot of experience being around people, Nix. I don't know why my Sight keeps latching onto you, but I swear I'm trying to stop."

"I'm not angry." Reve glanced up at Nix, her worry clear in her eyes. Nix's face crumpled with concern. "Reve, I'm not going to send you away over this. If anything I'm more convinced you have to stay. If that's what the Choir can do to you in a dream, I don't want to think of what their Songs would do to you on land."

Nix expected Reve's usual steely demeanor to return, putting up walls between them. Instead Reve looked up through her blonde hair, still mussed from her dream, her emotions laid bare. She looked just as delicate as she had in her dream. She was haunted. She was scared. Nix drew a sharp breath between her lips. Sometimes Reve seemed more creature than human, a being of magic withdrawn from the rest of the world.

Nix had never seen Reve look more real.

"Thank you, Nix."

"I told you as long as you're here you're family. I don't abandon my family, least of all to the Choir." Reve nodded slowly. "Are you going to be able to sleep?"

Reve snorted. "Not for a long time. I only let Sirena take me back to the room so she'd sleep herself. She worries too much about me."

Nix raised an eyebrow in surprise. "She wouldn't like that. She thinks she's watching out for you."

Reve glanced up at Nix again, humor in her eyes. A sly grin crossed her lips. "She's sweet. There's no reason to upset her."

"She's older than you."

"She hasn't lived my life. She doesn't know what it's like to suffer. To fight. She hasn't lost anything. Not really. I hope she never does."

Nix shook her head slowly. She didn't think Reve could get more confusing. "I can't sleep either. Do you want to help me? I'm trying to chart out our journey to the location you gave me, but a few things don't line up. Maybe you can answer some of my questions."

Reve nodded and Nix slid into her chair. Reve stood over her, one hand on the back of her chair, the other on the desk. She was so close Nix could smell her, still salty with sweat. The sound of Reve's gasp and the way her back arched flickered through her mind. She ran her tongue over her lips and pushed her thoughts aside.

"This is the location you saw. There's nothing here, not even close. What are we looking for? Are we meeting someone?"

Reve's lips pursed. "I don't know. I just know where we're supposed to go."

"What was your vision like? Did you see anything that might give us some kind of clue?"

Reve thought. "I was underwater. I saw lights and the shadow of a serpent. But I think I was just dreaming of Kana's story. I'd never heard of the serpents before."

Nix chuckled. "Don't take any of Kana's stories too seriously. Her pretty face hides a mischievous mind."

"You don't believe in the serpents?"

Nix shrugged. "I've never seen one."

"There are plenty of real things you've never seen."

"I didn't say I didn't believe in them. I just don't concern myself with much until it affects my life."

"Things do seem isolated on the sea. It would be nice to have the luxury of ignorance."

Nix smirked in amused shock. "You might be able to think of Sirena as a child, Reve, but don't mistake my focus for inexperience."

Nix turned to Reve, her eyes teasing, but tensed as she realized how close Reve was, how intense her eyes had become. "I don't think of you as a child, Nix. You know what it means to fight the Choir. You know how it feels to run. I envy what you've built here."

Reve held her gaze for a long moment. Nix cleared her throat uncomfortably and turned away. "We're going to need to stop for supplies before heading on. Will we have to wait at your spot for any length of time? I want to make sure we have enough inventory."

Reve released the back of Nix's chair and leaned forward over the map, resting on her elbows. "My instinct says we won't be there long, but it wasn't part of my vision. Sometimes when I meditate things become more clear. I just... I don't want to risk falling asleep."

"I can keep make sure you stay awake," Nix promised.

Reve nodded slowly. "Alright. It might take a while."

Nix glanced at the sky out her window. "Well, we still have a few more hours until sunrise. Let's see what we can get done before everyone wakes."

Nix woke slowly. Her back and neck were stiff from sleeping at her desk. A rosy red imprint from her arm was pressed into her cheek. She took a moment to remember her surroundings and sat up with a gasp. Reve.

She spun around. Reve was draped across her bed, sound asleep. Nix rushed to her side and touched her shoulder. "Reve?" Reve drew a deep breath and her eyes opened. She looked up at Nix in surprise. "Reve, I'm so sorry. I fell asleep."

Reve shook her head. "It's fine. I didn't dream."

Reve slowly stood and stretched. She didn't look fully rested, but she looked better. There was color in her cheeks and her eyes were focused and clear. Nix glanced out at the sky. It was already noon.

"I keep sleeping in like this and my family will think I'm getting lazy," she grunted.

"Just tell them you were up with me. They couldn't blame you after last night."

"That's probably why no one tried to wake me for breakfast."

Nix opened her door and strolled out into the daylight.

"Good to see you up, Nix!" Tlaloc called down from the helm. "We should be docking before nightfall. I sent Enyo ahead with details about the repairs we need. Hope they won't take long."

"Thanks, Tlaloc. It was a long night."

"I assumed as much. How are you feeling, Reve?"

"Better. Just a bit of a lingering headache."

"You should see Agwe. He'll want to check in with you after your seizure. At least make sure you didn't break or strain anything when convulsing.”

Reve nodded. “I needed to talk with him anyway. Thanks.”

Nix watched as Reve disappeared below deck. “She really doing better?”

Nix glanced up at Tlaloc and joined zir at the helm. “I think so. She didn’t have another attack in her sleep.”

“Do you think the Choir has really left her mind alone or was it something else?”

“What do you mean?”

Tlaloc made a minor adjustment at the helm and shrugged. “Your presence seems to have an affect on her. Maybe she was safe because she spent the night with you?”

“I slept at my desk. She was helping me chart our course. We fell asleep before we could do much.”

Tlaloc smirked. “I wasn’t implying you did anything else. You were close to her. That may have kept her safe.”

Nix leaned forward over the railing, staring out to sea. “Maybe. Whatever it was, I’m glad she was able to sleep a bit. We need to figure out how they reached her in the first place and take precautions. We almost lost her.”

“The wind seems to help. Maybe we could set up a hammock above deck? It should be fine until the rainy season.”

Nix nodded. “I’ll talk to her about it.”

“Nix?” Kana called up to the helm as she crossed the deck. “You said you wanted to help Doris with zir fencing lesson?”

Nix let out a deep breath. She’d completely forgotten volunteering to help with lessons the day before. She closed her eyes. She was still so tired. “Yes, of course.”

Kana eyed her suspiciously as she climbed down from the helm. “You sure you’re up to it? I don’t mind taking charge.”

Nix shook her head. “You’ve been managing the brunt of their lessons for close to half a tenmoon. You deserve a break.” Nix grinned. “Doris could also do with some variety.”

Kana wrapped her arm around Nix’s shoulders. “All your smugness aside, you’re right. Doris is growing in leaps and bounds. I think she might consider becoming an Amazon someday.”

Nix’s smile faded. “Are you serious? Zi’s so young. We don’t even know if zi’ll decide to identify as a woman. It could just be a phase.”

“Absolutely. But I’d rather zi have the training necessary when the time comes for zir to decide. Would you be willing to take zir under your wing?”

Nix nodded. “Of course, Kana.”

Kana kissed her cheek. “Thank you.”

Nix smirked. "Tease."

"A little bit." Kana released Nix. "I'll send Doris up. Zi's just transitioning from zir staff, so the lesson shouldn't be too intense."

Nix unpinned and rolled her sleeves to her elbows. "I'll be ready."

"Keep practicing those drills. Do them over and over again until you can do them without thinking about it. Tlaloc and Lyr will help you with your lessons from now on as well. Tlaloc will teach you form, Lyr will help train you physically and eventually teach you other weapons. It will take a lot of time and focus, Doris."

Doris nodded and carefully sheathed zir new short sword. Nix had made sure the blade was dull in case Doris decided to play with it alone with Pan, but to her surprise Doris was focused and careful. Zi already treated zir blade with respect. "I want to learn. I can work hard."

Nix ruffled zir hair. "I know you can. You worked hard today! Go get something to eat. We'll have Sirena start adjusting your meals for your training."

Nix smiled at the child as zi walked away. Perhaps Kana was right. At the very least, Doris had the markings of a warrior.

"It's been a long time since you were a trainer. It was nice to see you like that again," Briza announced.

Nix smiled softly. "Zi's more focused than my children ever were. At least in fighting. Sirena was wild and Agwe was more interested in his books."

"Sirena found her way."

Nix nodded. "She's always preferred to learn on her own."

"Nix?" Lyr shouted down to her from the crow's nest.

Nix glanced up at the changling, still smiling. "What is it, Lyr?"

The look on Lyr's face stole Nix's good mood. "There's something coming. Fast. I think it's a storm but it's not moving like any storm I've ever seen."

Nix breathed in through her mouth. She'd always been able to sense a storm. There was no electric taste in the air. No tingle on the back of her neck or apprehension in her heart.

She grabbed her telescope and quickly scaled the ratlines, looking out to sea. A billowing storm slipped across the sea like an ebony fog. Nix slowly lowered her telescope. "It's moving faster than the wind."

Lyr shook his head. "I've never seen anything like it. It's coming right for us." Lyr's ears flattened against his head. "And it's making a strange noise."

"What kind of noise?"

"Just... high pitched."

"Nix!"

Nix spun around. Reve stepped out onto the deck, holding her head in her hand. Nix scrambled out of the nest and slid down the ropes. "Are you alright? Are you dreaming again?"

Reve shook her head. "I don't know how they're doing it."

"Reve?"

"The Choir knows where I am. They're coming for me."

Nix took her shoulders. "We're at sea. They can't reach us here."

Reve shook her head. "Anywhere I go. They can always find me."

The rustle of the sails fell silent. The wind disappeared. Nix looked to the sky. The storm clouds she'd barely been able to see with her telescope were spreading, covering the once cloudless sky. Within moment they'd were plunged into darkness.

Reve whimpered and held her head. "We have to go. We have to run!"

"All hands!" Nix howled, her voice carrying over the rumble of the storm. Her entire crew raced to her. "Volt! Activate the thrusters! We have to get to land now!"

Volt sped back below deck. The ship shuddered violently, swaying in the rising waves despite the absence of wind. Thunder and lightning crashed around them, illuminating the choppy sea. Nix looked up at the sails in fear. They still hung limp and useless.

"Secure your lifelines! Tie down the sails! We have to depend on the boosters!"

Her crew ran to do her bidding. Nix wrapped her arms around Reve's shoulders and led her to the captain's quarters.

"Stay here. We can outrun them."

Reve shook her head, her eyes squeezed closed. "Not on this ship. They've already found us. They've fought through the wind. They'll sink the ship."

"The Choir can't stop the wind, Reve. They have to be using everything they have to create this storm. They can't do it for long."

"Nix —"

"Reve. I promised to keep you safe and I will. Trust me."

Reve slowly nodded. "I trust you."

Nix shut Reve inside her room and raced to join Tlaloc at the helm.

"I can't see anything," Tlaloc warned, zir muscles tense as zi strained against the helm, trying to keep the *Niachero* on course as the storm became more violent.

Nix slid as the ship tipped violently to the side. "Just focus on outrunning it."

The ship pitched forward, launched on a violent wave and crashed back into the sea. A flood of water washed over the deck, sending her crew sliding across the slick wood. Kana tripped, nearly falling overboard, but her lifeline tied around her waist kept her secure.

The thrusters shuddered and sputtered. Nix grit her teeth. They hadn't put the thrusters under so much pressure before. If they overheated, they'd be at the Choir's mercy.

Thunder rolled, vibrating the ship. A streak of lightning narrowly missed the ship, sending a charge of electricity through the air that made the hair on Nix's arms stand on end. Nix growled at the sky. The Choir had tried to kill her in the desert. They'd abandoned her and she'd abandoned them. She wasn't going to die here, not at sea. She wasn't going to lose her home a second time. She wasn't going to bury any more friends.

As if in response to her rebellious thoughts, a massive wave slammed into the side of the ship, nearly capsizing them.

Tlaloc and Nix fought together with the helm to keep the ship on-course. "Nix, we can't hold much longer. The *Niachero* can't take it!"

"She can hold and she will!"

"Reve!" Sirena's scream rose over the sounds of the storm and Nix turned to the starboard rail, her eyes wild. Reve stumbled out of her room and slid, hitting the railing hard.

"Reve! Get back in the cabin!" Nix called. Her heart pounded wildly in her chest. Was Reve having another nightmare? Did she even know what she was doing? She turned to Tlaloc. "I'll be right back!"

Nix sprinted down from the helm, careful to keep her footing as the ship swayed.

"M'Sormee, be careful!" Sirena cried.

"Reve!" Reve didn't seem to hear Nix's call. Another wave crashed over the edge of the ship, swiping Reve's feet out from under her. "Reve!"

Reve stumbled back, hitting the rail hard and flinging her over the edge. Nix lunged forward, grabbing her arm. As if by the invisible hand of the Choir itself, the ship tipped, sending Nix and Reve flying overboard into the darkness of the sea.

Chapter Five

Reve sat up slowly. She could feel soft, woven carpet under her hands. She could smell old paper. She opened her eyes and pressed her lips in a tight line. She was in the library again, the library she'd dreamt of in the Triad's monastery.

She glanced around, but Hecate was nowhere to be found. Her head swam, her thoughts blurred and confused. She couldn't remember anything. How had she gotten here? She had fought so hard not to sleep after the Choir had caught her in her last dream. What could put her in such a deep rest she could return to this mysterious place?

She stood on trembling legs and took a few steps forward. Her right knee gave out and she caught herself on her bookshelf. She breathed heavily, her lungs burning as if she hadn't breathed in minutes. She ran her hand over her neck and shoulder. Her muscles ached.

Her strength was steadily returning, but her thoughts were as tangled as ever. She threw open the wide double doors that led to the endless expanse of bookshelves. The last time she'd been here, the Triad had unlocked her mind and the truth of her heritage. There had to be something else she needed to learn, something else to see. In her confused stupor, she didn't have the strength or will to fight the dream. The library would show her where to go.

She wandered through the stacks, careful not to touch any of the books. She still couldn't come close to understanding the proportions of the library, even with her Sight, but she sensed that it had grown since the last time she'd been there. There was something living about the place, constantly shifting and changing, adding new books and rearranging the shelves.

She reached a grand, spiraling staircase and began to climb. She climbed for dozens of stories, until she lost count and the library below extended on in every direction like the sea. Despite her climb, she never lost breath or grew tired. She moved as if in a trance.

Finally, as the tallest library shelves seemed as tiny as insects, Reve left the staircase. She stepped out onto a winding balcony lined with doors. In the distance she spotted a simple, rough wooden door glowing with a pale red light. Reve moved to it, every step bringing back memories and sensations.

She pulled open the door and was instantly enveloped in the warm, red light. She the glow faded, Reve could feel cool, dewy grass and thick, sharp pine needles prickling under her palms. Tall evergreen trees rose high overhead. The twin moons chased each other across the night sky. She drew a deep breath and the heavy scent of pine and damp bark flitted through the air. She hugged her arms closer to her chest and shivered as her breath escaped her lips in puffs of steam.

Reve looked around in shock. She knew these woods. She'd spent a ten-day hiding in its trees. She'd nearly died from exposure before she'd learned how to survive without a roof over her head.

The last thing she could remember was falling off the *Niachero*, twisting and tumbling in the stormy sea. How had she ended up in the forests near her family home?

Hecate bounded toward her through the foliage, tackling her to the ground and licking her face. Her breath was hot and wet on Reve's cheeks, but her nose was like ice. Reve smiled and hugged her tight. The hair on the back of her neck stood on end with worry.

"What's going on?" Reve questioned. "Where are we?"

Hecate's thoughts and impressions were so clear Reve knew they had to be sharing a dream. She wasn't just a creation of her mind.

Reve paused, looking into Hecate's eyes. "Am I dead?"

You wouldn't be dreaming if you were dead.

Reve blinked, momentarily filled with thoughts of her body tumbling in the ocean, slowly drowning. Surely she'd be dead by now if she was still in the water. "Am I still on the ship? Did they drag me back?"

I don't know where your body is. I barely found you in sleep.

Reve held her friend closer, burying her face in her warm fur. Everything felt so real. She could smell the musk of Hecate's skin, feel the cold clinging to her coat. She could feel the deep, thudding pulse of her heart in her chest and hear the ground crunch under the curl of her paws. She'd only had one other dream that felt so real.

"Is everyone else on the ship safe? Did the Choir let them live?"

The storm has abated. The ship still stands.

Reve breathed a sigh of relief. "At least the Choir didn't take me."

A deep, mournful howl split the night air. Reve and Hecate looked deeper into the woods as one.

"Another wolf?"

Not my kind.

Reve stood. She clenched her jaw to keep from shivering. Another howl, deeper than the first, echoed closer.

They're looking for something. Hunting.

"Should I run?"

Hecate sniffed at the air. *You're dreaming. Nothing can hurt you but the Choir. Do you hear any Songs?*

Reve shook her head. "Just the wolves. Can you make out anything they're saying?"

Hecate glanced back at her, amusement in her glowing, golden eyes. *They're howling, Reve. They're not talking.*

Reve smirked. "I don't speak wolf."

I'm well aware.

The howling was drawing closer, but there was no malice in the sound. Reve didn't understand her lack of fear or desire to run, but she didn't question it. Dreams didn't have to make sense.

The sound of pounding hooves rumbled in the distance and Reve caught a glimmer of sparkling, white light in the distance. She took a step back. She recognized the light, the cloudy consistency. There were Songs in the forest.

Reve instantly turned and ran. She didn't hear the Song, but she could feel it nearby. She wouldn't give it the chance to catch her trail. Hecate pounded behind her, speeding through the dense underbrush with a practiced ease. They both dodged in and out of the shadows, blending with the darkness. They were both creatures of the night, back in the forests of their birth. There was no way a Song would catch Reve in her own forests.

The steady beat of hooves continued. Reve grabbed the rough, low-hanging branches of a nearby tree and pulled herself up into the tree. In the depths of the pine bows, she was virtually nonexistent. Hecate sped further away, crouching low in a thistle.

The pounding grew to a roar and a massive stag raced beneath Reve's tree, its mighty horns curling up and around themselves in a spiral. Reve leaned out of her tree, her eyes wide. The stag wasn't flesh and blood, but a solid mass of Song, woven from glowing white mist and echoing the Choir's mournful tune in time with the beat of the stag's hooves.

As the Song disappeared into the distance, two sandwolves bounded after it. The muscles in their massive shoulders bunched and rippled as they ran. Their powerful, slender hind legs pushing them faster and faster in the hunt. The larger of the two howled, spurring the other on. What were sandwolves doing in the north?

Reve dropped heavily out of the trees, landing in a crouch.

Hecate scuttled out of the brush. Reve pursed her lips. She'd never seen a Song take such solid form, particularly not the form of something so alive. She briefly wondered if it was a real Song or if it was a figment of her dream, a creation made up of her subconscious fears.

"Are you lost?"

Reve spun around. A rider on a blood mare rode forward, a longbow in her hands. Reve instantly guessed the stranger to be the hunter working with the sandwolves. She'd heard from desert tribesmen the wolves could be convinced to leave the warmer southern continent if they took a human as packmate.

"Who are you?" Reve demanded. The rider slid from the horse. Reve glanced up. The hunter was half a head taller than her. "You're... you're an Amazon?"

The hunter grinned slowly. "Are you a Sister? A Shadow?" The Amazon drew closer, her long, crimson and gold quilted coat swaying around her legs. She caught a glimpse of Reve's eyes in the moonlight. "A Blue Sight?"

"I asked you first."

The Amazon chuckled and extended her hand. "Gwyn n'Athena. Royal Marshal. Are you lost? Forgive me for saying it, but you don't look well enough to be a hunter." Gwyn noticed Hecate as she circled around Reve's legs, her eyes scanning the Amazon. "Your packmate?"

"My friend."

Gwyn crouched low to be at eye-level with Hecate. Reve could sense Hecate's surprise and sudden ease. "I've never heard of a forest wolf bonding with another creature."

Reve glanced down at Hecate. *She speaks wolf better than you do.*

"You're a Royal Marshal?"

Gwyn looked back up at Reve and stood. "Yes."

"Which kingdom?"

Gwyn's brow furrowed. "The Ramains, of course. You're in the heart of the Ramains."

"I've never heard of it."

Gwyn took a cautious step forward. "What's your name?"

"Reve."

"Where do you hail from, Reve?"

"Nowhere."

"Reve?"

"You're just a dream."

A sharp howl split the air and the sandwolves returned, their tongues lolling and their eyes filled with joy. They leapt up at Gwyn, wrapping their slender legs around her shoulders and waist as they pawed at her. She grunted and laughed as she wrestled them away, patting and holding them like a fellow wolf.

"Did you catch it dumauzen?" The sandwolves shuffled, urging Gwyn ahead. "Ah. I see."

Gwyn swung back into her saddle and reached down to Reve. "My packmates and I are hunting for dinner. My family is waiting not far from here. You're welcome to join us if you like."

Reve remembered her dream of the Triad and the way they'd opened her mind. There was something about this dream that was similar. There had to be something to learn.

Reve reached out and took Gwyn's hand. The Marshal easily pulled her into the saddle behind her. Reve wrapped her arms around Reve's waist. Gwyn's short, silken copper hair was tied back in a short braid hanging to her shoulders. Gwyn smelled of dust and pine. She'd been hunting for a while.

"I don't know how to hunt," Reve admitted.

Gwyn fit an arrow into her bow. "Just hold on."

Gwyn nudged her mare with her heels and they took off, speed through the forest after the sandwolves. Reve glanced over her shoulder, afraid Hecate would fall behind, but the forest wolf sprinted, keeping time with her cousins from the south. Her eyes flashed joy and Reve realized it must have been a long time since she's been able to run at full-speed, to hunt in a pack. It made sense that she enjoyed chasing Nix's eitteh so much.

The larger sandwolf howled and Gwyn growled low in the back of her throat. She was primal. Pack. For a moment Reve envied her obviously intense connection with her wolves.

Gwyn urged her horse forward faster and soon the Song stag was I sight again. Reve held tighter to Gwyn, her stomach lurching at the sensation of running toward the Songs. Gwyn couldn't possibly think her bow could kill a Song.

"Don't!" Reve cried.

Gwyn glanced back at her in shock. "It's meat. Game."

"It's a Song! It'll take us all!"

Gwyn frowned. She drew her bow and let an arrow fly. It embedded in the stag's back leg. The Song staggered and tripped forward, crashing into the brush. The sandwolves were on it in an instant, biting its throat out, instantly killing it.

The mare slowed to a stop. Reve couldn't take her eyes off the Song. Its tune had ceased, the familiar glow dimming and still. Reve shuddered. It wasn't possible. Nothing could stop a Song, especially not something as mundane as an arrow.

"Reve." Gwyn gently touched Reve's shoulder.

"I don't understand." Reve released the Amazon. She felt sick. She tried to remind herself she was dreaming, nothing had to make sense in a dream. Was this the message the dream was trying to teach her? Was there some way to fight back against the Choir's most deadly weapon?

Gwyn looked back at the stag. "It's dead. It won't hurt you."

Reve shook her head. "You can't kill it."

"Are you opposed to eating meat? I'm sorry if I scared you. I thought you realized we were hunting."

"It's not meat."

Gwyn slid off her horse and moved to the Song. She studied it and pulled out a long hunting knife. She quickly severed one of the stag's legs and threw it to her wolves. "Thank you for your help, dumauzen."

The wolves claimed their treat with joy. Gwyn nodded to Hecate. "And for you, Sister. There's plenty to share."

Hecate joined in their feast. Reve watched as the glow of the Song started to fade, evaporating like morning fog until only a real stag remained. It was far less impressive than the Song stag, smaller in every regard. Gwyn used her hunting knife to part and clean the stag before storing it in a series of game bags. The wolves had quickly eaten the stag leg down to the bone.

Reve held her face in her hands and breathed deeply. She felt weaker, more scared than she'd been in many tenmoons. She wasn't herself anymore. Before, she would have just run away. She wouldn't have even thought about it. She didn't panic. That wasn't who she was. What could possibly have changed her so intrinsically?

"Almost done," Gwyn called, tying off the last of her game bags. The stag was nothing more than a stripped pile of wet bones. Gwyn had even severed the antlers. She tied the game bags to her saddle. "Do you have any family nearby? Anyone who would be worried about you?"

"No one."

Gwyn climbed back up into her saddle. "Well then, you should come meet mine."

Gwyn whistled and the wolves raced into the woods. They rode through the forest for more than an hour, following an invisible trail only Gwyn seemed to know. Reve scanned the trees as they rode, searching desperately for any other sign of Songs of the Choir, but there was no mournful tune in the air. There were no stags made of glowing mist. There was nothing but the pounding of hooves and the baying of the wolves.

They broke through a thick line of brush into a wide clearing. Two caravans and a line of horses surrounded a blazing fire. The wolves raced into the clearing and Gwyn slowed and finally dismounted.

"Gwyn! Welcome back!"

Two more Amazons stepped out of one of the caravans. A spry, slender woman wearing a billowing blouse and yellow tunic ran to Gwyn. Reve instantly recognized her as a desert nomad, the fire casting long shadows across her sharp cheekbones and slender chin.

Her honey-brown eyes sparkled as she clasped hands with Gwyn. "We heard your packmates in the distance. Did you catch anything?"

Gwyn pulled the stag antlers from her saddle. "We're going to feast tonight."

"I see you caught more than game." The second woman walked toward Reve. Her voice was gravely and soft. Her dark, graying hair was so short it bristled, but her eyes were kind.

Gwyn glanced back at Reve. "Reve, this is Brit and her bondmate Sparrow. I found Reve in the forest. I told her she could join us for a meal."

Brit waved her down. "More than a meal, come down near the fire, Reve. You look chilled to the bone."

Reve slid to the ground and let the amazons lead her to the warmth of the campfire. Hecate ran to sit beside her, the wolf's tongue lolling with joy. The run had been good for her.

The other caravan door opened with a sharp creak. "Gwyn?"

Gwyn turned, her eyes growing soft. "Llinolae. It's been too long"

Reve felt an electric warmth and an immediate connection with the newcomer, like she had with Adrian. She didn't have to see Llinolae's eyes to know she was a Blue Sight.

Gwyn dropped the game bag she'd been carrying to the fire and tenderly kissed her lover. Llinolae's long, silken ebony hair fell free, brushing Gwyn's cheeks.

Llinolae grinned. "It took me a while to get away. I've been wrapped up in meetings

Llinolae instantly spotted Reve. "We have a guest?"

"This is Reve. I think she's lost."

Llinolae and Reve caught each other's eyes. A moment of understanding passed between them. Llinolae's lips pressed tightly together. "I see."

Gwyn looked between Reve and Llinolae. "Do you know each other?"

"No." Llinolae rested her hand on Gwyn's shoulder and smiled. "We should start the meal. Reve looks hungry."

Llinolae strolled to Gwyn's horse to help untether the game bags. Reve thought she moved like nobility, her back straight and her eyes intelligent. She glanced once over her shoulder at Reve, studying her, but she didn't say anything.

"Here. Let us know if you need anything." Sparrow wrapped a thick quilt around her shoulders.

"Love?" Brit stepped out of their caravan, a small child bundled in her arms.

Sparrow let out a heavy breath. "Feeding time again?"

Brit smiled. "She'd growing fast."

Sparrow squeezed Reve's shoulders and returned to her family.

"Just give us a moment, Reve, and we'll get you something warm to eat." Gwyn announced as she stoked the fire.

Reve hugged her blanket tighter around her shoulders. She watched Llinolae as she delivered the last of the game bags to the fire. "It's alright. I have time."

Sparrow and Brit's child laughed and clapped, the sound bubbling and bright as Sparrow bounced the baby on her feet. The Amazon curled her toes and the arches of her bare feet, expertly balancing the child. Reve watched the display in shock, both at Sparrow's dexterity and the way the other women ate, seemingly unconcerned if the child would fall.

Gwyn noticed her concern and laughed. "Sparrow won't drop her."

Brit tossed a bone to the wolves. "She's determined Cas will at least be a tumbler. As long as she stays away from trick-riding I'll be fine."

"With you and Sparrow as mothers? You'll be lucky if the craziest thing Cas gets into is trick-riding."

The warmth of the moment wasn't lost on Reve. There was so much camaraderie between the Amazons and wolves that Reve couldn't help but think of the crew of the *Niachero*. Clenched her jaw and pushed the thought away. After the Choir's storm, there was no way she could go back even if she had survived her fall.

Reve nibbled at the meal. She didn't even know if the food could fill her in a dream, and she couldn't get the memory of the stag made of Songs out of her mind.

"Reve?" Reve glanced up into the darkness as Llinolae approached. "Could I speak with you? Privately?"

The other Amazons glanced up, trying to hide their interest. Reve sighed and stood. She knew this was coming. "Of course."

Llinolae led her deeper into the woods. Hecate joined them, refusing to leave Reve alone even in a dream. Llinolae didn't bring a torch. She knew none of them needed light to sense their surroundings.

Llinolae paused once they were out of earshot. "Where are you from, Reve? Or perhaps a better question would be when are you from?"

Reve leaned back against a nearby tree. "You guessed?"

"It's a rare gift of the Sight, being able to project through time and space."

"You speak from experience?"

Llinolae's eyes sparkled. "When I was a child, my Sight help me seek others like myself outside of time. It's not an ability gifted lightly. You must come from a time when it's hard to receive guidance from your fellow Blue Sights."

"There are no other Blue Sights. Not that I know of, anyway."

Llinolae's brow furrowed. "What happened to them?"

"They're all dead. Killed the moment they're born."

Llinolae's eyes widened in fear and disgust. "And the people allow this? The Amazons don't intervene? What about the Marshals?"

Reve shook her head. "Things are very different. I don't know what year this is. The fact that the Ramains still exists makes me think many centuries have passed. Perhaps millennias."

Llinolae clasped her hands behind her back, her hair falling into her eyes. "I see."

"You're not the first Blue Sight I've met in my dreams. I think the Sight is using the dreams to guide me in my quest."

"What's your quest?"

Reve shook her head. "It's a very long story."

"Then how am I supposed to know how to help you?"

Reve slid to the ground. "I'm just tired of having people in my mind."

Llinolae sat beside her. "Then tell me. I have the time. I don't need to see your past to feel the fear and chaos in your amarin. Perhaps speaking aloud will allow you some release."

Hecate curled up beside Reve, resting her head on Reve's knee. *She doesn't know you. You can speak openly with her.*

Reve closed her eyes and nodded. "I'll tell you my story."

Llinolae listened to Reve's story until dawn began to break over the horizon. Reve had felt Gwyn and Brit stalking along the forest edge for a time, checking to ensure that the Blue Sights were safe, but they left upon hearing their voices. They wouldn't infringe on Reve and Llinolae's privacy.

Llinolae barely spoke, interrupting just to clarify facts and offer support when the memories became overwhelming.

"You fell off the ship?" Llinolae questioned as Reve reached the end of her story.

Reve hesitated. "Yes."

Llinolae's lips formed a thin line. She could sense the truth. "I see."

"I didn't have a choice. They were going to die or worse."

"Reve... has it occurred to you that it's not your duty to save them?"

Reve looked her over. "I don't know what you mean."

"There's a particular hardship, being alone with the Sight. We see and feel so much more than the people around us. But they aren't blind. If someone chooses to be with you, to help you, you should be with them. There was a time I thought I had to fight alone. But then I met Gwyn. We're both strong, but we're far stronger as a family."

Reve shook her head stubbornly. "I can't afford to think about family. I have to destroy the Choir."

"And what will you do after?"

"There's no reason to think past the battle."

"Reve... there's more to life than revenge. Trust me."

"I can't involve them. Just being near me almost got them killed. I'm not underestimating them. I just know what the Choir is capable of. They won't die for me."

"It sounds like they know what the Choir is capable of after they lost their homes."

"They know the Choir is unmerciful, but allowing their village to burn wasn't vindictive. They didn't give a second thought to Nix's village. The storm was just a taste of the Choir's targeted wrath."

Llinolae rested her arms on her knees. "You told me you thought the Sight was leading you to Blue Sights from the past to help you on your path. I'm not sure what you're supposed to learn from me. I don't know enough about your world to give you strategy. But I would encourage you to let them help you. Blue Sights weren't meant to be alone. We're tied to the emotions, to the heart of Aggar. No matter how powerful we become, we are weakest alone. You need family. You at least need someone worth surviving for."

Reve grunted, her stomach turning at Llinolae's truth. Nix's face flashed through her mind and she ran her fingers roughly through her hair. She could feel the power in Llinolae's words as powerfully as if they had shared a connection through the Sight. No matter how hard Reve fought it, this was the lesson the Sight wanted her to learn.

A shuffle in the trees caught their attention. Reve's mouth opened in shock. Nix stood in the shadows, almost transparent. She was pale, water dripping from her hair and clothes. Reve couldn't feel her with her Sight.

"Your Amazon?" Llinolae questioned.

Reve stood cautiously. "Nix?"

"Reve."

Reve ran to Nix and the forest faded around her, disappearing like a lifting fog. Reve reached out to Nix. The moment they touched, the world solidified. They were both transported to the stone caverns of Reve's dream. The Songs blared loudly just behind her. Nix looked around in confusion, her eyes wide. Reve took her hand. "Run!"

They sprinted through the twisting caves, Hecate bounding ahead of both of them. Reve clenched her teeth. She'd never had anyone, not even Hecate, follow her into her dreams of the caves. She was certain the Choir could find her here, that the Songs were real. So much more was at stake when she had people to protect.

As they rounded a particularly sharp corner, the tunnel opened up into a massive cave. Reve gasped and her breath caught in her throat. She could feel them near. She could feel the presence of the Choir, more real and physical than ever before. Could it be she wasn't in a nightmare, but had somehow passed into the realm of the Choir? "They're here. I can't believe they're here."

"Reve!" Nix screamed as the Songs poured into the cavern after them. The sound was deafening. Hecate howled in pain.

"Not yet. You can't take me yet," Reve growled and closed her eyes, using every bit of her will and Sight to shift the dream to its natural conclusion. Every dream of the caves ended the same way.

They were instantly absorbed in darkness Reve expected the pressure on her lungs, the ache of needing to draw breath as they all sank beneath the sea. Reve had stopped panicking long ago. She couldn't die here. She couldn't drown. She just had to wake up.

She spotted Nix out of the corner of her eye, swimming down toward the sparkling lights. Her powerful muscles and precise strokes cut through the water like a fish. Reve watched her in shock. She didn't seem scared, but she also didn't seem aware. She was moving as if compelled.

Reve floundered to get to her, but Nix sped away. Hecate grabbed Reve's sleeve in her jaw and pulled, tugging Reve back. The sea wavered and blurred as Hecate dragged her and Nix disappeared into the depths. Reve's mind swam and her eyes closed.

The sea around her became more rough and gritty. The darkness turned to sunlight on her eyelids and the cold of the sea turned to heat. She could hear the roll of the tides and the cry of gulls. Her strength instantly disappeared. She was heavy and sore, every muscle spasming. Her lungs burned.

Reve coughed as she woke, sea water exploding past her lips and running down her face into the sand. The pull on her arm stopped.

"Reve?" Nix's voice, heavy and gruff, called out to her.

Reve opened her eyes, but couldn't find the strength to do much more. Nix released her arm and collapsed into the sand. Water lapped at Reve's ankles. It was clear Nix had carried her out of the sea to shore.

"You saved me?" Reve whispered.

Nix gasped for breath, her body trembling. She locked eyes with Reve and the connection they shared shot between them like lightning. "I dreamed of you."

Nix passed out, collapsing into the sand. Reve summoned what was left of her strength and crawled forward, her muscles screaming with every movement. She fell back to the ground as she reached Nix and held her hand to her lips. To her relief, she could still feel her breath and warmth returning to her skin.

Reve allowed her weakness to overcome her. Nix was alive. She would be fine. Reve's head swam, exhausted from the dream and nearly drowning. She took Nix's hand and closed her eyes. It didn't matter if she passed out. She knew with a strange certainty that she wouldn't dream. Hopefully, the Choir had lost her in the torrent of the storm.

They were together. They were both alive. For a moment at least, they were safe.

PART THREE

SONGS OF AGGAR

Chapter One

Reve woke slowly, the heat of a fire warming her cheeks. Kindling crackled and the thick scent of smoke filled her nose and lungs. Her clothes were dry and stiff with salt. She pushed off the ground, her billowing blouse rough against her skin. Her eyes fixed on Nix as she stoked a small fire. She moved with confidence and health. There was color in her cheeks. She was alive.

Nix dropped her gathered wood and raced to Reve's side, helping her sit up. "How do you feel? Are you alright?"

Reve glanced up at the night sky, her mind spinning for an instant, but steadily calming. "How long have I been out?"

"We've both been unconscious. I only woke a couple hours ago. Just long enough to pull you out of high tide, start a fire, and explore the island a bit. It's bigger than I expected and there are a few fruit-bearing trees. That's more than we could have hoped for."

Reve remembered the way she'd passed out, holding tightly to Nix's hand. If Nix had found it unsettling, she didn't show it. Reve smiled. "I'm just happy you're alive."

Nix smirked. "It takes a lot to kill me, Reve. Can you stand?"

Reve nodded. "I think so."

Nix pulled her to her feet and steadied her as she nearly toppled over. "You should find your balance again soon. You were pretty waterlogged."

Reve's mind was steadily clearing and her legs were growing stronger. "I'm feeling better."

Nix carefully released her, her arms hovering around her waist until she was sure Reve could stand on her own. "Good."

As her senses returned, Reve grew increasingly more aware of Nix's presence. The touch of her hands was like electric fire on her waist. She could feel Nix's worry, a emotion she was desperately trying to hide under a mask of confidence.

Reve had been able to feel Nix more than anyone else she'd ever met since the day she boarded the *Niachero*, but that connection paled to the bond she felt now.

Reve glanced up at the Amazon, avoiding looking directly into her eyes. Instead she watched her lips. The soft, pink lines of her mouth were pressed tightly together as Nix clenched her jaw. The muscles in her cheeks spasmed. There was so much she wasn't saying.

"We were both unconscious for a long time. Did... did you dream? After we reached the beach?"

Nix shook her head. "Nothing. Just sleep. Did you?"

"No." Nix seemed so uncomfortable, so unsure, Reve wondered if her hypersensitivity to the Amazon went both ways. "When you pulled us ashore you told me you dreamed about me."

Nix tensed. "I don't think we should talk about that right now. It was just a dream, right?"

"Nix—"

"Reve. Please." Nix's voice was sharp, unwavering. "We have a lot of things to worry about right now."

Reve let out a sharp breath. Nix wasn't going to talk with her. "Like survival?"

"The island is small. There's no source of fresh water, limited food. We need shelter. More stable warmth."

"We need to get off the island," Reve replied.

"When the stars come out I'll have a better idea of where we are, but I know we're no where near land. The Niachero has no way to track us. They'll send out Enyo. She'll look for smoke, messages written in stone. I'll set up the signals, but there's a minuscule chance that we'll be found."

"Hecate can join me in some of my dreams. If I know where we are, I can try to reach her in the dreamscape."

"You're the only one who can communicate with her."

"Between Briza, Agwe, and Enyo Hecate will find a way. It's our best chance."

"Do you feel safe going back into your dreams? After the Choir crossed the sea after us?"

"The Choir will be spent after an attack of that magnitude, especially since they attacked my mind the night before the storm. They won't come after me for a while, and even if they did I doubt they still know where I am. This is the safest time to dream if I can find a way back into that space."

"You can't control when you go into the dream?"

"No. I can project as far as my Sight can sense, but my visions and dreams come without warning."

Nix sighed heavily. "I'll do what I can to give you a safe place to rest."

Nix threw another handful of dried twigs and grass on the fire.

The kindling went up instantly, warming the flames around the large pieces of driftwood.

Reve watched the fire burn. "Tlaloc told me you've been stranded before. How did you survive then?"

"Pure luck. I swam out as far as I could, and eventually found a ship that was willing to take me on. It was pure fate I survived and had the strength to swim as far as I did. We'd do better to try to set up a livable situation here. My family won't stop looking for me. We'll signal as long as we can."

Reve nodded. "It's as good a plan as any."

"I'm going to try to find us something to eat. Do you feel healthy enough to be alone for a bit?"

Reve nodded. "I feel fine. I'll build a shelter."

"I'll be back soon."

Reve watched her stand and wander back into the cluster of trees on the opposite end of the island. It was going to be a long night if Nix continued dodging the questions that were on both of their minds. If they were going to die together, starving on a deserted island, Reve hoped they'd be able to clear the air.

"Her brooding is going to give me a headache," she grunted to herself as she turned to a nearby palm she recognized from her travels in the desert. Its bark could be stripped and braided into makeshift rope. It wouldn't be quality, and it wouldn't last long, but it was something.

She grabbed a sharp rock out of the sand and stabbed it into the trunk. There was something horribly familiar and somehow comforting about living for survival again. She knew how to survive in harsh conditions. It's what she was built for. If she was going to die, she wanted it to be like this. Fighting.

The savory scent of roasting fowl filled the air. The fat from the bird dripped into the fire in thick drops.

"Seems destiny is still on my side." Nix smiled as she turned the make-shift spit. "There are enough birds on the south side of the island to keep us alive for a bit. We get a good rainstorm, and we'll be set as long as we have driftwood to burn."

"Hopefully we'll have been rescued by then." Reve finished braiding a fourth loop of rope. She'd be able to use it to bind the large, waxy palm leaves into a make-shift covering.

Nix glanced at her from the fire. "You make a lot of ropes in your time? You're getting a lot done."

Reve tied off the rope and tossed it aside. "Focused. Angry. Every day I'm stuck on this island is another day the Choir rules unchecked.”

“You’re worried about your mission?”

“I’m always thinking about the Choir.” Reve could feel Nix’s eyes on her, lingering. Reve didn’t meet her gaze. “But you know that. You heard me talking to Llinolae.”

Nix looked away, instantly falling silent. Reve clenched her jaw. Nix had been closed off to any talk about the dream all day and it was frustrating Reve to no end.

“Dinner’s almost done,” Nix announced.

“Great. My stomach’s bee in knots all day.”

Nix chuckled. “Makes sense. Most can’t get tossed around in the sea without feeling a little sick.”

“It was pure luck I wasn’t more than a bit nauseous.”

Nix touched her back, her fingertips gentle. “You’re lucky you had a strong swimmer to pluck you out of the sea.”

Reve tensed. “You should have stayed on the ship.”

Nix cocked her head to the side in confusion. Reve turned to face her. Nix searched Reve’s face in surprise. “Reve, you would have drowned.” Reve glanced away. Nix let out a sharp breath of surprise. “You wanted to drown.”

“The Choir didn’t care about the *Niachero*. They were using all their energy to get to me. If I had died, they’d retreat.”

“So you jumped? You would have risked your entire mission for my family?”

Reve shook her head. “They had us trapped. It wasn’t about the mission anymore. They would have taken me. I’d rather die.”

“Reve —”

“Don’t feel sorry for me, Nix.”

“I don’t.”

Reve met her eyes. “You think you can hide anything from me anymore?”

A heavy silence fell, full of everything that had gone unsaid between them.

Nix spoke cautiously. “Can you really sense everything I’m feeling?”

Reve leaned forward, resting her arms on her knees. “No. But sometimes you look at me and your thoughts are so clear they practically echo in my mind.”

Nix stared at her hands, intentionally trying to keep her mind blank. “That must be awful. Invasive.”

Reve shrugged and picked at the patchy, long grass that grew across the island. “It’s not so bad.”

“Do you think it’s because of the dreams?”

"No. I think we're sharing dreams *because* of the connection."

"Is the connection so unusual for you? You were never taught to control your Sight. I'd think reaching out to other people would be natural."

"It might be. I haven't been around enough people to know. But it's not the same with anyone else on the *Niachero*. I spend more time with Agwe and Sirena and I've never shared a dream with either of them. Briza's a seer. You'd think if anyone would connect with me like this it would be her."

Reve could tell there was more Nix wanted to say, but she was intentionally trying to shield herself from Reve's Sight. She shifted uncomfortably. "I'm not trying to connect with you."

Reve looked her over. She seemed so sad, even insecure. She had never seen Nix so emotionally raw. She was so different than the Amazon captain Reve had come to know. Something had unsettled her, and the knowledge pulled at Reve's heart.

"Maybe I'm trying to connect with you."

Reve felt the explosion of confusion, panic and fear in Nix's heart. Reve was surprised by the strength of her reaction. She pulled their dinner out of the fire, the skin crisp and dark. She fought to keep her voice even."Why would you want to do that?"

"I want to talk about the dream, Nix."

"It was a dream. You're a Blue Sight. We were both half-dead. It would be odd if we didn't share a dream."

"You know it was more than that. My dreams – my lucid dreams – are visions. They tell me what I'm supposed to do next. And the entire point of my dream was to trust someone. To care about people. There's a reason you were there."

"Reve."

"Nix, I know you feel a connection to me, too. You wouldn't have jumped from the *Niachero* to save me if you didn't."

"Stop. Please."

"I'm not asking anything from you. I just want to talk to you. I want to know why we were in the same space, why you could find me in a vision. Are we supposed to fight together? Are we supposed to be some kind of family? I don't know what to do. I don't know what my vision was supposed to tell me. You have to be the missing key."

"I'm not anything to you, Reve. I already told you I'll fight the Choir with you. I told you my family is yours or as long as you want it. That's all I have. I don't know why we're dreaming together."

"I can sense your feelings, Nix. I know you're hiding from me."

Nix's cheeks grew rosy with anger, her eyes flashing dangerously. "Just because you have the Sight doesn't give you the right to sift through my brain. Stay out."

Reve was unmoved by her anger. Nix didn't scare her. She knelt beside Nix, taking her hand. She felt the same hit, electric thrill race through her body at Nix's touch. She felt her throat close and her heart pound. It was like the night after the Choir caught her in the dreams, spending hours in Nix's cabin, so close and alone. Being with Nix was like running. It made her feel wild and free, far from the grasp of the Choir. Pure adrenaline.

Reve had felt it since Nix had reset her fingers in the brig. She'd tried to ignore it, but it was getting harder. It didn't help that they were trapped alone on a deserted island. The mission was on hold for the foreseeable future. They would most likely die together, never to be found.

"Tell me. Please. You know something. Feel something."

Nix's words were clipped and sharp. "My feelings don't matter."

"They matter to me."

Nix let out a defeated sigh. She turned to face the fire and popped her jaw, relieving tension. "Sirena likes you."

Reve sat back in surprise. "I know. But what does Sirena have to do with this?"

"I won't fight my daughter for a woman's affection."

Reve snorted a laugh. Nix whipped around to meet her eyes, her face twisted with shock and incredulity. Reve hid her laugh behind her hand. "I'm sorry. I couldn't help it. I'm not interested in Sirena."

"What's wrong with Sirena?"

"Nothing at all. She's just so – young."

"She's older than you are!"

"We've had this talk, Nix. She's never fought the Choir. Never gone hungry. Never lost anything important. She's not like you and me. She's a child to me. I could never have true feelings for her. Nothing more than a sister. You're not fighting her for anything."

"It would break her heart if I..." Her words trailed off and she clenched her jaw.

Reve leaned closer. "If you what?"

"If I told you how I feel about you."

"How do you feel about me?"

"Reve."

"Please. I need to know. You're the next key to my mission. My arrow. What are you feeling?"

"I... care about you, Reve."

"Like a sister?"

Nix searched her eyes, apprehensive. Her breath came quicker in her lungs, her chest rising and falling in a rapid rhythm, a thin sheen of sweat forming along her brow and across the swell of her breast beneath her leather vest. She was scared. "Not like a sister."

Reve felt a swell of emotion radiating from her core. Curiosity. Excitement. Desire. She hadn't allowed herself to think Nix might share some of her feelings. In a flash she understood what Llinolae had been trying to tell her, what the dream had been pushing her to do. The Blue Sights of the past, the ones who had changed the world – none of them had been alone. Perhaps her feelings were more than an idle fantasy. Perhaps Nix was meant to be more than her captain.

Reve leaned forward and kissed Nix, their lips connecting for a brief moment before Reve pulled away again, searching Nix's face for response. "I care about you, too."

Nix sprang to her knees, pulling Reve into another kiss, her muscles taut and her hands clenching at Reve's clothes with tight fists. Reve wrapped her arms around the Amazon's neck, pressing tight against her, her body crying out for comfort, for touch.

Nix reared back, pulling away just enough to speak. "Wait. We shouldn't. You should eat and sleep. Try to dream, to reach Hecate."

"I'm not tired," Reve growled and kissed her again.

Nix held her tighter, her hands trembling. Her tongue flicked out over her lips. "Reve..."

Reve shook her head and kissed her once more, slower, deeper. "Please. Be with me."

"Are you sure?"

Reve rolled her eyes and they kissed again, the urgency in her embrace quickly breaking down the last of Nix's willpower. She led Reve back, never breaking their kiss. They reached the pile of leaves they'd gathered to string into a roof and Nix laid her back out of the sand.

Reve's hands fumbled with the clasps of Nix's vest as Nix left a trail of rough, wet kisses down her throat and collar. The leather was tough and stiff after being soaked in salt. Reve grunted in annoyance and Nix laughed, loud and genuine. She grabbed Reve's hand and kissed her fingers, her lips feather-gentle against her skin.

"Tough time, Love?"

Nix undid her own vest and tossed it aside with her shirt. The twin moons reflected pale blue light off her skin, her curves and the lines of her sculpted muscles. It caught on the silver in her hair until she seemed to glow. Reve was caught in the beauty of her, the wonder of another woman who had seen so much, who knew the pain of the Choir's rule.

Nix grinned and crouched down low over her, laying a soft kiss on her lips. "What are you thinking about? I can't read minds like you can."

"You're beautiful."

Nix blushed. "That's a very nice thing to be thinking."

Reve took Nix's hand and guided it over her body, over the swell of her breasts and held it over her heart. "Try reading my mind now."

Nix nipped softly at her jaw and eased her shirt up, her hands exploring the ridge of Reve's hip bones and ribs, tenderly roaming her slender frame. "I don't need to read your mind to understand you."

Soon their clothes lay strewn across the sand, Nix's arms wrapped around Reve's thighs as she kissed and licked hungry lines across Reve's body. Every touch was a caress, tender and loving. Reve drifted in a warm, floating cloud of Nix's emotions. Her Sight drowned out the rest of the world until all that existed was Nix's touch, her love, her determination to be careful with the younger woman.

Nix nipped at Reve's thigh and Reve's back arched, a gasp of pleasure spilling past her lips in a warm rush. For a moment in time, Reve didn't think of her mission. She didn't think of the Choir or dreams. There was only Nix. Only love. Only connection. And for the first time in her life, Reve could imagine a future with someone by her side.

As Nix slipped between her legs, driving her higher into ecstasy, a window opened in Reve's mind. An understanding. And as she came down from climax, both women collapsing in exhaustion from passion and the intensity of their connection, Reve slipped into sleep and willed herself to dream.

Reve sat in the library of her dreams, waiting. There was no vision waiting for her. No journey into the past. With Nix's help, she'd once again been able to transcend past her astral form and walk into the dreamworld. If Hecate was going to find her, it would be here. The doorway to the rest of her dreams, where not even the Choir could catch her.

Reve had been coming to the library nearly every day for a tenday. The situation was becoming more desperate as she and Nix ran out of wood and the birds they'd been hunting had started leaving the island. If they weren't rescued soon, they'd starve.

Reve sat cross-legged on the library table, her eyes closed, and willed Hecate near, calling out to her in the void. She sighed. She had already been waiting for a full night. There was such a slim chance she'd even be able to reach her friend it seemed foolish to keep getting her hopes up.

Just as she was about to give up, to return to Nix and the island, she heard a scuffle at the door followed by the hollow sounds of nails pawing at the wood. Reve jumped to her feet and opened the wide double doors and Hecate bounded in, tackling her back and licking her face. Reve laughed aloud and held Hecate close, kissing the side of her furry face.

"You heard me!"

You've grown in power.

Reve grinned. "Much has changed. Nix and I are alive. We're stranded on a deserted island not far from where the storm hit. Nix needs Tlaloc to know we're about twenty miles south of the storm point. She's not exactly sure where, but we're sending up smoke signals. Enyo should be able to see us and if not, I'll keep coming here every day."

I'll do my best to guide them. Enyo will help. She knows their ways better than I.

"Please hurry. We're quickly running out of food and we barely have any water."

We shouldn't be far. Tlaloc and Sirena have been sailing in overlapping circles searching for any sign of you.

"Everyone is still safe?"

Safe and worried. They haven't given up hope.

Reve held her tighter. "Thank you for finding me."

I didn't give up hope, either.

Reve rested her face against Hecate's fur, stroking between her ears. "Thank you, dumauz."

Hecate licked her cheek. *Don't die on me, pup. We'll come for you. Keep you Sight on the horizon.*

"We'll be waiting."

Reve woke, rustling in her sleep and sitting up, pulling out of Nix's embrace. Nix opened her eyes, already used to Reve's sudden wakings. Her short, dark hair clung to the sides of her neck, damp from sweat from the heat and their lovemaking. Her eyes sparkled.

"Any sign of Hecate?"

Reve grinned. "Yes. They're coming for us. Hecate says they aren't far."

Nix pulled Reve back down to her, kissing her softly. "I always knew you'd do it."

Reve threaded her legs between her lover's, the shade of their leafy shelter casting long shadows across their bare bodies. "Only with your help."

Nix let out a slow, contented hum and nipped gently at Reve's collar bone. "A rather pleasant duty."

Reve rested on Nix's shoulder. "I'll miss this, when they come back."

"Why miss anything? I'll talk to Sirena. She'll understand. You can come stay with me."

Reve sighed almost sadly. "It won't be the same. The mission will begin again. The Choir won't stop looking for me."

"You jump overboard again and I'll never forgive you."

Reve smiled. "No. I've already resigned myself that I can't keep you out of my fate. I just hope, when the time comes, you won't share my demise."

"You're so sure you won't survive the confrontation?"

"I've never let myself think otherwise. I'll hope once they're ash at my feet."

Nix looped her hand under Reve's chin, catching her eyes. "Our feet." They kissed again.

Reve laughed, low and cynical. "You have no idea what you're getting into, sharing my bed."

"It can't be worse than sharing your dreams. And perhaps you'll find my life isn't as sane and simple as you think."

"There's nothing about you that could rival the mission."

Nix arched one sculpted brow. "So arrogant in your youth."

Reve felt a tickle in the back of her mind, a sense of something approaching along the corners of her Sight. She sat up again and crawled out from beneath their leafy canopy and stared out to the horizon, shielding the sun with her hand.

"What is it?" Nix called as she joined Reve on the beach.

"Something is coming. Just there." She pointed to the north.

Nix squinted into the dawn sunlight. "I don't see anything."

Reve glanced over her shoulder at her, her mouth quirked in a wicked grin. "Of course not."

Nix shot her a good-natured glare. "Is it the Niachero? Hecate said they were close. I'd think we would have seen Enyo first, though."

Reve shrugged. "It's too far away to tell, but it's moving fast and it isn't a sea creature. What else would be coming at us with such speed?"

Nix rushed to pull her clothes back on and gather more wood for the fire. "I'll send up a signal. They may not have spotted us yet."

Reve dressed as Nix went to work building their small cooking fire to a roaring blaze, sending a cloud of smoke into the air. Within the hour, Reve wandered to the tide, stopping when the ocean lapped at her feet. In the farthest distance, just barely more than a blur on the horizon, she could see a ship.

She raced back to Nix, who was now covered in sweat and soot. "They're coming!" she cheered.

Nix ran with her to the beach. The ship was quickly becoming more clear. Her smile slowly faded and her eyes widened. She cursed, sharp and low under her breath and ran to put out the fire. "What's she doing here?"

"Nix?" Reve chased after her. "What is it?"

Nix threw sand on the flame, trying to dampen its smoke. "That's not the *Niachero*. That's the *Zephyr*."

Reve stumbled as she was carried aboard the foreign ship, the chaotic tumble of emotion and energy on the Zephyr overwhelming her. Nix watched her, nervous, but her hands were bound behind her back and she couldn't reach out to comfort her.

"Nix n'Niachero. What a surprise."

A tall woman with dark skin and a beaded sash sauntered down from the helm. She flicked her long, black hair over her shoulder, her eyes smoldering. She was obviously an Amazon like Nix, their past connection so clear it was nearly palpable. Reve didn't have to use her Sight to know the women had a complex relationship.

"Gale," Nix acknowledged.

Gale stepped closer to Nix, her hand on the hilt of her sword. "I saw your signals a day ago. Didn't even imagine it was you. Did your crew finally throw you overboard?"

"My crew is on their way, Gale, just let us go. We don't have anything for you."

"Nothing for me?" Gale's voice was sharp as her blade. "You jumped off my ship, Nix. You left my bed in the night and you risked drowning rather than staying with me."

Nix shifted uncomfortably, glancing at Reve out of the corner of her eye. "You would have stranded of killed me and you know it."

"I would never have killed you, Nix. You know that."

"I wasn't going to stay your prisoner, either."

Gale popped her jaw. "We'll see about that."

She nodded to Reve. "Whose she? A friend of Sirena's? I've never met her before."

"She's not important."

Reve's ears grew warm with a blush at the dismissive tone in Nix's voice. "I'm Reve." Reve's voice was soft and shallow. She wasn't sure what had prompted her to speak, but as she watched the unspoken words pass between Gale and Nix she felt the first stirrings of jealousy.

Gale rounded on her, her boots clicking hard against the wooden deck. "Reve, hmm? And why would you be left on such a forsaken little island with Nix?" She glanced at Nix. "You're going after children now?"

Nix struggled against her captor, but Gale's crewmate held her tight. "Let us go or lock us in the brig."

Gale sucked a sharp breath between her teeth. "So impolite."

"We're not doing this again, Gale. I'm done. I'm not playing anymore."

"You think it's so easy to leave me? I decide when I'm done with you." Gale waved her hand. "Lock them in the brig. We'll see if a few days doesn't soften Nix's attitude."

They were dragged deep below deck and locked in a tiny cell. The bilge water lapped sluggishly at their bare feet and the smell of mildew made Reve cough. Compared to the sun and fresh air of the island, Reve thought she'd rather risk starving.

Nix growled and pounded at the bars as their captors left, leaving them alone in the dim lantern light. "I can't believe this!" Nix growled.

Reve felt her heart sink in her chest. They had been so close. Now she was even further from the mission. From Hecate. From her family.

"What's going to happen now?" Reve questioned.

Nix leaned back against the bars, her eyes twin flames. "I'm going to beat some sense into Gale and she's going to take us home."

Reve glanced away cautiously. "And who's Gale?"

Nix's fury momentarily abated. "Reve..."

"I understand."

"She means nothing to me, Reve. I promise."

"You seem very familiar with each other. I could feel her emotions."

"We were lovers. Rivals. I left her behind."

"She's very beautiful."

Nix snorted and gathered Reve into her arms, kissing her gently. "And she's absolutely nothing to me. Not anymore."

Reve smiled softly. "I could dream again. Contact Hecate. If the *Niachero* can track us, they may be able to free us."

Nix glanced around the filthy cell with barely a dry place to sit. "You want me to help you sleep here?"

Reve grinned and looped her fingers through Nix's sash. "We could be careful."

Nix's grin was crooked as she kissed her again, pushing her up against the wall, her hands wandering under her shirt. "Very careful."

A sharp, strangled gasp echoed through the room. Nix and Reve turned as one as Gale stepped down into the hold, her face twisted with rage.

"Gale..." Nix's voice was a warning as she pulled away from Reve.

Gale shook her head, her words slipping past clenched teeth.

"You're going to rot in here, Nix n'Niachero." Her eyes raked across Reve. "Both of you."

Without another word she turned on her heel and stormed away.

Chapter Two

Nix sat in the only dry corner of the cell. Reve sat on her lap, resting against her shoulder. Reve wasn't asleep; she'd only been able to sleep once since they'd been locked in a cell by Gale. She said she'd been able to find Hecate, but with no idea where they were, her directions had been vague at best.

They didn't talk much anymore. They didn't need to. They'd been in a cell for nearly a ten-day by Nix's calculations, provided only the barest of necessities. Their connection was growing every day, their ability to sense each other's emotions and thoughts bordering on magical. Sometimes the silence was more intimate and comforting than words.

Gale hadn't visited, but Nix could tell by the looks her crew gave them that she was in a rage. The *Niachero* and the *Zephyr* had come to blows more times than one, but there was a twisted sense of family between them. A dependability. A drive that gave them focus when the nights at sea grew long and dark.

Gale had crossed a line. Not in putting Nix in the brig, but in her determination to watch Nix suffer. She wasn't playing a game anymore. She wanted Nix dead.

Nix ran her fingers through Reve's dark-blonde hair and over her slender neck. It was one thing to Nix for Gale to threaten her, it was another entirely to pull Reve into their feud. Despite her barriers and strength, Reve was still new. Still soft to the ways of people. She didn't show her emotions easily, but Nix had learned to recognize her confusion and fear.

Reve shifted uncomfortably, pulling slightly away from Nix. Nix grinned mischievously. "Did I do something wrong? I know I smell like mildew, but everything does anymore."

Reve didn't take her teasing bait. Nix sensed a dark seriousness about her. "Have I stepped off my path?" Reve's voice was soft and rough with disuse. She gripped Nix's shirt tighter, balling the limp fabric in a tight fist.

Nix tipped her face to to look into her eyes. The pale blue irises didn't have the same power over her they once did. They no longer scared her or made her swept her away. In the past few tenmoons they'd grown warm and stable. They'd become home.

"What do you mean?"

"I'm meant to fight the Choir. I'm meant to free the people of Aggar. But the visions led me to the island. Now here. I can't run. I can't fight. Was I unworthy?"

Nix smiled softly. "You've been so strong for so long. You run and claw and tear after your revenge. Are you going to crumble when fate decides to carry you for a while?"

The fear in Reve's eyes shifted to an incredulous glance. Nix felt a jolt of love and desire. There was her Reve. That fire. That passion. "I never crumble, Nix."

"I believe you." She kissed Reve's brow. "You live as much in your mind and your Sight as you do the physical world, Reve. Don't dwell too long on dark thoughts. They only twist you up. Your visions led you to a deserted island and a brig. They also led you to me. And together, we can do anything."

"I suppose."

Nix ran her thumb over Reve's chin, her fingertip skimming her bottom lip. "If you insist on wallowing, I could remind you that this started when you chose to jump overboard instead of trusting me to keep you safe."

Reve snorted. "You'll never let me forget."

Nix shook her head. "Never." They kissed, the embrace gentle and comforting.

"How disgustingly sweet."

Nix slowly pulled away from Reve and glanced at the door. Gale moved slowly, her skirt swaying around her legs with every click of her heels. Her eyes were black in the dim light, her skin flushed with rage. Nix held Reve possessively, meeting Gale's eyes with an unspoken challenge.

Gale scoffed. "Don't look at me like that, Nix."

"What do you want, Gale? I thought we were supposed to rot."

Gale leaned back against the wall, cloaked in deep shadows. She crossed her arms over her chest, her mind spinning. Nix watched her carefully. Gale wasn't stupid, but she was passionate. Impulsive. She was most deadly when she fell quiet.

Reve tensed in her arms. She was sensitive to Nix's energy and Gale was acidic even without the Sight. Nix gently released Nix, giving a silent request to let her stand. Reve slid from Reve's arms and Nix stood, letting Reve slide into the dry corner. The young Blue Sight tucked her knees to her chest, curling into a tiny ball, and watched as her Amazon moved to the bars toward Gale.

"If you have something to say to me, Gale, then let me out. We've never talked through bars."

"You think I want to *talk* to you?"

"Then fight me. Upstairs."

Gale curled her lip in disgust. "You just don't want your new toy to overhear us."

Nix shook her head sharply. "Leave Reve out of this. She has nothing to do with us."

Gale kicked off from the wall. "She has everything to do with us. Is she why you left me? Why you decided not to finish our race?"

"You attacked me. You kidnapped me."

"It was a game. Just like every other move we've made against each other. How many times could I have killed you? I never did. And you never did."

"We were hurting people. Our families. I didn't even know Reve when I let you go. I left you for Sirena and Agwe. For my family. For *your* family. We're toxic, Gale."

"You didn't even know her? We've been together for half our lives and you choose someone you met a handful of ten-days ago?"

"We were never together. We were rivals. We... we shared a bed. I've bedded a lot of people since we met and you never acted like this."

For a split second Nix spotted a spark of sorrow in Gale's eyes, but it was immediately swallowed. "You never looked at a lover like you looked at her. And you've never looked at me like you are right now."

Nix spread her arms wide in surrender, hoping she was reading the brief warmth in Gale's eyes correctly. "What do you want me to say?"

Nix took a step back in shock at the sudden seething that exploded from Gale. She took a bounding step forward and grabbed the bars of the brig, baring her teeth.

"I don't want you to say anything." She spun away from Nix and stalked around the brig, crouching beside Reve. "You think you know her? You think you've seen her true self? Innocent little waif of a girl. Do you want to know what kind of darkness she's capable of?"

Nix spun and slid to her knees, her hand shooting between the bars and grabbing Gale by the throat, stopping her words short. "Don't listen to her, Reve."

Reve gently touched Nix's arm, her face perfectly still. "It's fine." Nix loosened her grip on Gale. The rival captain gasped for breath. Reve turned, kneeling in the water to meet Gale's eyes. Her voice was cold and hard as steel. "What makes you think I'm so fragile?"

Gale's eyes grew wide in shock and fear as Reve's Sight filled Gale with the full weight of Reve's capabilities. Her potential for ruthlessness. She intentionally kept Nix out of the interaction, but Nix could sense the nature of their silent conversation, like the scent of sulfur and heat of a bonfire. Nix regarded her lover with pride and new respect.

"Goddess," Gale gasped, her skin pale.

"Perhaps it is Nix who should be warned about me."

Gale struggled out of Nix's grasp and forcefully turned away, covering her eyes with trembling hands. "What are you?"

"I want you to let us go. I have other things to do than watch you sort out your jealousy."

Gale shook her head, carefully avoiding Reve's eyes. "You think I'm going to unleash you on my family?"

"You brought us here in the first place," Reve countered.

Gale glared at Nix. "Those demon blue eyes. You're even more twisted than I thought."

Nix grinned and shrugged. "I've been accused of being attracted to insanity. And I'd recommend doing what she says. You have no idea what those eyes are capable of."

"Maybe I'll blind her and this won't be a problem anymore."

Nix grabbed the bars of the brig. "Just try, Gale. I'll snap your neck."

Gale looked them both over, considering.

"*Niachero*, coming fast off the starboard bow!"

The cry rose through the air, cutting all the way to the brig. Gale tensed. "Impossible."

Nix grinned wide. "You're having a lot of trouble judging what's possible today." The resounding boom of cannon fire shook the ship, knocking Gale against the wall. "Better hurry. My family won't go down easy tonight and your family wants us of the *Zephyr* so badly they might just surrender."

Gale held Nix's gaze a moment longer then raced up the stairs and out of the brig. Nix fell back against the wall and slid to the ground beside Reve. Reve wrapped her arm around her lover's shoulders and kissed her brow.

"You were amazing," Nix whispered.

"I wanted —"

Reve's words stopped short. She gasped and grabbed her face, her palm covering her eyes. Her fingers squeezed at her temples and she groaned with pain.

"Reve?" Nix spun around, crouching in front of her. She held Reve's arms as the Blue Sight started to seize, trembling violently.

The water on the brig floor sloshed and splashed as Reve's legs flailed, her toes clenching and digging at the wood. "Reve!"

Reve grabbed at Nix's shoulders, her nails biting into Nix's skin. She slowly forced her eyes open a sliver. Nix's breath caught in her throat. Deep red blood trickled from her tear ducts down her cheeks in slender, wet trails.

"The Choir is coming."

Nix shuddered. "Help! We need help!" Her screams boomed through the brig, her voice ragged with panic. "Help!"

The ship shook with another exchange of cannon fire. Reve grabbed at her head again and screamed. She violently pulled out of Nix's arms, falling to her side and curling into a ball.

"Please!"

The pound of boots and the clash of steel swept through the *Zephyr*. Nix heard the familiar cry of Lyr in battle, his mind lost to the fight in a berserker rage. Nix felt a flash of hope. She ran as close to the door as she could, grasping the bars in tight fists. "Help! We're here! Reve needs help!"

A dry sob burst from Nix's mouth as she heard boots racing toward her. The door to the brig flew open. Sirena and Tlaloc raced into the room, their swords aloft.

"M'Sormee!" Sirena cried as she raced into her mother's arms.

Nix held Sirena through the bars, smelling her familiar scent, feeling the strength of her arms. "I missed you, Soroe." She pulled away from Sirena. "Reve is having another attack, we need to get her out of here."

The deep thud of tumblers rolling into place filled the room as Tlaloc unlocked the brig door. Zi instantly ran inside, standing over Reve as she trembled and cried. "This is bad."

Nix hugged her friend. "We need to get her home. What's the fighting like?"

"Still ongoing. Gale's certainly in a mood," Tlaloc growled.

"Then cover me." Nix pulled Reve into her arms, willing her with every bit of the connection they shared to be at peace. "Stay with me. Please." She breathed the words against Reve's ear and for a moment Reve stopped seizing.

Sirena eyed her mother suspiciously. "Something's differe—"

The ship trembled and pitched violently to the side, knocking everyone off-balance. Nix grunted as she fell hard into the brig bars. "What's Volt thinking? We're too close for canon fire!"

"We're not firing canons." Tlaloc grabbed zir sword tighter.

The shipped rocked a second time and Reve cried out. "Do you hear it? Do you hear it?"

Nix grit her teeth. "Let's go."

They stumbled up the stairs and through the Zephyr sleeping quarters. The ship jumped and pitched violently. Nix wondered if the Choir had sent another storm, but as they approached the main deck there was no rain or thunder. The sky was clear, the sun drifting toward dusk.

Nix and her family reached the stairwell to the main deck.

"Nix!" Kana screamed as she ran toward the doorway. She pitched to the side as the ship swayed, but her acrobatic grace kept her on her feet. "Get below deck!"

Nix froze in horror as the water rippled and bubbled around both ships. Shiny, lifestone scales glittered under the water and hooked metallic ridges sliced through the surface of the water. Every member of the *Zephyr* and *Niachero* stood along the edge, shooting arrows into the sea.

"Sea serpents?"

Kana burst through the door, dripping wet, her eyes wide with fear. "They came out of nowhere."

"They?"

"Two of them so far. I don't know how to fight them, Nix. There aren't any specific tactics in the stories. They haven't attacked anyone personally, but they seem determined to sink the ships."

Nix nodded sharply, trying to form some strategy in her mind. "It'll be alright. We'll figure something out."

Reve screamed and seized, nearly falling out of Nix's arms. Kana reached out in horror and touched Reve's cheek, her finger coming back wet with blood. "Reve."

They struggled to keep their feet as a serpent rammed the *Zephyr* again. The waves split in a wild cascade of water as one of the serpents raised its massive head from the sea. It hovered for a second, its metallic body directing the sun into glaring beams. It scanned the deck, its unblinking, lifestone eyes glittered. In the distance, like a whisper in the back of her mind, Nix could hear a Song. It wasn't like the Songs she'd heard with Reve, these were sharp, violent, chaotic. They were driving the serpents mad, confusing them into doing the Choir's bidding.

"The Choir can control them?" Nix held Reve tighter and sank back into the shadows of the hold. "They're getting far too powerful."

Tlaloc shook zir head. "They must be looking for something. If they wanted to sink us, it would be over in seconds."

Nix looked down at Reve.

The serpent bared its teeth, the edges like swords, and sank back beneath the waves. Sirena touched her mother's arm. "I don't think they can sense Reve if they can't see her."

Nix slid down the stairs back to the living quarters. "Then we keep her hidden until we can kill them." She pulled Reve into the closest room and laid her in a hammock.

Kana followed close behind. "Kill them? The Amazons who have killed one serpent are legendary. No one has even seen two together, let alone survived the encounter."

Nix spun around, her hands clenched into fists. "We don't exactly have another option, do we? You think we can outrun them? Even with Volt's thrusters, we're dead if we can't fight them off."

"They might leave us," Sirena suggested. "If they can't find Reve, they might return to the depths."

Nix snorted. "They're controlled by the Choir. We've taken care of her. Guided her. The Choir will kill us."

Kana clenched her jaw in determination. She tossed Nix her sword. "We'll always follow your lead, Captain."

Nix ran from the room and shut the door. She leaned her head against the door as the sound of Reve weeping echoed through the walls.

"Nix?" Reve called out in her nightmare.

"I'll be back, Love," she whispered to the wood and led her family to the main deck.

"M'Sormee?"

Nix turned. Sirena watched her, the echo of a question in her eyes. Nix sighed softly. Sirena clenched her jaw in understanding. "We'll talk later?"

Sirena nodded.

"Nix!" Lyr bounded toward her and pulled her into his arms. "What do we do? How do we fight them?"

"We need to draw them out of the water. We can't do anything with them tossing us around under the water." She ran to the port side that lined up with the *Niachero*. She leaned over the rail, calling down into the *Niachero's* powder room. "Volt! Direct all cannon fire at the serpents!"

"Nix?" A canon withdrew and Volt leaned out the opening. "You're alive!"

"We need to draw the serpents out of the sea before we can find a weakness. Redirect your fire."

Volt paled. "Are you sure?"

Nix drew a sharp breath past her teeth. "No. But do it anyway."

Volt nodded slowly. "Alright, Captain."

"Tlaloc, take the helm on the *Niachero*. I trust you to keep her afloat."

"Right." Tlaloc ran on long legs, leaping the short distance between the vessels and landing hard on the *Niachero*'s deck.

Gale ran up to Nix and grabbed her shoulder, spinning her around. "What are you doing giving orders on my ship?"

Nix shoved her away hard, another pound from the serpents sending her crashing to the ground. Nix grabbed her hand and helped her back to her feet. "Do you want to survive? We need to work together. Great Amazons have killed serpents before. And we are both great Amazons."

Gale sucked a breath through clenched teeth, the sound like a serpent's warning hiss, but she nodded. "We are."

They clasped arms. "Together?"

"Aye." Gale spun around, addressing her family. "Redirect cannon fire! Draw them out of the sea!"

The canons on both ships blasted as one, surrounding both vessels in fire and gunpowder as they shot at the writhing coils of the metal serpents. Nix and Gale shouted orders, directing their families as the serpents shifted and rolled, annoyed by the fire.

"Keep going!" Nix called. "They can feel it!"

Kana swung up the ratlines, gaining a better view of their assailants. She reached into a pouch at her waist and pulled out a small bomb. Nix recognized Volt's experimental phosphorus bombs, said to be able to burn even under water.

"Be careful!" Nix cried.

Kana grinned and lit the fuse, throwing the bomb into the sea. Nix stared in awe at the explosion, the fire burning underwater, clinging to the serpent's skin. The fire ate through the metallic surface and Nix gripped the rail of the *Zephyr* as the creature started to bleed black. If they could bleed, they weren't invincible. They weren't even truly metal. They could be killed.

The beast reared out of the sea, screaming to the sky. Its cry shook Nix to the bone, setting her teeth on edge. The acrid stink of the creature's blood, more oil than living, filled the air with the stink of death. Nix winced as the creature thrashed, sending blood flying. The droplets burned like acid as they struck the skin of her hands and cheeks. She growled and glanced over her shoulder, meeting eyes with Gale. The other Amazon gripped her sword tighter, lifting her chin with fearless pride. They were thinking the same thing.

"Kana! Get back home and gather more of those bombs. Work with Volt on the other serpent.

Kana turned to climb back to the ground, but the serpent turned on her with vicious rage. Kana screamed as the beast opened its jaws after her. Faster than Nix had ever seen her, Gale raced across the deck and leapt into the air, kicking off the rail of her ship and throwing her sword into the wound Kana's bomb had opened in the beast's belly. Gale cried out in pain as the beast's burning blood gushed out over her like a tidal wave, but she turned the scream into a war cry.

Nix twisted around the ratlines and pulled Kana to the ground. "Go!"

Kana regained herself instantly and ran fort he *Niachero*.

Nix fell back to the deck, stained black with serpent gore. Her skin was red a beginning to blister but the blood didn't seem lethal.

"I could only stab deeper, my sword couldn't break its outer shell," Gale gasped. "What was in those bombs?"

"Only Volt knows. Pray to the Goddess he can make more quickly."

Gale popped her jaw. "Not since the Terrans of old has anyone had such control over fire and electricity."

The serpent shook its head and the Song grew louder. Nix winced, but Gale didn't seem to notice. The beast was rebelling, drawing on its pain to fight the Choir and the Choir was responding in kind, reaching such a vicious pitch Nix knew the beast would either submit or go mad.

"Nix!" Gale called as more explosions rippled under the sea on the opposite end of the *Niachero* and the second serpent roared.

"All the stories say to cut off their heads!" Nix shouted.

The serpent threatening the *Zephyr* charged for Gale and Nix ran, leaping up and wrapping herself around the creature's neck.

"Nix!" Gale howled, her voice full of panic and grief.

The serpent bucked, trying to shake Nix free, but she found a solid grip in the ridges of the creature's armor. The beast reared up tall, lifting Nix high above the topsail of both ships. She refused to acknowledge the height and scrambled along the beast's side. She grabbed at its dorsal fin, searching for any sign of weakness or tenderness she could exploit. She stabbed uselessly at its head and neck, her blade even catching its lifestone eye only to rebound against the stone.

The creature screamed in annoyance and Nix cried out with it in frustration. How could such creatures even exist? What had animated them? They couldn't really be metal and stone!

She stabbed wildly at a thin seam at the base of its skull and her sword caught in the joint. The creature arched its neck and Nix's blade snapped in two. Nix stared in horror as her only weapon fell helplessly to the deck of the *Zephyr* far below.

Lyr looked up at her in terror and launched himself at the

serpent, slashing and clawing like a wild animal. The serpent bucked again, throwing him back, and tipped. Nix's stomach twisted as the creature dove, tipping her upside down and pulling her down deep into the sea.

Nix tried to swim away, but the creature wrapped around her, squeezing her like a vice. She continued to stab at it with the shattered remains of her blade, her lungs screaming for air as the creature twisted and coiled, trying to drown her. Her sword finally caught its eye, the slender fragment wedging under the stone and prying it free.

The serpent's wail echoed even in the water, matching the Song in its mind, and Nix felt it lose what little was left of its sanity. It released her enough for her to slip away and she swam for the surface, dodging its flailing body. She broke through the ocean's surface and gasped for breath. A rope lowered along the side of the vessel.

"Climb!" Gale called.

Nix caught the rope and sped back to the main deck, falling in an exhausted heap on the ground. She held her chest, her breath burning even after returning to the surface. Gale and Lyr helped her sit as she spat up a lung full of sea water. "Is it dead?"

Nix shook her head. "No. Just angry."

A dull clunk echoed as the serpent's eye, a diamond-shaped lifestone, fell from Nix's boot. Nix stared at it in surprise. It must have gotten caught in the folds when she was swimming away.

Lyr picked up the gem. "You got its eye?"

Nix forced herself back to her feet, tucking the lifestone in her belt-pouch. "And next I'll have its head."

Lyr handed her his short-sword. The other serpent screamed as another explosion boomed. It was pocked with oozing wounds. Nix nodded to the *Niachero*. "Get another weapon and help the others. Volt's bombs can hurt them. You have the fearlessness to finish what Volt's fire starts."

Lyr met her eyes with equal determination and hope. He grabbed her shoulder, a fellow warrior, and nodded. "Good luck."

Nix grabbed his shoulder in return. "And you."

Lyr turned and raced away, leaping from the rail of the *Zephyr* to the *Niachero* on all-fours, his changling heritage taking full control.

The sea started to ripple once more and Nix's serpent reared its head, black blood spilling from its empty eye socket. She could barely hear its Song anymore. The Choir didn't need to urge it into a rampage. The beast was consumed with chaos and destruction.

Whatever wisdom or sentience it had once possessed had been destroyed.

Nix and Gale stood side by side, their swords flashing in the light reflected from the creature's metallic hide.

"Fight with me, Sister?" Gale asked, her voice sincere.

Nix grabbed her hand. They screamed a war-cry and charged as the serpent dove after them, snapping its massive jaws. Without the will of the Choir to keep it focused on finding Reve, the beast seemed bent on massive destruction. Its head crashed into the rail of the *Zephyr*, sending splinters of wood flying through the air.

Gale lashed out like a bolt of lightning, her sword singing as she stabbed at the phosphorus wounds at its throat as Nix swung around on its back and aimed for its other eye. Her short sword caught its bare eye socket, barely scraping the metal of its skull. The creature thrashed, barely missing Gale's mast. It reared back, preparing to dive again. It shook its head, throwing Nix back to the ship. She groaned as she slammed into the stairs leading to the helm.

"We need more bombs," Gale called, her cheek cracking, leaving a trickle of blood down the side of her face as her burns festered.

Nix shook her head and watched as the water bubbled, the serpent preparing for another attack. "We don't have enough, not for both of them. We need a miracle."

The slow scuffle and fall of feet dragging across the hardwood floors echoed from the stairs to the living quarters.

"Nix?"

Nix spun around. Reve pulled herself up the stairs, her body trembling, dried blood rimming her eyes and staining her cheeks. Her voice was soft and distant, her eyes clouded as if she were far away. She was still asleep. She seemed to glow with a pale blue light.

Nix tensed, ready to run to her lover, but the serpent burst from the ocean, sensing Reve's presence.

"Reve!" Nix screamed as the serpent went straight for Reve.

Reve didn't flinch or fall back. She raised a single hand and the beast froze in front of her as if she were surrounded by some kind of force field.

Reve turned to Nix, her eyes blank. Nix shrank back. She felt like she had a hole in her heart. She didn't recognize the young woman before her. She didn't feel their connection. In less than an hour Reve had transformed into something otherworldly and alien. Someone Nix didn't recognize.

Nix took a short step forward, her eyes wide in shock. "Reve?"

Reve lifted both arms. "We are one."

Nix doubled over as if she'd been hit, all her energy fleeing her body like a gust of wind. Twin beams of light burst from Reve's hands, streaking through the air and consuming the serpents. The beasts howled in agony, glowing molten red for an instant and then evaporating. The dust of their corpses rained down on the ships like ash from a fire.

Nix collapsed to the ground, followed by dozens of other thuds as everyone on both ships fell unconscious. Reve had drained them all. Nix's vision swam. Reve swayed on her feet. Her glow dimmed and disappeared. Her eyes closed and she crumpled.

Nix tried to crawl forward, but she only pulled herself forward a body's length before her limbs gave out and she hit the ground hard. She didn't even have the energy to lift her head. She watched Reve, unable to comprehend what she'd just seen.

The waters stilled and night fell as if there had never been a battle. Reve lay motionless, broken like a doll, but their connection had returned and Nix knew she was still alive.

"Who are you?" The words slipped past her lips in a final sigh before Nix fell unconscious.

Chapter Three

A low, guttural growl echoed in the darkness. Reve drifted in the void, her mind warm and blank. She had no concept of time or place. She had no memories of what had happened. All she knew was she was dreaming.

A distant howl beckoned Reve, calling her back into light and understanding. Reve willed herself to go to the sound and the darkness shattered. She stared up at the ceiling of the library, cradled in the cushion of the carpets. She felt too light, almost insubstantial, and warm. It was as if her blood and bones had been replaced with dying embers. She wondered briefly if she'd somehow left her body behind.

Hecate prodded her with her nose, the cold sharp against Reve's hot cheek. It was a sharp contrast to her warm breath against Reve's skin.

"What happened?"

You know what happened.

"Hecate?"

It's time, Reve. Time for you to know the truth.

Reve sat up slowly, staring at her friend in confusion. There was a wisdom and stillness about Hecate that she's never sensed before. Memories started to return. Reve slowly reached up to her cheek. Her fingers were covered in dried blood.

"I killed the serpents."

They had gone wild. Forgotten their purpose.

"How could I do that? Where did that power come from? Not from me."

You are a piece of art. A finely crafted vessel created by Aggar to save her children. You come from generations of heroes and daughters of fate who fought and died to create every facet of who you are. You are capable of power you'll never understand. Power you'll never control on your own. You are an agent of chaos. And it's time you met the first of your line.

Hecate moved through the library, the wide double doors opening for her as if by invisible servants. Reve used the table in the middle of the room to pull herself to her feet and followed her friend.

Unlike every other visit to the library, there was no sense of wandering or exploration. Hecate knew exactly where to go and Reve followed. They walked out into the endless stacks, traveling for what felt like hours to the deeper parts of the library.

The polished wooden shelves and moldings turned to carved stone. The air became distinctly colder, the smell of the books turned older, more musty. Reve could taste the dust in the air, an earthy quality in the back of her mouth.

Reve had the distinct feeling that this was the heart of the library, the roots of what had stretched on to become an infinite archive of moments. Reve knew the memories stored here would be ancient.

Hecate stopped in front of a great wooden door bound together with wrought iron.

You will find some of the answers you seek behind this door.

Reve hesitated. There was something unsettling about the sudden change in her first companion. "Are you really here, or are you just another part of the dream?"

Reve thought she could see a hint of smile on Hecate's muzzle. *You and I were brought together for a reason, Reve. There is much we don't know about each other.*

"Will you follow me inside?"

I will follow you to the end.

Reve drew a deep breath, but the confidence in Hecate's amarin brought a slight smile to her lips. "Thank you, my friend."

Reve pushed open the heavy door and was absorbed in a flash of pure, white light. As the light dimmed, she stood in the center of a wide, grassy plane. The moons floated high in the sky, casting the world in deep blue moonlight. Reve turned slowly. Pine trees stood tall, casting their sweet scent into the air. Ivy and thick, spindly brush tangled around the trunk and roots of the ancient evergreens.

She held up her arms. She was no longer in the salt-stained rags she'd worn when battling the serpents, but in a soft, billowing white shirt that reached down to the middle of her thighs. She could smell the lingering perfume of herbs and pine along the collar. It was Nix's shirt. Her bare feet curled over the wet grass. Something had changed outside the dream.

Reve hugged her arms close to her chest. There was something deeply familiar about the space. Something that almost smelled like her first home. Still, she knew she'd never been there before. There was a foreignness, even in the tapestry of amarin among the trees and plants. For a moment she even wondered if she'd somehow stepped into another world.

"How long ago is this?"

Thousands of years.

"I can feel it in the air. With my Sight."

I can, too.

Reve arched a single brow. "You can sense amarin?"

Hecate grunted low in her chest, a wolf's imitation of a laugh. *No. But I can smell more than you can. Hear more. This age is very different.*

"The way you were talking in the library, I thought you'd know where we'd end up."

I have a very confident presence.

Reve laughed hard. "So you don't know where we are?"

It is always your dream, not mine.

They wandered through the field, searching for a path. In the distance, Reve could make out a massive stone building but she knew it wasn't their destination. As they moved, the world continued to feel more and more off. Imbalanced. She felt her attention drawn in many directions. The air felt heavier, almost oppressive. It wasn't until they reached a small bridge that led to the grounds of the building in the distance that she realized she was sensing the amarin of other Blue Sights and seers. There were dozens of them nearby, living without fear or shame. They were simply existing.

"Was there ever a time when Blue Sights weren't hunted?"

There were times when Blue Sights were the ruling class. Other times when the fear they incited made their enemies flee.

Reve's brows rose in surprise. "Were we just and fair rulers?"

Is there any group that isn't eventually corrupted by power?

Reve hugged her arms closer to her chest. Her mind spun, but she was quickly acclimating to the new world. She couldn't imagine a time where her eyes would incite not just fear, but respect. She had always been seen like a rabid animal that needed to be put down.

"Are you alright, Ona?"

The voice came from the trees in the distance, the sound was low and rough, heavy with sleep.

"Someone is coming."

Reve hiked away from the bridge to a manicured, cobbled courtyard. Crimson flowers bloomed, casting their fragrant sweetness into the air. There was something meditative about the yard, something that calmed the fire in Reve's heart.

Reve blended with the shadows, keeping herself carefully guarded.

A Blue Sight stood in the middle of the yard, her hands folded gently behind her back. The moonlight glanced off silver in her long, ebony hair. Everything about her amarin was open, drifting in gentle waves off the air. Reve had never met a Blue Sight in her dreams with such steady control over her power. Reve realized it was because she had never known real terror because of her abilities.

The Blue Sight's Amazon stood in the shadows of a cascading willow tree. Her cropped hair looked gray in the darkness. A baggy, deep green sweater and tan breeches failed to hide the strong lines of her muscles.

"Who's coming, ti Soroi?"

"I don't know."

Reve took a step closer, coming out of the darkness, and the Blue Sight turned. Hecate pressed against Reve's leg, her fur warm against Reve's bare knee.

"I think you're waiting for me."

The Blue Sight smiled softly. "I suppose I am."

"Elana?"

Elana placed touched her Amazon's cheek. "It's alright, Diana. She's dreaming." Elana beckoned Reve forward. "You're safe here."

Reve walked toward them, the stones were smooth under her feet. She could feel the imprints from the boots of generations of Blue Sights. Her eyes flicked across the lawn. "Is this where we come from?"

Elana grinned and sat on a wooden bench. "No. But this is a haven for us. A place of study and peace. You're a shadow as well?"

"Yes."

"Trained at the Keep?"

"There is no Keep anymore. Not when I'm from."

Elana's lips formed a tight line. "I understand."

"You're a shadow as well? Are all Blue Sights?"

"Not all. And not all shadows have the Sight. At least not in my day. But yes, I am a trained shadow. It's why I was able to bond with Diana. What's your name, Child?"

"Reve."

Elana offered her hands, palms up. "I welcome you to this Keep, Reve."

Reve stared at her hands, uncertain of what to do. Diana chuckled and rested her hand on Elana's shoulder. "She seems to be a good deal out of time as well. I'm Diana n'Athena and this is my bondmate, Elana n'Shae."

Reve's eyes flitted to the lifestones embedded in their wrists. "Not from the same family?"

Diana and Elana exchanged glances. "We are family."

"N'Athena. N'Shae. From different ships?"

Elana shook her head. "I'm afraid I don't understand."

"Our names denote our house. I'm of house Athena. Elana chose house Shae. We don't take surnames as the people of Aggar."

Hecate prodded Reve's knee with her nose. *Much has changed since their time. Traditions have shifted with age.*

"Your pet?" Diana indicated Hecate.

"My friend."

Her guide.

Reve glanced at Hecate in surprise. The wolf's golden eyes were locked with Elana.

Elana nodded. "I see."

Reve and Diana looked between Blue Sight and beast in confusion.

Diana sat behind Elana, wrapping an arm around her waist. "The dreams?"

Elana nodded. Elana met Reve's eyes, linking their emotions. It was a sign of good faith, proof of honesty. "There was a time I used to dream of Diana. The dreams led me to her. To my destiny." Elana took Diana's hand and gazed into the eyes of her beloved. "To my home." She turned to Reve again. "Much has changed because of our bonding. Much I didn't foresee. But I've started dreaming again. My destiny isn't finished. The story of Aggar is just beginning and I feel it will be my responsibility to help the women chosen to save Aggar. I fear the time of peace I live in now won't last."

Reve sat beside Elana, tugging the hem of Nix's shirt further down her legs. "You've been dreaming of me?"

"Of your wolf."

Hecate sat at Reve's feet. *Aggar does not only choose humans.*

"You are not the first to have an animal companion to protect and comfort you."

Reve stared down at Hecate with new eyes. She had always wondered why a wolf of the north would find her way to Karatan. She'd never considered her friend had been running as long and hard as she had.

Diana shook her head slowly. "You never cease to amaze me, ti Soroi. Though I'd hoped our dealings with destiny had ended. I could do with retiring from fate."

Elana kissed her Amazon's cheek. "There is no retiring from fate."

"Not with you as bondmate."

Elana smiled.

"What else have you seen in your dreams?"

Elana shook her head. "I can't control the dreaming. It's not my power."

Reve grunted. "Just once I wish the dreams would send me to someone with answers."

Elana and Diana laughed together, their voices blending in a harmonious chorus. Diana glanced at the stars. "Fate doesn't give answers, Reve. Only choices to make. It's up to us to walk the right path."

"Fate takes a lot of risks, trusting us like this."

"There are always people ready to take up the call of destiny. If one of us fails, another is chosen. We aren't all that different in the end. Terran, people of Aggar, even changling and wolf."

Reve cocked her head in confusion. "You can't be serious. I know the stories of the time before the Choir. You were constantly at war. The terrans invaded and pillaged. The changlings were wild, raiding and massacring across the land while the people of Aggar gave in to pride and cruelty. It's how the Choir was able to infiltrate the world. The people sacrificed their free will for peace."

Elana reached out and took Reve's hand. Her blue eyes seemed to glow in the moonlight. "I've seen wars, Reve. Cruelty. Pain. I fear it's nothing compared to what will come, but I've seen Terran and changling. Amazon and the capability for cruelty among my own people. We fight because our cores are the same. By all accounts, Diana and I shouldn't be together. But look at us. Really See."

Reve glanced between them. She had never felt two people so in love, so dedicated to each other. "You were the first, weren't you? The first to bond outside of your race. The first Amazon and Blue Sight pairing."

Diana nodded. "First of many."

"And we were the first to create children together. The first to share homeworlds."

Reve fell quiet, letting herself process everything the dream was trying to show her. She shook her head. She thought of the battle with the serpents and the enormous power that had used her as a conduit. She thought of Nix. What had happened to her? "I don't understand. Things are so different when I'm from. Everything has changed. There's nothing you can tell me that still holds true for my people."

Elana smiled knowingly. She carefully ran her finger over Reve's wrists. A lifestone had appeared. "Not everything has changed. Who are you bonded to, Shadow?"

Reve stared down in shock at the stone glowing at her wrist. The moment Elana had touched it, bringing it to her attention, she'd felt the weight of it, the tender heat around the fiery stone where it fused with her flesh. She felt its pull on her heart and an image of the lifestones in the masthead of the *Niachero* flashed through her mind.

"What did you do?"

Reve looked up but Elana and Diana had vanished. Reve leapt to her feet, spinning around in fear. A crackle and hiss echoed in the distance and she turned to the Keep. The building was on fire, the flames leaping high to the sky as the stones crumbled to ash and dust.

"Hecate?" Reve cried as she stumbled back.

She tripped and fell, hitting the ground hard. She groaned in pain as she landed on stone, not grass. She held her throbbing head in her hands until the pain receded. When she looked up again, she was no longer in the courtyard, but in the caves of the Choir.

She rose carefully, reaching out with her Sight, but there was no sign of the Songs. She could feel a heavy exhaustion in the air like a physical weight. The Choir was weak. They'd used too much power trying to control the serpents after sending a storm. There would be no Songs for a while.

Hecate raced around a nearby corner. *Come with me. I found something.*

Reve ran with Hecate through a winding trail to a small cavern illuminated with an eerie light that didn't seem to have a source. Reve froze in the center of the room. The walls were decorated with dozens of glyphs and symbols.

Reve moved to the first and ran her fingers over the simple etching of a mountain. Electric power bit at her fingers and gripped at her Sight. She groaned at its power, blinking back tears of pain before the sensation faded, replaced with an understanding of the images.

She ran her fingers along the walls, the images transferring their story as if she were meeting eyes with another Blue Sight.

She Saw the halls of the Triad's settlement in the mountains, long after the Triad had passed. She felt a divide between the powerful students and a splintering among the seers. A faction split away from the school, closing themselves into the roots of the mountain and collapsing all entrances and exits from their catacombs. Reve watched as they retreated into their dreams, their powers growing and mutating as their bodies withered away.

She saw the birth of the first Song and the Choir's experiments on the minds of their fellow seers outside the tomb they had built for themselves. As they starved to death, their spirits and powers melded and coalesced in the dream world.

Reve felt tears stream down her cheeks as the origins of her enemies were laid bare. She could hear the ancient Songs as they swept across a war-torn Aggar. The land had fallen into chaos, broken by civil and race wars. The Songs seemed to be a gift, promising peace, unity, and protection. The cities and villages that embraced the Choir were protected as if by the hands of the Gods.

The Choir ended the wars. They slowly changed hearts and minds through the power of their Songs. Tyrants stepped down from their thrones. The races forgot their quarrels. But with the peace came more adjustments to the minds of Aggar. Within a generation the Choir had eradicated their rivals among the Triads and had turned the hearts of the world against the Blue Sights. Within two generations, they'd destroyed every Triad believer and massacred all but the most hidden Blue Sights.

There were moments in time when groups of people tried to revolt against the Choir, but every time they either failed or were destroyed by the people. Even some who knew the truth about the Choir had dedicated themselves to stopping revolutionaries, preferring the forced peace of the Choir's control to the wars and destruction that had been prevalent before. Atrocities that the Choir whispered would be inevitable without their Songs to control the inherent differences between the races.

Finally, her hands came upon the last image, the paint faded and the marks in the stone shallow, older than then others. A series of stars and waves surrounded by the coils of the serpents. Reve's dream of the lights in the depths of the sea returned and she suddenly understood the lights were the secret the Choir was most desperate to protect.

Reve pulled away from the wall and collapsed on the floor. She trembled, the memories and emotions of the people who had come before filling her almost to insanity. The glyphs had connected her to the Choir, training her Sight on them as creatures and not a source of power. The Choir were still here, their power and astral consciences wandering the dream caves reminiscent of their tombs in the mountains.

She could feel how they possessively hoarded their secrets, afraid of losing their power. Reve grit her teeth, filtering through everything she'd learned. If they were afraid, then there was a way to defeat them. At least in the first years of their power, they had relied on the belief and acceptance of the people. Reve would find what they were hiding. She'd expose it. Their secrets would be their undoing.

In a moment, the inborn fear of the Choir that had gripped Reve her entire life vanished. The Choir was no longer an unseen force, crafting lethal Songs to destroy her. They were physical beings. They were the astral ghosts of beings that had once been human. And they could be killed.

Reve locked eyes with Hecate. "Thank you for bringing me here."

Did you find what you were looking for?

Reve nodded. "Yes."

"Reve?"

Reve stared up at the ceiling. "Nix."

She's calling for you. Scared. You should go back to her.

Reve glanced down at her arm. The lifestone was still pressed into her arm. She nodded and closed er eyes. The dreams were easy to control now.

For a moment she felt herself slip away, becoming nothing but the thought of her ship, her Amazon; her family. Reve opened her eyes and hot tears rolled down her cheeks. Her arm ached and she knew her lifestone had followed her into the waking world.

She instantly recognized the energy of Nix's room She felt like a different woman. Everything had changed. Everything but the wood grain patterns in the slats of Nix's ceiling, the softness of her quilt, and the firm grip of Nix's hand.

Nix knelt beside the bed, holding Reve's hand tightly between her own. Reve smiled gently. Nix had fallen asleep, exhaustion from battle and her fear for Reve's safety overcoming her. Reve slowly ran her fingers through Nix's hair as if for the first time. Her amazon.

Nix stirred in her sleep and held Reve's hand tighter.

"Nix."

Nix looked up, her eyes still clouded from a deep, dreamless sleep. "Reve?" Nix leapt up onto the bed and pulled Reve into her arms. "Reve."

Reve sank into Nix's arms, finally allowing herself to trust the connection she felt, to lose herself in her lover's arms.

Nix kissed her brow and pulled back to look into her eyes. "I was so afraid I was going to lose you."

Reve could feel Nix's pain and fear. She felt the old emotions and trauma her sleeping had awakened in Nix. Old pain at Briza's abandonment. The horrors of watching her friends and family die of thirst and disease.

Reve shook her head and held Nix's face in her hands. "You'll never lose me."

Nix kissed her, her fingers curling in Reve's hair, her body trembling, pressed tight against Reve. "I love you."

Reve kissed her back, infusing all her care and intention into the embrace. "I love you."

Nix ran her fingers over Reve's arms and paused. "What —?" She turned Reve's arm over and gasped. "A lifestone? What happened?"

Reve searched for the words to explain what had happened, but she couldn't find the turn of phrase that would fully encapsulate her dream. "I know... everything now. Everything has changed."

Nix ran her thumb over the stone, carefully avoiding Reve's eyes, but Reve could feel her sudden emotional withdrawal. "Who are you bound to?"

Reve chuckled and pulled Nix forward for a tender kiss. "Don't be jealous."

Nix shot her a playful glare. "What am I supposed to think when you wake bonded in such an ancient way?"

"Do you remember what you told me about why Amazons mount lifestones into the eyes of their mastheads?"

"I told you it's symbolic of the bond of the family."

"And now I'm part of that bond. Forever linked with the crew of the *Niachero*."

Nix shook her head. "Why would you agree to that? You never wanted to be tied to the ship."

"I didn't understand what I wanted." Reve met Nix's eyes, hoping she could feel her desire. "And I don't just want to be bound to the Niachero."

Nix tensed. "Reve..."

Reve squeezed Nix's hands. "You don't have to. You told me you didn't want to be bonded. I know you don't want to hurt Sirena. I'll still be your shadow. The Blue Sight of the Niachero. But if you ever —"

Nix shook her head and silenced her with a kiss. "I never imagined bonding with a lover because I never found someone I wanted to give so much of myself to. But you had more of me the first time we shared a dream than anyone ever has. Sirena knows. I couldn't hide it. I'll bind myself to you, Reve. I never want to be far from your side."

Reve's lips quivered, a surprising surge of emotion washing over her. "You want me?"

Nix folded her in her arms and kissed her ear. "I want you forever and for always. Stay with me?"

They kissed as if for the first time, their hearts and minds entwining in a molten embrace that forged their hearts into one.

Nix pulled away. Reve's hands clutched at her shirt, trying to keep her close. Nix laughed and kissed her briefly. "A moment, Love."

She moved to her desk and drew a stone from a jewelry box. She crawled back onto the bed and held open her hand. A perfect, almond-shaped lifestone rested in her palm. "The eye of the sea serpent."

Reve touched the stone gently. "You did this?"

Nix grinned with pride and passion. "Deep under the sea. It broke my sword."

Reve wrapped her arms around Nix's waist. "My Amazon."

Nix rolled up the sleeve of her left arm. "If I'm to carry a stone, I'd like it to be this one."

"A battle trophy?"

"A symbol of a time I fought to keep you safe."

Nix sat up slowly, her eyes sparkling mischief. "A battle that I won."

"You certainly did, my darling."

Reve took the stone gently in her hand, running her fingers over the smooth surface. Reve shivered. The moment she touched the stone, she could feel the icy depths of the sea, feel the metallic power of the creature that had once used the lifestone eye.

She met Nix's eyes again. "Are you sure? You know what a true bonding entails? We would be joined in body as well as in our hearts. We'd live together. We'd die together. Do you want this?"

Nix held out her left arm. "With all my heart."

Reve pressed the stone against Nix's forearm. The Amazon stared at it in wonder as it sank into her arm. She seemed to be in a kind of trance as her skin around her stone turned red and burned hot. Reve felt her heart jolt at the new, unbreakable bond between them.

As the stone became a part of her, Nix looked up, tears in her eyes. "Reve."

Their kiss consumed them. Nix hesitated, her hands grabbing at Reve's shirt with tight fists. "Are you alright? Not hurt?"

Reve sprang forward, knocking Nix back on the bed, straddling her hips and leaning over her. "Look into my eyes, beloved. Tell me what I'm feeling."

Nix cupped her face, her fingers mapping the lines of Reve's cheeks and brow. Nix's eyes grew dark with desire. Her hands tangled in Reve's short hair and her breath escaped past her lips in sharp gasps.

Reve bent over her, running her lips over the long lines of Nix's neck and jaw. "Did you feel me? Did you see it in my eyes? My Amazon. My bondmate."

Nix undid the ties of Reve's shirt, slipping it over her shoulders and pressing her mouth to Reve's navel. "How could I not?"

Reve hummed low in her throat, her muscles leaping and burning at the intimate touch. "Then what are you going to do about it?"

Nix's kiss became a bite and Reve yelped in surprise. Nix laughed and laid her back, licking a long line up Reve's waist and ribs as her hands worked the clasps of her breeches. She looked up at Reve, meeting her eyes with hungry desire. "You're a Blue Sight. Read my mind."

Reve draped back against Nix's chest, the sheets tangled around her legs. The air was cool against her damp skin. The rise and fall of Nix's chest, the pounding of her heart, beneath Reve's head was soothing. She wrapped an arm around Nix's waist and her lover trembled beneath her touch.

Reve leaned over her, kissing her softly. "So exhausted and you still respond to my touch?"

Nix lifted Reve's hand, nipping and kissing at her fingers. "I could be unconscious I'd still react to your touch."

Reve leaned forward and rested in the crook of Nix's neck, breathing in the scent of her, basking in the softness of her skin. Nix ran her hands over her back, soothing and comforting her as they rested.

"Tell me about your dream. After that show of power, I can only imagine what fate had to show you."

Reve kissed her shoulder. "It's hard to put into words."

Nix chuckled. "Since when have we communicated just with words?"

Reve smiled against her skin and arched up on her elbows, meeting Nix's eyes. She explained everything she'd seen in as much detail as she could. She relied on her Sight to get her full intention across.

"Then I saw the lights under the sea. The same lights we saw in our dream together. I used to think it was symbolism, some image conjured up in my mind, but now... I think it's real. There's something the Choir is hiding. Something important. We need to find it while they're still weak from attacking us and use it against them."

Nix shook her head. "Reve, Love, we have to head to land. The ship was damaged before you boarded. The storm and the serpents have only made our temporary fixes break down even more. If they attack again —"

"They can't attack. They're paralyzed. They're exhausted. If we wait to fix the Niachero, they'll regain their strength and we'll go through this all over again. The lights are far away. If we delay, we'll never make it in time."

"We don't have the supplies. The food."

Reve took her shoulders, the sliver of her nails biting into Nix's skin. "We can do it. We have to. This is our best shot at taking them down. Destroying the Choir. We can set everyone free." She hesitated, afraid to let the words slip past her lips. "If they're dead, we can be together without being afraid."

Nix brushed her fingers through Reve's hair, tucking the golden locks behind Reve's ear. "Do you know where the lights are?"

Reve nodded. "I know the way."

Nix paused. "I remember serpents in the dream."

Nix smiled. "Not the kind that attacked us. The lights are guarded by the serpents who remember who they are. The guardians of wisdom. The Choir can't control them."

Nix drew a deep breath and nodded. "I trust you."

Reve crawled out of bed and pulled a map off the wall. "Then come. I'll help you plot out a course."

Chapter Four

Nix glanced over her shoulder. The *Zephyr* skimmed over a short wave, the smaller ship keeping time with the *Niachero* as it cut through the choppy open water. She grunted as she swept Enyo's wing aside. "You're getting too big to sit on my shoulder, Enyo."

The eitteh only grunted in annoyance and blinked as she scanned the distant horizon.

"I didn't think she'd follow us this far," Kana announced as she leaned over the rail. "I thought she'd abandon us. Gale was never one to let go of a grudge."

Nix glanced at the sails and made a minor adjustment to the helm. "She's as obsessive as ever, she's just aiming her focus somewhere else."

"Are you sure she's not trying to keep an eye on you?"

Nix snorted. "She's upset the Choir nearly sank her ship. She's going to see this through. And if we run into trouble, It'll be nice to have her on our side."

Kana held her chin in her hand. "I don't think it's just about anger. When you fought together the serpent together... It was the stuff of legends, Nix."

"We didn't save everyone." Nix glanced across the deck to where Reve stood at the prow, gazing out at the open sea. Hecate stood at her side, even more vigilant than usual. Her blue eyes scanned the horizon, trying to sense their final destination. Even across the ship Nix could feel her steady energy, her intense focus as she cast her Sight as far out into the sea as possible.

"Still, something changed between you and Gale."

Nix rubbed at the lifestone set in her arm, hidden beneath the sleeve of her voluminous black shirt. "Everything has changed."

Kana followed Nix's eyes and grinned. "I suppose it has." Kana wrapped her arm around Nix's shoulders. "I'm glad you didn't let your pride get in your way. I knew you liked her from the moment you met her."

"I put her in the brig."

"You let her on board."

Nix grinned to herself. "I was outvoted."

Kana laughed. "You were curious! You've never let a vote sway you before. If you'd really thought she was dangerous to the family, you would have left her in Karatan."

Nix looked Reve over lovingly. She could barely remember a time when she hadn't known the Blue Sight. They had merged with each other's memories and dreams so many times she felt like Reve had somehow been beside her as a child, walked with her when the village had been destroyed, had been there for the births of her children. She couldn't comprehend that they had only known each other less than a tenmoon. "I really didn't expect to love her."

"That's why you have me. I know you better than you know yourself."

Nix leaned forward, resting her arms on the spokes of the helm. "Most seem to lately."

Reve turned away from the prow and jogged back to the helm, Hecate at her heels. "We need to turn south."

Nix straightened in surprise. "Are we getting closer?"

Reve shook her head. "I can barely sense the general direction. Everything comes in snippets and visions."

Nix took her hand. "Be careful."

Reve smirked. "I won't break."

"Nix?"

Nix turned to Kana. Her friend's eyes were wide, her cheeks dark with shock. "What's wrong?"

Kana reached out and took Reve's arm, running her fingers over the lifestone. "When did this happen?"

Nix sighed softly and rolled back her sleeve, displaying her stone. "I was going to tell everyone together."

Kana covered her mouth with her hands, her eyes flitting between the two stones. "You're bonded?"

Nix rolled her sleeve back down to her wrist. "Please don't tell anyone yet?"

Kana nodded slowly. Her hands fell from her face, her smile dazzling. "You have to tell the family. Nobody ever thought... And so fast!"

"Kana."

"I have to tell Volt."

"Kana! I asked you to wait."

"I can't keep secrets from my husband."

"Yes you can."

"Fine, fine. I won't say anything."

Kana hugged Nix and Reve and scampered below deck. Nix watched her go and sucked at her teeth. "She's going to tell everyone."

Reve wrapped her arm around Nix's waist. "We should tell them first."

"Are you sure you want them to know yet?"

Reve tugged on her shirt. "Are you embarrassed? Or afraid they won't accept us?"

Nix glanced down at her in surprise. "Of course not. We just haven't had a lot of time to figure this out ourselves."

"Having second thoughts?"

"Of course not."

"Ah. You'll miss having a secret." Reve kissed her gently, her eyes teasing.

"Reve."

Reve's gaze grew serious. "We should at least tell Agwe and Sirena. They deserve to know."

Nix let out a sharp breath and glanced at the sky. A dozen different scenarios unfolded in her mind. Sirena had been understanding enough when Nix had explained her relationship with Reve, but bonding was completely different. "You're right. I just wish I knew how they were going to take it."

"They'll understand. They might already know. You can't hide much from Agwe or Briza."

"Luckily they've both been distracted caring for our injured. We could wait until they figure it out on their own."

Reve only patted Nix's arm and pulled away, running down to the deck and returning with Tlaloc.

"You needed me?" Tlaloc questioned.

Nix glanced at Reve, pleading to further delay the inevitable, but Reve's eyes were hard and unforgiving. "I need to talk to Agwe and Sirena. Can you take the helm for a while?"

"Of course. Where are we heading?"

"Just keep a steady course."

Tlaloc glanced at the sky, zir lips forming a tight line. "We're pretty far from land and we need to make critical repairs." Zir voice was even and logical, verging on critical. Nix hesitated. Things had to be more dire than Nix realized to shake Tlaloc.

"I know. Just a little longer." Tlaloc nodded and took the helm. "Thank you."

"Stay with Enyo? This should stay private." Reve knelt before Hecate, scratching the wolf between the ears. Enyo leapt off Nix's shoulder and landed beside Hecate. "Thank you both."

Reve took Nix's hand and led her down to Agwe's healing room. "Everything will be fine," she whispered.

"I hope you're right."

Nix quietly opened the door to Agwe's room. The heady scent of lavender permeated the air, violet smoke trailing to the ceiling from a steel incense burner. Most of the crew had been in and out of Agwe's room since the attack. Even Doris had cracked zir head open falling out of zir hammock during the attack.

Agwe sat beside his cot, watching over Lyr. Lyr had faded in and out off consciousness since the battle, where he'd led the fight against the serpent attacking the *Niachero*. He had nearly decapitated the creature himself, but the fight had taken a toll.

"How's he doing?" Nix whispered as she sat beside her son.

Agwe looked Lyr over sadly, his eyes unreadable. He carefully finished changing the bandages of a burn that snaked up Lyr's arm. "He'll be fine. He's lucky he got as far back from the bomb as he did. Any closer and he would have lost his arm."

Nix rested her hand on Lyr's leg. Memories of holding Lyr as an infant, his downy-soft changling ears twitching as he reached up to her flashed through her mind. He was fiercely independent. He'd never fallen back on Nix or Briza's motherly concern. He had never called Nix mother. Still, in many ways, the fierce warrior changling had been her son since she'd guided him from his mother's womb.

"I should have been there to fight with him. He's usually better with his timing."

"He was burned saving me."

Nix turned to Agwe in surprise. Her son didn't take his eyes off Lyr. "Agwe?"

"The serpent lunged at me. I froze. He ran at it, nearly dove into its mouth shoving the bomb down its throat. His arm was caught in the beast's teeth. He could have died."

Nix's hand on Lyr tightened. She felt a fresh swell of gratitude fill her heart. "He's always been selfless with his family."

Agwe shook his head slowly. "I had a vision when he screamed. I never saw—" Agwe's voice broke. "I never understood him. I wasn't paying attention. I thought we were just friends. He almost died, m'Sormee."

Nix pulled her son into a tight hug. "He'll live. He's in the best of hands."

Agwe tensed in her embrace. "You came to tell me something."

Nix pulled away and laughed to herself. "Of course you'd feel it."

Agwe glanced back at Reve. "Is everything alright?"

Reve nodded slowly. "Everything is wonderful."

"We should get Sirena. I want to talk to you at the same time. Do you want to talk in my room?"

Agwe shook his head. "I can't leave Lyr for long. I have him in an induced sleep until the worst of his injuries heal. I need to be here if he starts to wake."

"We can talk here. We'll be quiet," Reve promised.

Agwe nodded slowly, suspicion in his eyes. He washed his hands thoroughly and dried them on the towel tucked into his belt. "I think Sirena's in the kitchen. I'll be right back."

He slipped out of the room. Nix's breath caught in her throat and Reve squeezed her hand. "Breathe, Love."

"He wants to get Sirena so he can talk to her first."

"Then it will be easier for us to talk with her. I've never seen you so tense before."

Nix shifted uncomfortably. "They're the most important thing to me, Reve. I should have talked to them before the bonding."

Reve squeezed her hand. "They'll want you to be happy. They're both grown. You have the right to make your own decisions."

Nix cast her a sly glance. "You sound like a mother."

"I don't think Sirena and Agwe would take to that notion."

Nix laughed loud and instantly covered her mouth to keep from disturbing Lyr. "No they wouldn't."

They stood in warm silence as Agwe fetched his sister. Nix's mind was a jumble as she tried to plan what she was going to say. Was it really a good idea to speak to them together? Should she speak to Sirena privately first? They didn't even truly understand Blue Sights and traditional bonding. The only lifestones they'd seen were embedded in serpents or worn as promise rings.

Nix glanced at Reve, drawing comfort from her effortlessly calm companion. "I never imagined having to do this."

"Telling your children you're bonded?"

"And to a woman my daughter was pursuing."

Reve glanced at her, their eyes meeting for a moment. A warm, comforting touch of Reve's Sight blossomed beneath Nix's skin, steadying her heart and calming her breath.

"What's done is done, Nix. We're bonded. If we were to stray far enough from each other for too long, one or both of us would die. They all have to know eventually. They all have to accept this. Sirena loves you far more than she ever could have cared for me. She'll understand." Reve laughed softly. "If Gale can accept us, Sirena should be no challenge."

Nix smiled as well. "Sirena and Gale have more in common than you think."

Reve tensed and looked to Nix, her eyes narrowing. "Nix, Gale's not…"

Nix caught Reve's implication immediately and she had to cover her mouth to stifle another burst of laughter. "Sirena's other parent? No. Never."

Reve relaxed. "Good."

Nix bent and kissed her soft cheek. "You have nothing to fear from Gale. Honestly, I think she's more afraid of you than she ever was of me. Between your attack with the Sight in the brig and the way you decimated two sea serpents, Gale will be on her best behavior around us from now on. Or at least until she gets to know you better."

Reve grinned wider, showing her teeth. "I like that."

Agwe and Sirena slipped into the room. Sirena's black eye and collection of stitches were steadily healing. Nix silently thanked whatever deities might be listening that both of her children had survived the battle with minor injuries. Sirena always put herself on the frontlines. She could easily have been killed.

"You wanted to see us?"

Nix leaned back against Agwe's work table, unsure of where to start.

Nix pulled two chairs forward for her children. Sirena crossed her arms over her chest and arched a single brow. "Did someone die?"

Nix held the bridge of her nose, warding off a headache. There was a reason she'd avoided serious emotional connections her entire life. "Sirena, I really don't need your sarcasm right now. This is serious."

"You bonded with Reve."

Nix's eyes widened in shock. "How did you know?"

"Besides the fact that you've been mooning over each other like adolescents?"

"Sirena."

"Agwe told me."

"I felt it the moment I touched you," Agwe remarked.

"When did you start reading amarin?" Nix demanded.

Sirena laughed. The genuine, lilting sound wiping away the worst of Nix's fear. "You were really nervous about this, weren't you?"

"Of course I was. I knew how you felt. I didn't expect to bring anyone into the family for me."

Sirena's arms fell to her sides, every hint of teasing gone. "M'Sormee, you're right. I did like Reve." Sirena glanced at Reve.

"You're a mystery. But I see the way you two connect. The way you speak without even talking. You fit. My momentary infatuation doesn't compare to what you have. I've never seen you happy, not like this. Agwe and I supported you when chasing after Gale gave you a reason to live. You think either of us would have a problem with you finding someone to dedicate yourself to? Reve won't stab me."

Nix swept Sirena up in her arms, hugging her tightly. She felt like she could breathe for the first time since Reve woke. "Thank you, Sirena."

Sirena clapped her shoulder. "I want to see your stones."

Nix smiled and leaned back, rolling her sleeve up to her elbow. The fire of the lifestone in her wrist seemed to glow in the dim light of the healing room. Nix glanced lovingly at Reve, who rolled up her sleeve as well. "Reve's appeared while she was dreaming."

Sirena ran her fingers over Nix's stone. "Is that the serpent's eye?"

"The stone should have been lost to the sea, but it made its way back to me."

"It seems fate brought you together," Agwe agreed.

Sirena pulled Reve into a tight hug and for a moment the quiet intensity in Reve's eyes softened. Nix felt a surge of peace. Of home. Reve finally found a place she belonged.

"Welcome to the family."

"She was already family," Agwe remarked as he hugged Reve as well.

Sirena braced her hands on her hips. "Now I need to get back to dinner. I suspect you'll tell the rest of the family then?"

"Kana knows," Nix commented.

"So the announcement will just be a formality."

"Basically."

Sirena smiled. "I'll make something special for desert."

Reve tensed. "We probably shouldn't feast. We'll want to conserve rations."

Sirena's brow furrowed. "Why? We're going to head back to land soon. We have to repair the ship."

"We still have a long way to go before we can turn around."

Sirena looked between Reve and Nix. "M'Sormee? What's going on?"

"Reve had a dream. A discovery that could take down the Choir, but we're not exactly sure where it is. The mission is too time-sensitive for us to turn back now."

Sirena's eyes narrowed, her lips parting for a moment as she chose her words carefully. "We're already running low on supplies. I coordinated the resupply to coincide with our repairs."

"We'll have to be more conservative until we reach Reve's destination. Once we do, we'll be able to plan out the return trip in more detail."

"M'Sormee —"

Nix raised her hand. "It'll be alright. I promise. This is something we have to do."

Sirena and Agwe exchanged nervous glances. "We trust you. I'll adjust our meal schedule. Let me know as things change."

"Thank you, Sirena."

Lyr rustled in his cot. He moaned in pain, his breath coming in sharper gasps. Agwe rushed to his side and cradled his head. He grabbed a cup off a nearby night table. "Lyr, listen to me. You have to drink this. You have to go back to sleep." Lyr whimpered, beads of sweat glistening in his golden curls. He tried to sit up in a feverish haze and Agwe struggled to keep him down. "Lyr. Please. You need to heal and I don't have the supplies to numb the pain."

Agwe helped Lyr drain the cup and held him until he fell back to sleep. Agwe stared down at Lyr's disheveled bandages.

"Do you need any help?" Nix offered.

Agwe shook his head. "I need to make sure he didn't tear any of his stitches and rewrap his bandages. He needs silence."

Nix stepped toward the door. "We'll leave you alone, then. Let me know if you need anything."

Agwe nodded, but his focus was already trained on Lyr's injuries. Nix led Reve and Sirena out of the room.

"About time he noticed Lyr," Sirena grunted as she jogged back to the galley.

"I told you it would go well," Reve commented.

Nix took her lover's hand and kissed her fingers as the strolled toward the helm to relieve Tlaloc. "Thank you for being there with me."

"Always."

Nix leaned forward over the helm, her eyelids drooping closed. Her muscles ached and her stomach rumbled. They'd been sailing for over a ten-day. Nix slept and ate as little as she could. They were running dangerously low on supplies. If they didn't reach the secret soon, they wouldn't be able to make the return trip.

"Sailing through the night will only make you sick. Come to bed."

Reve climbed the steps, sleep clouding her eyes. She wore Nix's shirt and breeches, the clothes baggy on her frame. With the Choir in hibernation regaining strength, Reve had been sleeping peacefully for the first time in her life.

"As we get closer to the secret, you seem better able to pinpoint our destination. And when I sail through the night, the crew doesn't seem as upset by how far we are from land."

Reve combed through her hair with her fingers. The moonlight caught on her lifestone. "If you pass out at the helm, it will cause more panic. We're getting closer. I can feel it. But you need your strength for whatever we disturb when we find the truth."

Nix sighed. Reve was right. She was in no shape to bolster her crew, let alone fight a serpent or the Choir. "Fine. We can drop anchor and rest. But I'm up at dawn."

Reve reached out to her and Nix moved into her arms. As they worked together to drop anchor, the *Zephyr* appeared in the distance. "Gale realized you didn't stop for the night."

Nix sighed, a surge of guilt welling in her stomach. "I thought she would have turned back by now."

"She seems very dedicated to you."

Nix nodded. "She does. But they have to be running low on food as well, and their ship took more damage. She should have gone back by now."

"Perhaps there's a reason she needs to be with us."

"I still wish she wasn't wrapped up in this."

Reve pulled Nix into her arms and kissed her, guiding her back to their room. "Come to bed. Sleep. You can worry about everyone else in the morning.

Nix sank into her embrace and allowed Reve to lead her back to bed.

Reve quickly falling back into a deep sleep, but Nix couldn't force her mind to calm. Laying in Reve's arms, Nix could faintly feel the call that constantly pulled at Reve's sight. It was becoming more clear, piercing through the waves, beckoning them on. But she knew the rest of her family, not even Briza and Agwe, could sense anything. Tlaloc was tense. Nix knew zi was spending hours every day trying to calm the rest of the family's fears. Their support was fraying. If they continued on much longer, Nix knew the family would demand to turn back.

Nix shifted uneasily, changing position. Perhaps she could convince Gale to ferry everyone back. Nix and Reve wouldn't be able to sail alone for long, but it would be better than watching her family starve.

Traumatic memories of living on land returned. She had watched too many people die of hunger and thirst. The Choir had taken so much away from her. She couldn't give them the *Niachero* as well.

Nix finally sighed and carefully detangled from Reve's embrace. She crept back out to the main deck and stared at the moons, wondering if her exhausted body would have enough strength to raise anchor on her own.

The rush of a ship parting the waves filled the air as the *Zephyr* caught up with her. Nix stood in the center of her deck and watched as Gale dropped anchor and moved a boarding plank between the two ships. Nix searched for Gale's expression in the darkness. She was nearly overcome with the urge to grab a knife, but when Gale crossed to the *Niachero* alone, her eyes filled not with rage, but with concern, she relaxed.

"We have to talk," Gale called.

Nix glanced over her shoulder at her quarters. Reve was still sleeping. "Fine."

Gale crossed her arms, a cocky grin rising to her lips. "Afraid I'll make your new lady love jealous?"

Nix crossed her arms over her chest. "Not at all. What do you want?"

Gale leaned back against the railing of the ship. "After we fought the serpents, you told me your mission was to defeat the Choir. You never gave me any more details then that, and I didn't push. But we've been sailing too long. My family thinks I'm insane."

"Then go back. Please. I might even be able to convince some of my family to go with you."

Gale hesitated. "Nix, is this some kind of suicide mission?"

"No. I trust Reve. But I don't know what this mission will entail. Lyr is awake again, but he's still injured. Doris and Pan shouldn't be under this kind of stress. Briza's salty as ever, but she's getting sick. My family shouldn't suffer for my quest. Neither should the *Zephyr*."

Gale pursed her lips, her eyes scanning the ground as she thought. "You really trust Reve? She can take down the Choir?"

Nix raised her arms, almost in surrender. "I trust Reve with my life. I'm just not sure I have the right to trust her with the lives of my family."

Gale clenched her jaw. "Then we'll continue following you. I won't leave you alone with the serpents and storms. I can't say how long my family will last, but I swear, if they don't lock me up in a mutiny, to take whoever will go willingly back to land if I leave. I was telling the truth before. I never wanted to see you or anyone on the *Niachero* dead."

Nix clasped Gale's shoulder in a sisterly embrace. "I know. It was the danger."

Gale lifted a single brow. "And the sex."

Nix grunted a laugh. "Yes. And the rage."

"The rage doesn't have to change."

Nix grinned. "I suppose not. But we're still sisters. Amazons. And I trust you to do right by the people I love. Promise me."

They clasped hands, Gale's humor replaced with seriousness. "I swear it."

Nix heard Reve shuffling in their room. It wouldn't be long until she woke. She nodded back to her room. "I have to go. I'm setting sail again at dawn."

"I'll be at your back."

"It's nice to have you as an ally for once."

Gale fingered the knife at her waist. "Don't get used to it. The moment the Choir is incinerated everything will go back to normal."

"Nothing will go back to normal, Gale."

"I'm not scared of your demon-eyed lover, Nix."

"You should be."

"We'll see what happens."

They shared another glance of understanding and Gale flitted back across the boarding plank to her ship.

"Nix?" Reve's confused cry was slurred with sleep.

"Coming, Love," Nix called back and slowly strolled back to bed.

"Nix, this is ridiculous. Everyone is going to die."

Nix held the bridge of her nose, warding off a headache. Briza paced in front of her door, her braid whipping about her plump frame as she trembled with frustration. "Gale has offered to take you all back. I'll give her the bulk of our remaining supplies. You'll be able to get back to land."

"And what will happen to you and Reve? You think I'm going to leave you out here to die? That Sirena and Agwe will be willing to leave you behind?"

"Yes. I expect you all to survive. Reve and I made a pact to take down the Choir. I don't know what secrets the sea will reveal, but we're both ready to die in the confrontation. There's no need for the rest of you to risk going down with us."

"You're not helping your case."

Nix reached out and took her mother's hands. "Briza. Please. You know why I have to do this. You know what I went through at the hands of the Choir and I know you can feel the connection between Reve and me."

"Reve's mind has nearly crumbled twice in a handful of ten-days due to the Choir. She might not be entirely aware of where she's taking us."

Nix's eyes narrowed. "You know there's nothing wrong with Reve's mind. The Choir wouldn't hide anything that could be used against them in plain sight."

Nix closed her eyes, digging her fingers into her temples. Her headache was getting worse.

"I'm not going to stand by and watch you kill yourself. You're our captain. Our Amazon. You have a duty to your family."

"I have a duty to the world."

"Nix—" Nix whimpered and squeezed her head harder. As the tension built, her vision blurred. Briza stopped mid-tirade. "Nix?

"Get Reve."

Nix heard Briza race from the room and soon return with Reve. "Nix? What's wrong?"

Nix cupped her hands to her ears as a high-pitched tone echoed in her mind. She could hear a soft melody drifting behind the sound, almost like a Song. "Do you hear it? Is it the Choir?"

Reve covered Nix's hands with her own, pressing their foreheads together. "I hear it, too. But not like you do. What are you feeling?"

Nix rose to her feet, led entirely by instinct. Her legs moved without her willing it, leading her out of her room and across the main deck. The sun shone down hot and bright on her face. She could hear the concerned voices of her family as she passed.

"Nix?" Reve called. Nix grabbed the railing of the ship and, without hesitating, vaulted over the edge, plunging down into the sea. "Nix!"

Reve's panicked scream was drowned in the depths of the sea as Nix swam. She was intensely focused, her muscles moving with a liquid grace, cutting through the ocean like an arrow through the air.

It wasn't long before her lungs started to burn, but she continued on. She had to go deeper. She had to reach the secret. Just when her head started to swim and her muscles cramped, she felt Reve's presence. Her need for breath disappeared and she moved as if in Reve's dream again, sinking into total darkness.

She could see a faint light pulsing in the void. As she drew closer, she felt a rush of the sea and the feeling of an immense presence. Her arm shot out in another stroke and the cold smoothness of metal brushed her fingertips. Serpents. She was in a serpent's nest.

She hesitated, floating in the darkness. Suddenly, dozens of glowing blue lights lit the darkness. More than a dozen serpents stared down at her, their lifestone eyes glowing like the moon. They rose up around her like the columns of a temple, standing ominous watch over the ocean floor.

Nix tensed, her heart pounding wildly as she looked for an escape, but they didn't attack. They only watched her. Nix remembered Kana's stories of guardian serpents, the ancient beings that guarded Aggar's darkest secrets. Were these the wise ones?

Nix continued on, following the lights. She hovered over a rocky outcropping surrounding a small, metallic tube. A light still flashed deep in the capsule, its song reverberating off the bodies of the serpents. Reve reached for it and the closest serpent sprang to life, twisting down before her and snapping at her arm.

Nix pulled back, holding her arm close to her chest. She locked eyes with the beast and her heart calmed. The beast exuded a wisdom and a warmth, the complete opposite of the wild monster that had attacked her ship.

The serpent studied her, its lifestone eyes searching with its own kind of Sight. Nix closed her eyes, hoping she wouldn't be found wanting. Just when she was sure the creature would swallow her whole, it snapped at the rocks, freeing the capsule and nudging it into Nix's arms.

Nix held the ancient device, the rough metal of its outer shell heavier than she'd expected. The serpent approached again but instead of scaring the Amazon, it bowed, offering the ridge of its dorsal fin. Nix slid into the grove of the serpent's fin like a saddle and the beast sped above its fellows, throwing Nix halfway to the surface.

She rocketed out of the water, the waves exploding as if from canon fire.

"Nix!" Reve's scream shocked Nix out of her shock at her encounter with the serpents. She gasped for breath, every muscle burning. Sirena, Gale, and Volt lowered a rope. Nix tied the rope around her waist and they pulled her back to the main deck.

The *Zephyr* floated beside the *Niachero*, both crews gathered on Nix's deck. Nix faintly noted how strange it was to see them working together.

Nix collapsed on the ground, still cradling the capsule. Reve knelt at her side, her eyes wide in horror. Nix grabbed her hand, looking deep into her lover's eyes. "I felt you. You saved my life."

"What happened? I thought it would be me, I never knew it would call to you."

Nix shook her head and kissed Reve. "I'm fine. It was..." Nix shook her head, remembering the eerie lights of the serpent's eyes. "In comprehensible. But I found this."

Reve took the capsule in her hands, running her long fingers over the rivets and jagged bits of stone that had melded with the metal long ago.

"It's an archive."

Nix shook her head. "I don't understand."

Reve wedged her fingernails under a sliver of a ridge in the center of the capsule. Her eyes flashed once, too similar to the serpents for Nix's comfort, as she ripped the top off the top. A bright light flared and the hiss of static filled the air.

"What is that?" Gale demanded. "A weapon?"

Reve placed the topless capsule on the ground and shook her head. "It's a story."

Chapter Five

Reve sank to her knees and Hecate raced to her side as a bright, blazing light erupted from the capsule, casting a holographic field in a perfect square, as tall as Nix on every side. Its pull on her Sight was intense, casting the holographic figures as complete beings. She could See their emotions, echos of their thoughts. It wasn't as strong as the people around her, but whoever had made the hologram had to have had some hint of the Sight to store such detail.

"It's Terran." Volt held his chin in his hand as he studied the figures.

"It's earlier than the first Terran landing," Reve argued.

The hologram followed a team of five explorers, walking through the forest. Reve studied each of their faces, searching for blue eyes, but the graphics had broken down over time. The colors were faded and hard to distinguish.

"They aren't of Aggar origin. Look at their skin," Kana pointed out. "Amazon?"

"If it's earlier than the Terran landing, they wouldn't be Amazon. The Amazons were more strict about gender identity then," Gale grunted. "They didn't even get a choice back then. Labeled their children before they came of age."

Reve studied each of them as carefully as she could. She couldn't make out much in their electric amarin, but she could feel determination and fear. She saw flashes and snippets of their thoughts. She saw a fleet of ships adrift in space. Ships every member of the team thought of as "family." She saw glimpses of other planets and primitive villages. She saw arguments and ships pulling away from the central cluster.

"There's something ahead. Stephen? Where's Pallas?" A woman with long dark hair raised an electric torch, shining its beam into the forest shadows. She was tall, her energy more curious than afraid. If she didn't know any better, Reve would think she was an Amazon.

"She's with the ship. There was a gas leak on impact. We can't risk contaminating natural resources," Stephen answered, studying a waxy ivy plant, scanning it with a hand-held electric device.

Everyone on the team focused on taking samples and studying plant life."

"It seems the reports were true. This planet doesn't just sustain life, it's thriving."

"The atmosphere is practically untouched. Some primitive animal life."

"From what I can tell, the geomorphology is within the acceptable range. The north is has volcanic activity, but nothing we can't handle."

The Amazon woman's eyes flicked through the trees. Her torch caught on an eitteh, who instantly hissed and flew away.

Stephen laughed. "Scared of the kitty cat, Athena?"

Athena grunted. "We don't know what creatures are out there. I can't believe a planet like this has no sign of sentient life. There may be predators."

"Of course there are predators, but I doubt they can handle a laser shot."

Athena clenched her jaw. "Don't get too trigger-happy."

One of the field team, a scientist who privately identified as unfettered, stood. "There's no reason we couldn't colonize here. We won't even have to terraform. We'll have to adapt some of our farming and game techniques. With time, we'll the human race will shift and alter to the environment, but we'll survive."

Stephen stood. "I concur. That makes six alternate planets."

"Five," a blonde woman announced. "I received word this morning that CX-43 failed. Spores. Took out the entire colony."

Athena ran her fingers through her hair in frustration. "The team should have been more thorough. I told them there was something wrong with the water."

"News also holds that CX-12 has been overrun with separatists. Killed their governors. Shipped all the men off-world."

"Damn," Stephen grunted. "CX-12 was our most stable base. Is it the pagans again?"

"They're calling themselves Amazons."

"Amazons?" Sirena exclaimed.

"Shh." Reve held a finger to her lips, completely entranced in the hologram.

"Terrorists," Stephen growled.

"CX-12 was becoming a slave colony. Their governors deserved to die. Let them keep their world in peace," Athena argued. "The Amazons have never taken the offensive. With the Earth in ruins, we don't have the strength to micromanage a slew of far-flung planets.

Colonies are splitting away from the fleet every day. Let them rule themselves."

Stephen eyed her questioningly. "You sound like a sympathizer."

Athena glared at him and returned to scanning the forest.

The sound of feet tearing through the forest and a voice gasping for breath sounded in the distance.

"Athena!"

"Pallas?"

A slender woman with long, black hair tied up atop her head ran into the clearing. Her silver jumpsuit was stained with oil. Reve felt an electric jolt in her chest and she crept around the hologram to see Pallas's face. Even in the faded colors of the display, Reve knew Pallas had blue eyes. A touch of the Sight. It was suppressed and weak, but it was there.

She held a chunk of raw lifestone in her hand, the stone pulsing with a hungry amarin. Reve had never felt a stone with amarin. It clung to Pallas, feeding off her abilities and Sight, strengthening them and imprinting on her.

It was reacting like an organism, latching to Pallas and strengthening her abilities in return. There was a feeling of adoration in the bond. Aggar was already claiming her favorite child.

"There's something... off about the landing sight. Look at these stones."

Athena looked it over and shrugged. "Pretty."

"No, there's something different about them. They're warm. They're... responsive? That's not the word."

"Any signs of radiation?" the unfettered asked.

"No, the scans show it's safe but I feel it."

"If the scans read them as safe, then we have nothing to worry about. We can break them down and study them later."

Pallas shook her head. "Just because our scans show safety doesn't mean they couldn't be emitting an unknown kind of radiation."

Stephen looked down at her, condescension barely hidden in his eyes. Reve could tell Pallas knew the way Stephen saw her, but she wasn't nearly as stupid as he thought. "You're a mechanic, Pallas. I know visiting a new world can be frightening, but we know what we're doing."

Pallas took a step back, her eyes flickering to Athena and for a brief moment they echoed a fierce familiarity and frustration. A shared image of the future Amazon homeworld was laced in the emotion. Reve didn't know if it was the Sight abilities of the programmer leaking through the encoded imagery, but in that single look Reve could feel impending tragedy. They would eventually be ripped away from each other. She saw flashes arguments, of war. Pallas would die on Aggar. Athena would die far away among the Amazons.

Stephen, oblivious to Pallas and Athena's connection, shut off his device. "I'm calling the Terra rep in the morning. We could get the first dozen colonies here in a month."

The voices and images faded and skipped. Reve's heart pounded. There was more information buried in the capsule, but the elements and age had tampered with it. She wanted more.

The images finally went black, but Reve could feel the imprinted messages through her Sight. She saw more flashes, each embedding a series of understandings in her thoughts. Se saw the first colonies on Aggar. She saw generations pass. The lifestones called and mutated the blue-eyed children of the colonizers. She saw peace, followed by fire raining from the sky: a civil war across planets. She saw explosions, pulses that destroyed technology.

"Is it done?" Tlaloc questioned hesitantly. "Why would the Choir be afraid of that?"

Reve glanced at Nix, their eyes meeting, and Nix instantly knew what Reve did.

"They were the first. Our ancestors. Everyone's ancestors."

"They said the Amazons split from their people," Gale pointed out. Amazons and Aggar have the same genetic roots?"

"It makes sense. They were so compatible in the past," Briza announced.

"Not just the Amazons." Tlaloc's voice was sharp. "They also said Terrans."

"Terrans were not of Aggar," Dane of Gale's crew hissed. "They were invaders. Nothing like us."

Volt clenched his fists and opened his mouth to argue, but Nix's voice cut them off. "This hologram claims we all came from the same place. Amazons, Aggar, Terrans... we're not alien to each other. We're all family."

"That's what scares the Choir." Everyone turned to Reve, her low voice, laced with her Sight was mesmerizing. "The Choir asserts control by fear. They insist that without their help, without submitting to their control, we'll all kill each other. They whisper we're too different, too foreign. That we never should have mixed in the first place. But we're the same. We carry the same root genes. Their logic is inherently flawed."

Another of Gale's crew shook zir head. "Having the same ancestors doesn't mean we'll get along. So much history—"

"History be damned!" Reve growled. "The fighting was because we made up inherent differences between each other, some warped sense of xenophobia, but it was a lie from the beginning! Yes, if the Choir dies there will eventually be war and disputes. There will be anger and resentment. But it won't be because we're incapable of blending peacefully. It'll be because we're human. The Choir knew it. The Choir found this capsule first and they hid it. This is the key to their undoing."

As Reve spoke, she heard a sharp, squealing whistle on the Wind. A storm of pure Song rose on the horizon. The Choir had sensed the capsule's discovery. Even with their strength weakened, they would throw whatever power they had left at burying the truth.

Reve stood fearless. She grinned, more feral than Hecate. It was time.

"Reve?" Nix called in confusion and fear. "Are those Songs?"

"I need to sleep."

"Now?"

Reve grabbed Nix's hand, pulling her into their room. "This is it, don't you see? Whatever strength they regained while we sailed to the capsule is being spent creating this Song. Everything has fallen into place. We have the truth. They're weak. Between the two crews we are representative of every race that ever spread across Aggar. We're meant to take a final stand. I can enter their caves. I can beat them."

"You're not going alone. I won't let you."

"You have to stay here with the family. Keep them safe. If the Song hits the ships, it will be fierce."

Nix shook her head. "If you're right and everything that's happened has brought us here, then there's a reason Gale stayed with us. She promised to help keep both families safe. She'll defend them now. We're bonded. We've both been to the caves. I can keep up with you. We do this together."

Reve let out a deep breath, her shoulders drooping as she relaxed. She hadn't realized how much she wanted Nix by her side until the Amazon had volunteered. "Thank you."

She wrapped her arms around her bondmate, kissing her fiercely. She closed her eyes and filled her mind with memories of the caves. She could smell the cold, stony walls. She could hear the way the Songs echoed of its halls and rough texture of the cavern.

"Is there something I can do to —" Nix glanced around in shock. They already stood in the caves of the Choir.

Reve grinned wickedly. "I've gotten better at shifting into the dream plane."

Reve released her lover as Hecate raced down the hall to stand with her. *You could have invited me along.*

"I wanted you to stay with the family," Reve rebutted. "I wanted you both to stay."

But you're glad we're here.

Reve smiled softly. She had never imagined this moment with friends, but now she was glad she they were by her side.

Reve patted Hecate's head and they sped down the tunnel. Reve reached out with her Sight. She could feel them nearby, focused on their Song. She slipped ahead of Nix and Hecate, leading them on. Her heart fluttered. Her skin warmed. She was back on her path. She was whole. This was the moment she had been waiting for since her parents were killed, since she understood what the Choir was doing to Aggar. And for the first time, she felt like she had the upper hand.

Reve slowed, melding effortlessly with the shadows as she approached the home of the Choir. She held up her hand to her friends, silently bidding them to remain behind for a moment. She crept forward, peeking into the darkness.

Her breath caught in her throat. The beings that had made her life a nightmare from her birth. The whispering tyrants of Aggar. The Choir stood in a circle, the folds of their long, black robes hiding their hands and faces. They seemed more mist than solid, their bodies long turned to dust, leaving behind only their consciouses and astral forms.

A deep, guttural hum echoed from their throats, the sound twisting and melding into the Song plaguing the *Niachero* and *Zephyr* on the physical plane. Reve's head spun and her mouth went dry at the wave of emotion assaulting her Sight. Their determination, their need for control, and aggressive lack of sympathy felt like needles stabbing at her skin.

In an instant whatever confidence she'd felt vanished. She could feel their combined powers pouring into the Song and the portal that unleashed it on the physical plane. It paralyzed her with doubt. She would need all the power she'd used against the serpents and more, but she'd never learned how to call on those powers. She was helpless.

Nix reached out and grabbed her shoulder, feeling her bondmates' fear and doubt. "It's a dream," Nix whispered, her words more a hot breath against Reve's ear than audible words. "Anything is possible."

Reve turned, meeting Nix's eyes. She didn't need words for Nix to understand her fear. If anything was possible, and the Choir were masters of the dreamscape, they didn't stand a chance.

Nix grit her teeth, her determination and protectiveness blazing like flame around her. She wouldn't listen to Reve's fear. She wouldn't let them retreat. They would fight together. They could do anything together.

In a flash of blinding light, a sword of flame appeared in Nix's hand. A symbol of her power and heritage solidified by the power of the dream. Reve drew close, kissing her with all her heart. An intimate touch Reve prayed wouldn't be their last. "I love you."

"I love you."

It's time.

Reve cast a look of gratitude to her animal guide and they charged into the chamber of the Choir.

The Choir turned as one, screaming out in a wordless hiss. Nix charged, her sword raised. She screamed a battle cry as she swiped at the first member of the Choir, the blade passing clean through it like through mist, but the mage howled in pain and pulled away. It was clear she couldn't kill them, but she could keep them at bay.

Hecate lingered behind Reve, her eyes locked on the Amazon. *You have to do something. The finishing blow can only come from you.*

Reve's mind raced as she tried to think of a way to attack. "I don't even remember battling the serpents, how can I use that power again when I don't know what it felt like?"

Perhaps that's not the power you're looking for.

Nix cried out as a member of the Choir grabbed her arm, the steam of an unformed Song exploding to life around the creature's boney hand, burning her. Nix pulled away and stabbed the creature in the void of its hood, aiming for a face but finding none. She glanced down at her arm, the fabric of her sleeve burned away and angry red welts forming across her skin.

"Just a touch can do that?" Reve hissed.

Did you think they'd be defenseless?

"Reve?" Nix shouted as the Choir moved on her as one. She fought with all the skill of a master, but the creatures only fell back, always returning.

Reve wished with all her heart for some kind of weapon, envisioning it and willing it as she had to come to the dreamworld in the first place, but nothing happened.

Her eyes flitted across the room, looking for anything that might help. The cavern was uncharacteristically smooth compared to the tunnels, without a sharp stone in sight. Reve's eyes were instead drawn to the portal over the Choir's ring, the swirling vortex still linked to the Song battering at her home.

Her eyes suddenly lit with understanding. Reve saw the Choir in their true forms for the first time. She stared in wonder. These were the creatures that had Aggar completely twisted to their will? These emaciated bodies, twisted by greed and pride until they were no longer human? They were of a hive-mind, losing all individuality and will until they were nothing but personifications of their previous ambitions. They were the will to dominate, to control, to preserve their power made whole. They were pathetic. They were weak. They were a parasite, clinging to the belief and unquestioning obedience of the people. They needed passive wills to feed their need for dominance. They needed to be obeyed to exist. If all of Aggar had a reason to turn their backs on the Choir and their rule, if the people saw through their whispered Song that they were perfect, infallible, incapable of lying, the Choir would cease to exist.

She locked eyes with Hecate and the wolf howled with glee at Reve's revelation.

"Cover me!" She raced for the vortex, dodging the hands of the Choir. She stumbled and fell to her knees as one grabbed her leg, burning her skin black before Nix chopped off its misty arm, the limb evaporating and instantly grew back as the Choir member flitted away.

"Are you alright?"

Reve grit her teeth. "I'm fine. Nix!"

Nix twisted back to block a blow ad stab the Choir member in the stomach. She glanced over her shoulder, not even meeting Reve's eyes. She didn't need to know the plan. She trusted her bondmate. "I'll watch you. Go!"

Reve crawled forward, her palms and leg scuffed and blood welling to the surface of her torn skin and burns as she scrambled over the rough stones. Nix growled with adrenaline and pain as the Choir surrounded her, recovering from her blade faster with every stroke. Hecate circled at Reve's back, snapping and growling at anyone who came too close to Reve.

Reve closed her eyes, moving purely by Sight. She couldn't look back and see what was happening to Nix and Hecate as they defended her. She could hear their cries and yelps. She could smell burning flesh and fur. This was her last chance. She couldn't give up now.

She reached the vortex, the portal a swirling pool of light on the ceiling. Her Sight instantly latched onto the lights. She could feel the Song roiling over the ships, battering the fragile vessels and tormenting both crews with their whispers of doubt and despair.

Reve reached out to the Song, connecting with it like the Choir would. Her mind was instantly sucked into a turbulent storm of Song. She screamed at the raw power of the manifestation of the Choir's will. The Songs weren't meant to be controlled by a single person. Reve could barely hold onto her sanity.

Hecate nuzzled against her, slipping between her arms. Reve felt her guide's abilities join with hers, giving her a brief moment of peace. With their abilities combined, she was able to wrestle control of her mind back from the violent storm of Song. She felt an exhilarating thrill at being in control of the force that had once hunter her. She wasn't a victim of the Choir or the Songs anymore. She was the master. The controller.

Don't get proud, Hecate growled in her mind. *These Songs would destroy you.*

Reve reasserted her control. Hecate was right.

She worked her way into the roots of the Song and embedded in it every image, every word, and feeling from the capsule. We are one. We are family. We don't need the Choir. We don't need rulers or tyrants to have peace. Stop giving yourselves to them. Stop believing their lies.

Reve poured herself, her heart, into her message. She infused it with her amarin, pleading with the people of Aggar to turn away from the Choir. The Choir wouldn't exist without their belief and obedience. No matter how powerful they were, they were still just wraiths standing on the backs of the willingly enslaved. If the people of Aggar stood up and rejected them, the Choir would fall.

Reve lost herself once more in the Song, but this time she led it. She pulled it away from the ships and cast it across the entire planet. The Songs whispered the truth to every citizen, working into their minds before they even realized it. In a matter of moments, everyone knew about the capsule and its contents. She felt them rising, casting away the Choir and its lies. They remembered the Triad. They remembered Blue Sights. They were reclaiming their willpower.

Reve's joy spread through the Song as she disintegrated into it. Of course she wouldn't be able to escape the storm. She knew her victory stroke would be her end. It only made sense that she would return to the ether, becoming one with the last Song.

"No."

Reve felt her physical body again, could feel desperate hands pull at her. She was losing her connection with the Song like waking from a dream. Her senses were returning, reminding her she was human.

She lost all connection with the vortex as Nix dragged her out of the Choir's old circle, both of them collapsing to the stone floors the instant Reve was free.

Reve looked around in a panic, but the room was empty. She reached out with her Sight, but she couldn't sense any sign of the Choir anymore.

"Is it done? Are they gone?"

"The disintegrated into dust. I don't know what you did."

Even in her pain and exhaustion Reve smiled. She laughed, the sound wild and ringing through the cavern. It was done. It was finally done and somehow she was still alive. "I spread their secret. The people of Aggar defeated them. They're gone. They're dust." She crawled forward, dragging her exhausted body to her bondmate. "You saved me."

Nix was covered in burns and blisters, her body trembling in pain. Her hands shook as she slowly raised her hand to touch Reve's cheek. "I wasn't going to give you up. We defeated them. They couldn't take you with them."

Reve held her hand, kissing her palm. "I couldn't have done this without you. They would have killed me instantly."

Nix smiled. "I told you as much."

Reve snorted and fell, wrapping Nix in a gentle embrace. "Come home with me."

The dream faded and Reve woke. She was still sprawled across Nix's floor where they'd fallen asleep. Nix sat up slowly, holding out her hands. Where once had been blackened burns, there was now only a warm blush.

She shook her head. "You're amazing."

Reve kissed her hard, overcome with her emotions. "We're amazing. And Hecate. Where's Hecate?"

Desperate scratches echoed on the other side of the door. Reve stood on trembling limbs and threw it open, falling back a step as Hecate launched herself at her. The wolf lapped at her face. It was over. They had won.

"M'Sormee!" Sirena cried as she ran into the room.

"The storm vanished. What did you do?" Gale demanded.

Briza smiled softly to herself. "You found each other."

Reve wrestled Hecate away and stepped out onto the main deck. The air felt somehow cleaner, the sun brighter. She smiled wide with pure, unadulterated joy. "The Choir is no more. There will be no more Songs. No more control."

"What was the damage? Is everyone alive?" Nix gasped as she glanced around the ship.

"No major damage, but minor injuries. The storm didn't last long," Tlaloc reported.

"Good. Tlaloc, take the helm. Gale, return to your vessel. Volt, I want you to power the thrusters, controlling for damage to the ship. We're returning to land."

Both crews cheered. Reve could feel their relief as they realized their Amazons weren't insane. That no one would die at sea.

Nix wrapped her arms around Reve's waist. "And you, come with me."

Reve gasped at the clear, heated intentions of her lover as Nix pulled her back toward their room. "Shouldn't we help with the sailing?" The words slipped past her lips despite her desperate desire to be with her Amazon.

Nix shook her head, her hands and fingers already roaming across her body. "They know what they're doing. We're free. You're finally safe. Mine. Come be with me?"

Gale grunted in false disgust. "Go celebrate elsewhere. And shut the door."

Briza waved them away and Reve allowed herself to be pulled back into the room with her bondmate. Hecate raced out of the room before Nix shut and locked the door.

They fell into a passionate embrace, still overcome with adrenaline from the battle. Their lifestones burned in time with their emotions and desire. They tumbled into the bed, wrapping around each other like serpents.

"Stay with me always," Nix whispered as she nipped at Reve's ear.

The request sent a thrill of love and excitement through Reve's heart. "Yes. Always. I promise."

And for the first time, Reve knew she could keep her promise.

Epilogue

Reve leaned back against the rim of the crow's nest, her arms tucked behind her head and her eyes closed. The sun beamed down on her, warming her skin and freeing her heart. It was the first beautiful day since the rainy season in Karatan had ended. Reve intended to soak up every blessed ray.

"I should have known you'd be here. Like a seal on a rock."

Nix climbed into the basket, straddling Reve's lap. Reve grinned, her eyes still closed, and wrapped her arms around Nix's waist. "You're blocking my sun."

Nix kissed her brow. "You're sending mixed signals."

Reve opened her eyes and kissed her bondmate, her lifestone warming against her skin. "Not mixed. I always want you close."

Nix slid aside, resting on Reve's shoulder and entwining her leg with Reve's. "You've been up here for hours. What are you thinking about, Love?"

Reve shook her head. "I'm just at peace. The sunlight. The quiet. Home. I never thought I'd find myself here."

Nix squeezed her hand, her love and happiness flowing from her amarin in gentle waves. "You still haven't sensed any sign of the Choir or their Songs? No dreams? No whispers?"

Reve shook her head. "They're gone forever. What happens next is up to the people."

"Do you think they'll maintain peace with what they know? Do you think this could be an end to the violence?"

Reve snorted softly. "I'm an agent of chaos, Nix. Not harmony. Knowing we're all kin won't stop the fighting. Nations will form. Boundaries will be drawn. There will be wars and misery once more. But it will be their choice, and it won't be because we're too different. It will be because we're family, and sometimes families fight."

"You're probably right. But there's peace for now. I received word from Ristol. Sects of Triads are rising again. Rumor says they want to start a school. Even more amazing, twins were born in the desert. Blue Sights, both of them. There was no rage from the village. They're being celebrated. It seems the capsule's message didn't just contain information about Aggar's origins."

Reve smirked. "Or the messenger righted a few wrongs along the way."

Nix turned to her sharply. "You added to the message?"

Reve only kissed her lover, silencing any further questions.

"Zephyr, coming fast from the north!"

Reve and Nix glanced over the crow's nest at Tlaloc's cry. "We probably should have seen that first," Nix mumbled.

"I wonder what Gale wants now," Reve grunted.

Nix laughed. "You two feud more than she and I ever did."

The two women scurried down the ratlines, landing hard on the main deck. Sirena, Lyr and Agwe raced up from the lower decks. Sirena instantly drew her sword. Agwe caught Lyr's hand.

"Be careful."

Lyr's eyes twinkled mischief as he lifted Agwe's hand and kissed his fingers. "I know you'll patch me up."

Agwe sighed in frustration, their eyes lingering long. "Fine. But I'm not numbing anything this time."

Lyr's ears trembled in amusement and he ran to join Sirena.

"Canons ready!" Volt called from the powder room.

"Mine, too!" Doris hollered in return.

"No it isn't!" Kana called sternly.

"M'Sormee!" Doris howled.

Nix laughed aloud. "Let zir load!"

"Nix…" Kana's growl was low with warning.

"Best not to tempt her. She's already worried Doris will one day be an Amazon," Briza warned.

"There's nothing wrong with being an Amazon."

"Perhaps she just doesn't want her child facing sea serpents, inter-dimensional tyrants, and mind-controlling storms."

"Then they shouldn't be n'Niachero," Tlaloc commented as zi drew her sword.

Reve wrapped an arm around Nix's shoulders. "That's why I joined up."

"You're insane?" Nix countered.

"As mad as you are."

They kissed.

"Still disgustingly bonded, I see." The *Zephyr* slid up beside the *Niachero*. Gale stood at the railing, her arms crossed over her chest. "Can you take a long enough break from mooning over each other for a competition?"

"What do you propose?" Nix called.

"A race to Ristol. Loser pays for the drinks."

"What say you?" Nix called to her family.

"Aye!" came the rousing cry.

Reve sighed, rolling her eyes. Nix held her tighter and kissed her cheek. "Humor me?"

"You already drink too much."

"You'll understand when you're older."

Reve glared at her. "Is that really what you want to have said?"

Nix kissed her.

"Are you going to try to blow us out of the water when you realize you can't beat us?" Sirena taunted.

Gale raised her sword. "I've stabbed you once, Sirena n'Niachero, I'll do it again."

"You can try in Ristol."

The two shared a fiery glance and Nix cocked her head to the side. "Gale, she's my daughter!"

"Let the girl make her own decisions," Gale returned as she turned on her heel and raced up to the helm. "I like straight ale, Nix."

"You can get yourself one when you buy my drink," Nix returned.

"If you're going to race, you better win," Reve called to her lover as she raced to the helm as well.

"What will you do when you disappoint your bondmate?" Gale shouted as the *Zephyr* pulled away.

"You better pray to the goddess no one upsets Reve!"

Reve's lips quirked into a smile as the Niachero pulled forward. Nix's warm, competitive energy thrilled her, wiping away any minor annoyances at leaving the peaceful sun of Karatan. She couldn't be angry, not surrounded by her family.

"Reve Serpent Slayer! Reve Choir Destroyer! Reve n'Niachero!" Pan cheered as zi bounced up from below deck. Reve caught zir in her arms and spun zir around.

"Yes, Reve n'Niachero." She caught Nix's eyes, a flood of love and hope for the future binding them together. "Always and forever. No matter what comes our way."

The End of Book Four

DICTIONARY OF AGGAR TERMS

amarin: The amarin is the essence of life, the empathic imprint of animate existence which results in a cumulative pattern of feelings, thoughts and reflexes. It is one's aura.

basker jackal: a sleek, scavenger canine, native to the Ramains' plains and renowned for its blood lust; semi-domesticated by militia for chase and guard chores

black glass: a ceramic-glass compound of especially durable strength that hones to a sharp edge; commonly used in making knife blades

blackpine: A valuable hardwood conifer with a black, barkless trunk and green-black needles which is common to Maltar's lands.

Blue Sight: The Sight or Blue Gift is a sixth sense genetically linked to blue eyes; an awareness of and ability to manipulate life auras and amarin. The terms also refers to a person possessing the Blue Sight.

bondmate: any eitteh, human, or sandwolf who has been empathically bonded into a sandwolf's familial unit (see pack bond; sandwolf)

boko: A food native to the Ramains, boko is a vegetable-meat paste wrapped in boiled leaves.

braygoat: a short-horned goat native to Ramians' southern districts

brushberry: an evergreen bush with a sweet-tart berry; a Ramains wine

bunt: A tall, stemmed grain which yields red-brown seedlings and whose husks are often used for animal fodder. The term also applies to the grayish flour produced from the seedlings.

buntsow: a carnivorous, hooved mammal; a scavenger native to the northern forests; a non-venomous cousin of schefea

"By the Mother's Hand": (idiom) "Done with the Goddess' blessings."

Changlings: Sentient half-human, half-feline beasts native to the Northern Continent, Changlings are a race of people known for their amoral selling and reselling of information. They are also miners of lifestones.

Circle, The: The elite soldiers of the Core, bands of bandits and warriors who do the Twins' bidding

Clan, the: people of the Clan's Plateau; descendents of off-worlders who were stranded on Aggar at the fall of the Galactic Terran Empire; renowned for their weapons technology and raiding activities

Clan Lead: legislative representatives chosen by and from among the Clan folk; (plural) a governing assembly; civil servant

Clantown: the governing settlement and militia corp of the Clan's Plateau; a village in the ancient Terran Quadrant, located at the edge of the eastern plateau adjacent to the Ramains' Great Forests

commons: A Ramains' term for a tavern housed by an inn.

Core, The: The nation risen from the ruins of the Clan's settlement, once the Maltar's realm.

Council of Ten: A collection of ten Masters and Mistresses educated in the history and humanity of Aggar who are guardians of the planet's integrity.

Crowned Rule: the designated heir of the Ramains' Royal Family; usually chosen for skills of statescraft rather than warfare

cucarae: A small, extremely poisonous scavenger, this crustacean is found in the wastelands of both the Northern and Southern Continents.

cucarii: A group or nest of cucarae.

Desert Peoples: Also known as The Southerners, the Desert Peoples are loosely organized nomadic tribes native to the Southern Continent and renown for their distilled liquors and merchant ventures.

Diblum: a small Ramains' village southeast of Khirla

dracoon: A governing marshal appointed by the Ramains' King.

Dumauz: (plural: — en) a kind-hearted individual; a concerned friend

early moon: The first of the twin moons to rise on any given evening.

eitteh: A sentient feline native to the Northern Continent. The term eitteh usually refers to the winged females of the species as males are never seen. See also winged-cats and men-cats.

Eldest Prepared: These individuals are the best of the Shadow trainees at the Council's Keep and are the preferred choice for assignments and lifebonding. They also instruct the younger recruits.

Fates, the: The male deities of evil mischief, the Fates are mystical rulers of the dark underworld. Their primary figures include Malice and Ambition while their secondary figures include War, Ire, Greed and others.

Fates' Cellar: The legendary home of the Fates, Fates' Cellar is the mythical place where evil souls go after death to suffer in a punishing afterlife. Also known as hell.

Fates' Jest: (idiom) A malicious turn of events attributed to the Fates.

Firecaps: These intersecting, volcanic mountain ranges comprise the northeastern third of the Northern Continent. They are uninhabited and controlled by Seers in order to stabilize continental land masses.

grubber: A generic term for ground rodents in the Northern Continent.   Grubber generally refers to smallish, nasty-tempered mammals.

harmon: a soul-spirit; self-image projected by a Blue Sight to another honeywood: a deciduous hardwood with rough, red bark; yields a golden grain of decorative value; common to the southern Ramains

Jezebet: Usually given to a woman, this title is bestowed upon someone who is a resident of the Council's Keep and is trained in the arts of lifebonding Shadowmates.

jumier: a fowl native to the Ramains' northern districts

Karatan: a jungle region in the southern-most continent of Aggar

Khirla: Dracoon's capital in the Ramains' southeasterly district Khirlan

lexion: A domesticated fowl common to farms of the Northern Continent which is raised for its meat.

lifestone: An opal-like energy stone often found in limestone deposits in the Northern Continent and used by the Council in the practice of lifebonding Shadowmates.

mala': A female slave or bond-servant of the Ramains whose duties are restricted to the household and the bedroom.

Maltar: The ruling family of the northern half of the Northern Continent. The term may refer either to the ruling family member or the country itself.

men-cats: The male of the eitteh species, these cat-like savages inhabit the mountain ranges on the Northern Continent.

mesta: A thick-skinned, amber fruit with a tart, meaty pulp in the seed pods that is cultivated by farmers in the Northern Continent.

midnight moon: The second of the twin moons to rise on any given night.

Min: A generic title given to free-born women in the Ramains. It is comparable to the Terran term ma'am.

milkdeer: middle-sized, long necked mammal native to the Ramains; frequently domesticated for its milk monarc: A standard calendar division, roughly equivalent to a Terran month, which is comprised of four, ten-day periods.

Mother, the: A nurturing female deity who is seen as the birthmother of the universe.   Aggar's twin moons are associated with her watchful light.

mumut: a spice leaf grown chiefly in the lower districts of the Ramains

pack bond: empathic understanding of personal commitments; empathic bond of sandwolves used to define familial units (see sandwolf)

pripper: A small, tree-dwelling mammal known for its comical antics and bushy coat.

Purge, The: The last attack on Aggar by Terran forces that culminated in the use of biochemical warfare that massacred nearly every Blue Sight. The battle also destroyed the Council's Keep and Valley Bay, scattered the seers and Amazons.

Ramains: The southwestern third of the Northern Continent which is united beneath a liberal monarchy and shares a border with the Council's lands.

Royal Marshall: special emissaries of the Ramains' Royal Family; originally banded to protect travelers; duties expanded to provide districts with legal and military resolutions, to supply the Royal Court with information from outlying districts

sandwolf: sentient canine, originally native to the Southern Continent, which instinctively imprints at birth to one or more sentient others to provide an emotional, empathic bond in developing protective behaviors and communication skills (see pack bond)

schaefea: A hoofed scavenger of middle size native to the northern mountains. The schaefea has protruding tusks and venomous saliva glands.

Seers: Those individuals gifted with the Blue Sight who are bound to Aggar's lifecycles and no longer capable of individual thoughts or actions. They are directed by the Council of Ten and are the crafters of Aggar's landscapes. Sometimes referred to as mystics.

silverwood: A hardwood conifer with a smooth, silver-green bark and gray-green needles which is common to the Ramains foothills and mountain regions. Also called silverpine.

single moon: The night at the end of each monarc in which only one of the twin moons is visible. Term is synonymous with monarc.

Songs: the unseen force that allows the Choir to manipulate the minds of the people of Aggar; named for the mournful tune that drifts through the air whenever they're near

Tad: Generic title given to free-born men in the Ramains which is similar to the Terran term sir.

tinker-trade: a traveling merchant member of the Traders' Guild

ten-day: A division of days within a monarc, roughly equivalent to a Terran week.

tenmoon season: A period of time roughly the same as two Terran years. The name comes from the fact that ten single moon nights will occur during the time it takes for Aggar to complete one orbit around its sun.

torin: An edible, broad-leafed fern commonly found in the wooded rangers of the Northern Continent.

Traders' Guild, the: a merchant union supported by membership dues that promotes the fair exchange of market goods; endorsed by the Desert Peoples, Ramains, Council and Valley Bay the union may provide arbitrators, bonded transport agents, and travel lodging to supplement regional resources

twin moons: Two planetoids orbiting around Aggar's globe. The term is also associated with the Mother's watchful care.

Twins: The tyrannical, magical rulers of the Core

Unseen Wall: An unidentified energy field which was ordered by the Council of Ten and is controlled by the Seers; the Unseen Wall comprises the border around the Terran Base Quadrant.

Valley Bay: the settlement of the Sisterhood; located near the White Isles, isolated from the Northern Continent by the Firecaps; governed by the Ring of Valley Bay and bound to the home world through the Blue Sighted gifts of the Ring's Binder.

waterferret: amphibious ferret with both scales and fur; often used to aide fisherman and common along coastal towns; very intelligent, but often sneaky and prone to theft.

White Isles of Fire, the: The group of volcanic islands off the eastern Firecaps of the Northern Continent. Sometimes called the Archipelago, it is the native homeland of the Council and the Seers.

Wine of Decisions: A spiced wine containing a natural drug which prompts the visions of the Blue Sight.

winged-cats: Generally used as another term for female eitteh.

DICTIONARY OF SORORIAN TERMS

Amazon: a Sister choosing to work/settle outside of the Sisterhood's jurisdiction

ann: (idiom) A word used to emphasize thoughts or ideas and function as a verbal exclamation point. Ann might also be translated as "Take note!" Other meanings include to be far away or distant.

be: far, distant

beasties: Large, hoofed mammals, these horned animals have copper-colored, wooly coats and are descended from the Highland Cattle of old Terra.

bin: A preposition meaning between. Sometimes means to or from.

Cee: A word that refers to the customs or ways of any given people.

cheroan: to make safe, to protect

Coramee: daughter

corean: A verb meaning to find precious, to treasure.

crone: a wise elder among healers n'Shea

dey: This word can be used as either an article as in "the" or a pronoun as in "we" or "our" and is meant to connote respect.

duen: to do kindly; to act with concern

Dumauz: (plural: —en) a kind-hearted individual; a concerned friend

Feast of Helen: This anniversary celebration of unity and independence marks the birth of the Sisterhood's firstborn child.

felan: A verb form meaning using, doing or creating.

Founding, the: the original planetary colonization of dey Sorormin under the Galactic Terran Empire; settlement of the home world

Helen: This name refers to the Red star of dey Sorormin's solar system, the firstborn of dey Sorormin's original settlement and the leader of n'Sappho during early negotiations to retain Sorormin independence. The word means "light."

Houses of dey Sorormin: surnames of Sisters, designating family and/or skills; six of Seven Houses recall ancient goddesses of Terran lore (n'Athena: guardians (Greek), n'Awehai: crafters (Iroquois), n'Hina: agricultural providers (Polynesian), n'Huitaca: artists (Chibcha), n'Minona: historians/teachers (Dahomey), n'Shea: healers (Irish); First House of dey Sorormin (n'Sappho: legislative leaders) recalls a Terran stateswoman of Greece

Kahmee: little daughter; a very young girl

kahn: A noun meaning sunrise or dawn.

kamak: A verb which indicates something is brought to completion or finished. It may also be used in place of is made.

kau: A pronoun referring to the second person singular (you).

ki: A word indicating possession (yours).

kumin: A verb meaning to join together.

m': A preposition denoting as or of (from).

m'Sormee: birth mother; (literally) from the woman's life

mae: A word indicating that something is dear or precious.

"Mae n'Pour":   (idiom) An expression which means "Give me strength." This term is often used as a curse to express frustration or anger but can also be used as a genuine prayer to the Goddess.

mau: A noun meaning heart.

mauen: The plural form of mau (hearts).

mee: A noun which denotes life.

minmee: A word meaning birth, minmee also carries the connotation of the sacred connection of life-giving or creating.

n': This expression denotes possession. It is usually used to indicate an individual's House.

n'Athena: One of the Seven Houses of dey Sorormin, members of this house are traditionally the guardians of the Sisterhood. The term also recalls a Terran goddess from ancient Greek lore.

n'Awehai: One of the Seven Houses of dey Sorormin, members of this house are traditionally the builders and craftswomen of the Sisterhood. The term also recalls a Terran goddess of Iroquois (Native Northern American) lore.

n'Hina: One of the Seven Houses of dey Sorormin, members of this house are traditionally the agricultural providers of the Sisterhood. The term also recalls a Terran goddess of Polynesian lore.

n'Huitaca: One of the Seven Houses of dey Sorormin, members of this house are traditionally the treasurers of music and arts of the Sisterhood. The term also recalls a Terran goddess of Colombian Chibcha (Native Southern American) lore.

n'Minona: One of the Seven Houses of dey Sorormin, members of this house are traditionally the historians and teachers of the Sisterhood. The term also recalls a Terran goddess of African Dahomey lore.

n'Sappho: First House of the Seven Houses of dey Sorormin, members of this house traditionally make up the legislature and leadership of the Sisterhood. The term also recalls a Terran stateswoman of ancient Greek citizenship.

n'Shea: One of the Seven Houses of dey Sorormin, members of this house are traditionally the healers and earthwitches of the Sisterhood. The term also recalls a Terran woman-deity and/or the white witches of ancient Irish lore.

n'Sormee: parenting mother or guardian; (literally) of the woman's life

nehna: (idiom) A prompt for more information meaning and then, then it happened that or so then.

Niachero: Daughter of the Stars; descriptive of Sisters who genetically resemble those n'Athena who negotiated the settlement of Valley Bay; Amazons who led the space protectors to save Aggar during the fall of the Galactic Terran Empire

nor: An word that indicates an event happened in the past.

puor: An word meaning strength, stability or virtuousness.

quinn: A word denoting peace, tranquility or the absence of violence.

quitan: to nurture; to tend with compassion

ret: A word meaning cruelty or harm.

sae: Another term for please, this word denotes a request.

sak: This word means intelligence or cleverness.

shea: This noun refers to a healing witch from the House of n'Shea. A member of this house will frequently be one who is closely bound to nature. She may also be a mistress of love potions and possess the evil eye. See the term n'Shea.

sheaz: A noun meaning the earth or world, this term may also refer to the components of a nurturing Earthmother Creator.

Shekhina: The moon of Helen's second planet. This moon is home to Helen's high-tech base where diplomatic contacts between the dey Sorormin and the Galactic Terran Empire occur. It is also the home of the Immigration offices and the orientation/screening facilities for new Sisters. Historically, the term refers to an ancient Terran goddess of Judaic lore and sometimes connotes the divine image of a woman.

sor: The noun meaning woman.

soroe: The noun denoting friend or dear companion.

Soroi: loved one; lover; beloved

Sororian: The woman-made language of the Sisterhood. The term derives its root meaning from the ancient Terran word which refers to sisters.

Sorormin: A noun that is synonymous with the word Sisterhood.

Sorormin, dey: The word which represents the proper name of The Sisterhood. The term also refers generally to the culture of women who settled on Helen's second planet. dey Sorormin are recognized members of the Senate in the Third Galactic Terran Empire.

sueht: A past tense form of the verb to lose or to misplace.

tau: A pronoun denoting me.

ti: A word that indicates possession (my).

tizmar: A verb which means to remain, to settle or to unite and/or join together.

vu: A term meaning very little, a small amount.

z': A term indicating for or with.

"Z'ki Sak, Diana": (idiom) An expression of regret or disbelief which translates as "By your wits, Goddess."

www.ingramcontent.com/pod-product-compliance
Lightning Source LLC
Chambersburg PA
CBHW071526120726
47907CB00013B/1086